M000318219

# THE CAVES OF SAN PIETRO

## SUSAN GAYLE

Black Rose Writing | Texas

©2021 by Susan Gayle

All rights reserved. No part of this book may be reproduced, stored in a retrieval system or transmitted in any form or by any means without the prior written permission of the publishers, except by a reviewer who may quote brief passages in a review to be printed in a newspaper, magazine or journal.

The author grants the final approval for this literary material.

First printing

This is a work of fiction. Names, characters, businesses, places, events, and incidents are either the products of the author's imagination or used in a fictitious manner. Any resemblance to actual persons, living or dead, or actual events is purely coincidental.

ISBN: 978-1-68433-739-2
PUBLISHED BY BLACK ROSE WRITING
www.blackrosewriting.com

Printed in the United States of America
Suggested Retail Price (SRP) $19.95

*The Caves of San Pietro* is printed in Sabon

*As a planet-friendly publisher, Black Rose Writing does its best to eliminate unnecessary waste to reduce paper usage and energy costs, while never compromising the reading experience. As a result, the final word count vs. page count may not meet common expectations.

I dedicate this book to all those who continue the fight for equality – the battle to overcome bigotry, misogyny, and hate – and to those who battle for our democracy and a better life for all. Thank you, Julie Johnson.
And to all adopted children – may they all be as loved as mine are.

# THE CAVES OF SAN PIETRO

*"Liberty costs a great price, and one must either resign himself to live without it or decide to pay its price."*
**–José Martí**

ITALY

Showing major cities &
key locations in the story

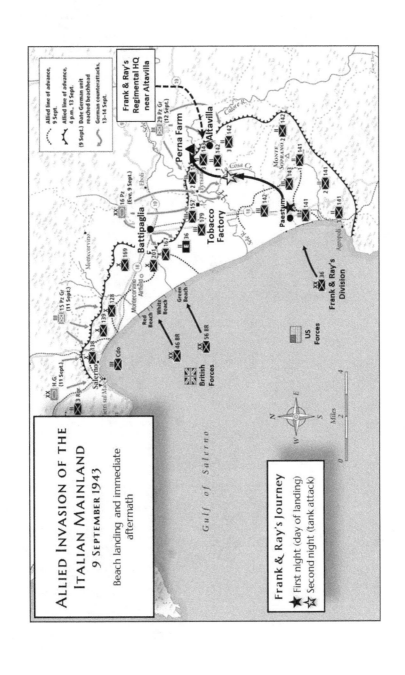

ALLIED INVASION OF THE
ITALIAN MAINLAND
9 SEPTEMBER 1943

Beach landing and immediate
aftermath

Frank & Ray's Journey

★ First night (day of landing)
☆ Second night (tank attack)

- - - - Allied line of advance,
9 Sept.
......... Allied line of advance,
4 p.m. 13 Sept.
〰〰 (9 Sept.) Date German unit
reached beachhead
〰〰 German counterattacks,
13–14 Sept.

Frank & Ray's
Regimental HQ
near Altavilla

Gulf of Salerno

US Forces

British
Forces

Frank & Ray's
Division

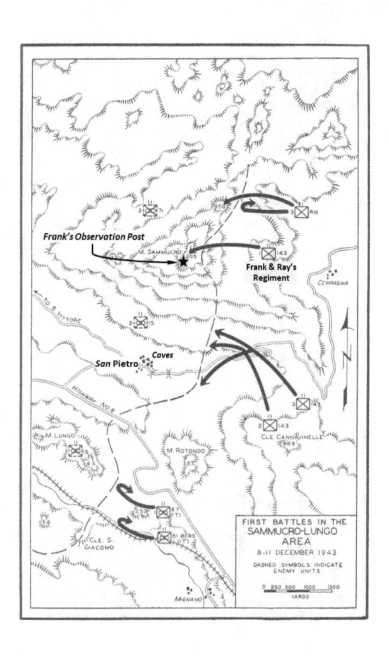

FIRST BATTLES IN THE
SAMMUCRO-LUNGO
AREA
8-11 DECEMBER 1943

DASHED SYMBOLS INDICATE
ENEMY UNITS

0  250 500    1000      1500
YARDS

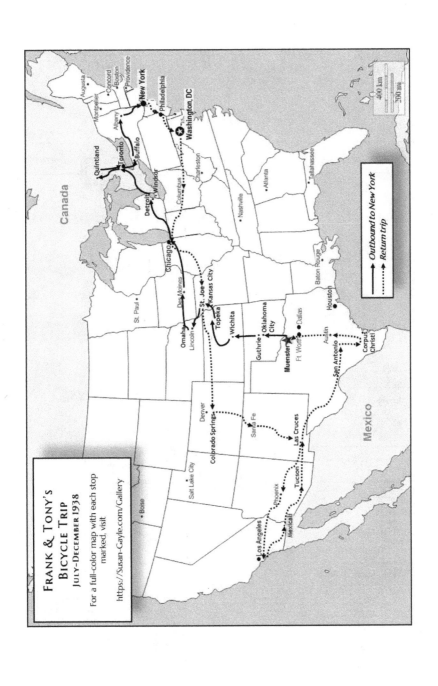

FRANK & TONY'S
BICYCLE TRIP
JULY–DECEMBER 1938

For a full-color map with each stop
marked, visit

https://Susan-Gayle.com/Gallery

Outbound to New York
Return trip

400 km
200 mi

Canada

Mexico

Augusta
Concord
Boston
Providence
Montpelier
Albany
New York
Philadelphia
Washington, DC
Toronto
Buffalo
Quintland
Windsor
Charleston
Detroit
Columbus
Chicago
Nashville
Atlanta
Tallahassee
St. Paul
Des Moines
St. Joe
Kansas City
Topeka
Wichita
Omaha
Lincoln
Guthrie
Oklahoma City
Dallas
Houston
Baton Rouge
Muenster
Ft Worth
Austin
Corpus Christi
San Antonio
Denver
Santa Fe
Colorado Springs
Las Cruces
Salt Lake City
Tucson
Phoenix
Mexicali
Los Angeles
Boise

—————— Birth ——————
– – – – – Adoption – – – – –
– · – · – Marriage – · – · –

# The American Families

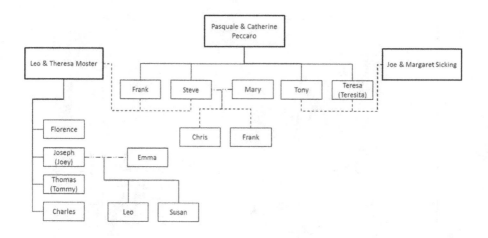

—————— Birth ——————
– – – – – Adoption – – – – –
– · – · – Marriage – · – · –

# The Italian Families

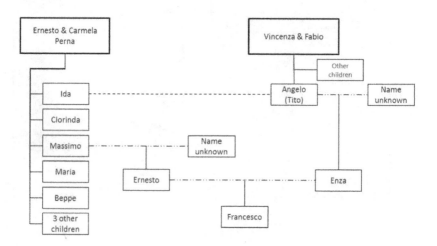

# CHAPTER 1

*Near Altavilla, Italy, September 8, 1943*

The sound was unmistakable – the powerful engine over-revving and gears grinding as the driver tried to get the car up the lane to the top of the hill. Wherever he learned to drive, Ida mused, they must not have hills.

It had been five days since she'd first heard that sound. Massimo, her twelve-year-old brother, had spotted them first – a truck and a car driving along the main road beyond the pastures, swastikas adorning the front door of each. When the two vehicles slowed, approaching their lane, her father sprang into action. "Ida, take the rest of the children to the barn – now. Get them up in the loft and hide behind the hay bales. Hurry! There's no time to lose. And no one can make a sound. Massimo, help your sister keep everyone quiet, understand?"

"Yes, Papa," Massimo replied.

"Your mother and I will be right behind you. Now go, Ida.

"Carmela," he called to his wife as he headed toward the kitchen, "throw all the food you can into some sacks and be quick about it."

"*Si*, Ernesto. Bring down that big water pitcher from the wash basin upstairs," Carmela replied.

Ida scooped up Beppe, the youngest, from where he was playing on the floor, and rushed out the door behind Massimo and her two younger sisters.

It wasn't easy climbing the ladder to the hayloft with Beppe in one arm, but somehow she managed. "Come on," she told her sisters, "let's get back here behind the bales. We're going to play hide-and-seek, all right? So no talking and no giggling. Not a word. Do you hear me?" The girls nodded. "If the men in those trucks decide to come up this way, we can't let them know anyone is here."

Beppe squirmed, but she held onto him. "Not now, *bambino*. You can play later."

"They've stopped at the lane," said Massimo, who was peering through one of the narrow gaps between the boards of the outer wall of the barn.

"Come back over here behind the hay bales, Massimo. And you be quiet too."

And then she heard the sound of the vehicles starting up the lane toward the farm house, one driver apparently having trouble negotiating the hill. Where were Papa and Mama? Surely Papa wasn't going to try to hold off two carloads of German soldiers with his old hunting rifle!

She sat rocking Beppe to keep him calm, brushing her fingers through his soft brown curls while she listened to the vehicles coming closer to the top of the hill. What was keeping her parents? Just as she'd decided to leave the rest of the children here and go look for them, they dashed into the barn and climbed up to the loft, lugging three flour sacks filled with whatever they'd been able to grab in their hurry to avoid being seen. Carmela was still wearing her apron – something she never did when she left the house. Her face, already careworn from the hardships of the war, now betrayed raw fear, and she gasped for breath after the frantic run from the house. Beppe wriggled free from Ida and ran to his mother. While Ida and her sisters helped hide the provisions, their father pulled the ladder up and spread hay from an open bale to hide it.

The noise of the trucks reached the top of the lane then stopped as the engines were shut off. Then came the clatter of opening doors, shouted orders, and the bootsteps and voices of men hurrying to secure the site. German voices. Some of them coming toward the barn. Ida held her sisters' hands. Mama cradled Beppe. Papa put his arm around Massimo and held a finger to his lips, exhorting everyone to silence.

Bootsteps below, walking around. Ida held her breath, afraid even the sound of breathing might echo through the barn. The sound of the old farm truck door being opened then slammed shut. Finally, after what seemed an eternity but was probably no more than three or four minutes, "*Heinrich, Gehen wir. Hier nichts.*" Let's go. There's nothing here. Followed by the sounds of two men laughing and talking as they made their way back toward the house.

That first night, Ida hadn't slept a wink, her ears alert to every sound, unable to shake the fear that some of the men might come back to the barn. The next morning, her father put the ladder back in place and ventured down to arrange a primitive toilet for them in the far back corner of the barn – really nothing more than a hole in the ground in one of the milking stalls, but the half wall of the stall provided a small bit of privacy, and the corner was dark enough that it couldn't be seen easily by anyone passing the barn door that the soldiers had left open. To close it would just alert them that someone was inside. They kept the ladder hidden in the loft when it wasn't absolutely necessary for someone to go down to the toilet.

Ida and her father alternated keeping watch through one of the narrow gaps in the wall. It was a good thing Carmela had been baking for two days – at least they had half a dozen loaves of fresh bread. But every night, Ernesto had to go down to the pump by the barn door to refill the water pitcher. On the second night, while her father was at the pump, Ida gasped when she saw one of the Germans making his way toward the barn swinging a flashlight from side to side. She put her finger to her lips, urging everyone to silence. Beppe whimpered and Carmela hugged him to her chest. The soldier froze in his tracks and shone the light toward the barn then resumed walking in their direction. Beppe whimpered again, and this time Carmela stuffed a piece of bread into his mouth to quiet him. The soldier slowed his advance, panning his light slowly around, looking for the source of the sound. Ida watched as the beam caught two eyes at the end of one of the rows in the vineyard – one of the farm cats out hunting. The cat yowled – sounding surprisingly like Beppe – then hissed and darted across the path in front of the soldier just as a harsh German voice shouted something from the house.

"*Jawohl, Unterfeldwebel,*" the soldier shouted back. He made one more quick sweep with his flashlight before turning on his heel and heading quickly back to the house.

No one moved. No one made a sound. Not until the lights were all off in the farm house did Ernesto finally venture back up the ladder with his pitcher of water. "Papa, thank God," Ida whispered, taking the water pitcher as he stepped off the last rung and into the loft.

"I caught a glimpse of the moving light and hid in a stall where I could watch," said her father, rubbing one hand over the top of his bald head. "No one . . ." He pointed first to his wife and then his eldest daughter. "Do you hear me, Ida? No one but me goes down that ladder for anything but the toilet. Do you understand?"

Carmela nodded and Ida whispered, "Yes, Papa," then helped him pull up the ladder and hide it once again.

After that, it seemed the soldiers had no further interest in the barn, but they never left the house and there were always two outside. From sunrise to sundown every day. One in the back, watching the valley below, now and then raising binoculars to his eyes for a closer look at something. Another one, usually lolling in the swing on the front porch, smoking cigarettes and occasionally glancing toward the road.

Until this morning, that is, when she'd heard the engine start and watched the car drive down the lane. For a brief moment, Ida dared to hope. Maybe the rest of them would pile into the truck and leave too. But the minutes passed and the truck remained stationary and now, the sounds in the lane told her the car was returning. She went back to peer through the gap.

Two uniformed men got out of the car and forced a third man out, pointing a rifle at his head. He was plump, wearing overalls and a jacket, his arms tied behind his back. The soldiers shoved their prisoner against the side of the car and then seemed to get into an argument of some sort, shouting at each other and gesticulating wildly. One of them started toward the porch and his companion kept shouting at him, turning his back on the prisoner – who took advantage of the situation and bolted toward the vineyard, perhaps hoping to find a hiding place among the vines. Ida could just make out his face as he turned to run.

"Papa – quick! Look!"

Her father scurried over to look out a nearby gap. "*Dio mio!*" My God! "Our neighbor!"

No sooner were the words out of his mouth than the soldier on the swing grabbed his rifle, and the crack of a shot resounded as the farmer fell to the ground, his jacket oozing blood from the wound in the back of his chest. Ida gasped and covered her mouth to keep from screaming, but she couldn't take her eyes off the gruesome scene. The soldier who'd fired the shot walked over, kicked the fallen farmer, then put a pistol shot through his head, just to make sure he was dead. Shouting something to the two who'd been arguing, he resumed his position on the swing while they dragged the dead farmer by the feet around the corner of the house and flung the body over the side of the ridge.

At the sound of the gunshots, Beppe jumped and tears rolled down his cheeks as he ran to his mother.

"Papa, what are we going to do?" Ida couldn't keep the petulance out of her voice. Why hadn't her father done something sooner? Why hadn't he tried harder to get parts for the truck? Why had he just assumed they'd be safe here? "We'll be next if they find us. We've got to get out of here."

"She's right, Ernesto," said Carmela as she stroked Beppe's head to soothe him. "It's been five days now, and we're running out of food. The little ones can't take this much longer."

"I know, I know." Ernesto hung his head and shook it back and forth, his despair obvious in the gesture. And then he seemed to shake it off as he got up, uncovered the ladder, and put it in position. "I'm going down to work on the carburetor of the old truck. Maybe if I can get it running, we can get out of here. Watch for anyone coming toward the barn."

Ida tried not to let her anxiety at the mention of the truck show in her face. "I'll come help you, Papa," she said as he started down the ladder. "Mama can watch."

As Carmela took her daughter's place at the gap in the wall, she grabbed Ida's arm to keep her from leaving right away. "Don't be cross with him, Ida. He's doing the best he can in these terrible times. I know you think he should have done more, but . . ." Her voice trailed off as tears welled in her eyes. "I'm sure you heard the planes last night. I thought I heard tanks in the hills too. The children are frightened and hungry. And I . . ." Carmela dropped her voice to the softest of whispers, not wanting the younger children to overhear. "Ida, I don't know how much longer I can go on like this. Help him find a way to get us out of here."

Ida patted her mother's hand. "Stay strong, Mama. Tonight, when the soldiers have gone to sleep, I'll go out and see what I can find. Maybe there are still some grapes in the vineyard."

"Oh, Ida, I don't know. That's too close to the house." Carmela wiped away the tears that had run down her cheek. "Just go help your father."

Ida nodded and told her mother, "Whistle if you see anything."

As she made her way down the ladder, Ida's anxiety returned. What if her father had found them? When she got to the back of the barn, her heart sank. There he stood, holding the stack of pamphlets she'd stashed behind the seat. He shook them in her face. Even though he spoke softly to avoid being heard, there was no disguising the anger in his voice. "I thought I told you, Ida. I thought you'd agreed. So why do I find *these* when I move the seat to get to the battery?"

"Papa, I can explain."

He cut her off. "How can you explain putting your family in danger? There is no explanation."

"Papa, I had to do *something*. I got those away from my friend just before the Germans caught him, and I was going to destroy them. I just hadn't had a chance."

"And what if *you'd* been caught? What then? You know what they're like. They wouldn't have taken just you – they'd have come for all of us."

"They come for anyone and everyone and nobody lifts a finger. My friend – just taken and put on that train – his brother left to bleed to death in the street – and no one seemed to care. Everyone just turned a blind eye. Well, not me! Not the rest of my friends. It was bad enough when Mussolini ran things himself, but now he's just Hitler's lap dog. This madness *has* to be stopped.

"I'm twenty-two, Papa. I should be teaching in a school – looking for someone to marry, to start a family with – not hiding out in a barn while my friends are imprisoned or God knows what! I *can't* just stand by and do nothing."

"Ida, your friends were taken because they were Jewish."

"So what?"

"Even more reason they shouldn't have been publishing these. You *know* the Nazis banned printed materials other than their own." He shook the pamphlets again. "Even more reason you shouldn't be involved."

"So what should I do? Turn my back like everyone else – like you – while our lives are torn apart?"

Her father's shoulders slumped. The hand holding the pamphlets dropped to his side. His expression changed from anger to defeat. And Ida realized she had gone too far. Her tone softer, she began, "Papa, I'm sorry. I—"

Her father held up his hand to cut her off. "I understand you, Ida." His whisper was now kind and gentle. "And in one way, I'm proud of you. But one little slip . . . one little mistake . . . and you're lost to us. I can't lose you." He hugged her tightly then held her at arm's length. "We'll find a way to stop what you call this madness, but it has to be a smarter and safer way. Until then, you're not to leave your mother. Do you understand?"

Ida sighed, knowing he was right. For the moment, anyway. "Yes, Papa."

"All right. Now go tear these up and put the bits in our little toilet." He handed her the pamphlets. "Then come back and help me with the truck."

Ida didn't argue. She wouldn't expose her family to further danger – but she wouldn't sit here and starve either. When darkness came and she was sure everyone was asleep, she shimmied down the post that supported the loft and crept out the barn door, careful to stay in the shadows lest someone on guard in the house notice something moving about. Hopefully, she'd find food tonight – but one way or another, she was determined to find freedom.

# CHAPTER 2

*Salerno Bay, September 9, 1943*

Hundreds of soldiers crowded the decks of the USS *Samuel Chase* as it plowed through the Tyrrhenian Sea toward the Italian coast. They all knew that some of them – many of them – wouldn't see tomorrow. Everyone was trying, in his own way, to push that thought aside – smoking, praying, chatting with a good buddy, laughing and bragging about the heroics they were sure they'd display on the beach.

Frank and Ray leaned quietly on the port-side rail, watching the bow wave that marked the ship's relentless passage through the water. They'd been friends in high school, but friendship had transformed into something akin to brotherhood when Ray had rescued Frank from a brutal beating at the hands of some of their fellow soldiers during boot camp.

Frank reached for the chain around his neck that held his dog tags, the silver cross that had belonged to his father, and a small key. "If I don't make it, Ray, remember – this key is for Florence. Make sure she gets it." He stuffed the chain and its contents back beneath his shirt.

"Sure thing, Frank, but we're *gonna* make it outta here." Ray slapped his friend on the back. "And you can give that key to your little sister yourself."

Just then, the ship's PA system came alive. "Attention on deck! Attention on deck! Sergeant Moster to the radio room. Sergeant Moster to the radio room."

Frank pushed himself off the rail. "Duty calls."

"I'll wait for you here."

Frank scrubbed what the army barbers had left of the red hair on top of Ray's head. "Pretty sure I can find this wherever you are."

Ray laughed. He didn't let many people get away with teasing him about his hair. "I'll be right here."

Frank had to elbow and nudge his way through the crowd to get to the stairs to the superstructure deck where the radio room was located. It was slow going – slow enough that the PA crackled to life again. "Hotfoot it, Moster. Cap'n's getting impatient."

When he finally got there, the tiny room was bulging at the seams – the two regular operators, the ship's captain, and the commanding officer of Frank's unit – the 143rd Infantry Regiment of the Army's 36th Division. The CO hurriedly returned Frank's salute and barked, "Get in here and listen. They're getting some mainland comms."

One of the operators handed Frank a spare headset while the other hunched over the controls, fine-tuning the frequency. The radio squawked and crackled in Frank's ears before he started hearing voices. The operator sat up. "Best I can do, sirs. We're still pretty far out to get it any clearer."

Frank listened intently and winced when a particularly loud bit of static assaulted his eardrums. The senior officers hovered, impatience obvious in their posture. Frank concentrated as the voices eventually began to fade and finally disappeared altogether.

"We've lost 'em for the moment," said the operator. "I'll try to get 'em back." He returned to fiddling with the dials.

"Well?" The CO couldn't contain himself any longer.

"There's a lot of static, sir," Frank said. "But from what I can make out, there seems to be a major quarrel going on. The Italians are trying to back down while the Germans are giving orders for an all-out push to the beach. Could be several *Panzergrenadier* divisions being diverted to the coast. Then something about Altavilla. That's all I could get before we lost the frequency."

"All right, Moster. Dismissed." The CO turned to the ship's captain. "Sounds like the Germans are expecting us. Let's get ready for all hell to break loose."

This wasn't the first time Frank had been called on for such things. The son of Italian immigrants, orphaned at an early age and adopted by a German family in Muenster, Texas, he spoke both languages fluently. In Algeria, where his regiment had trained, he'd been assigned to translate during the negotiations for Italy's switch from the Axis to the Allies. They'd given him sergeant's stripes for that. Frank never knew if the stripes were a reward for a job well done or just to demonstrate his importance to the visitors – not that it mattered, since no one ever asked for them back.

Back on the main deck, Frank side-stepped and elbowed his way to where Ray was waiting. But now Ray wasn't alone.

"Fran-*chess*-co, you're goin' home to your land of dagos." Jack Watson, an arrogant bully, also from Muenster, who despised Frank for being "different," had wandered up with a couple of his cronies. He shoved Frank in the chest, then, getting no response other than a withering glare, he shoved again. "Chicken-shit! How come you were in the radio room? Sabotaging us? Damned *eye*-talian."

Frank's blood was boiling. He'd taken more than enough from Jack, including that beating in boot camp. The swagger. The unlit cigarette hanging from his lower lip and the crumpled pack stuffed halfway into his shirt pocket. The grinning adulation of his sidekicks. Frank wanted nothing more than to punch the square-headed bastard's lights out, but Ray was shaking his head back and forth and mouthing "No."

As Frank clinched his fists and started to walk away, Jack stuck out a foot and tripped him. The sidekicks erupted in laughter.

Helping Frank up, Ray shouted, "Jack, you are *such* an ass. When are you going to grow up and stop being a bully?"

Jack snickered and spat his cigarette out at Frank. "Make me."

"We'll be watching our backs with you behind us, you wop," one of the sidekicks added.

Regaining his footing, Frank started to take a swing, but Ray held him back. "Get the hell outta here, Watson. You've made your point."

At first, it looked like Jack was going to stay and pick a fight. Then he put one arm around each sidekick and began to shepherd them away. "Come on, guys. They're not worth our time. They'll get what's coming to them on the beach."

Frank and Ray turned back to the rail. The outline of the coast was just coming into view. Frank raised his binoculars for a closer look.

Italy.

A broad sandy beach surrounded by mountains, like an amphitheater. A medieval stone watchtower overlooking the shore at the edge of a town. The opening at the top of the tower gave him an eerie feeling, like the eye of Poseidon staring back. Colorful fields of what appeared to be farmland surrounding the town but rising quickly into the foothills and mountains. From this distance, it looked serene. But it was ground-zero for their landing.

Frank handed the binoculars to Ray. "God help us if those mountains are full of Germans."

"Does the CO think the Gerrys are waiting?"

Frank nodded. "We are *so* screwed – like sitting ducks on a pond. Let's see if we can get out of this slaughterhouse alive."

The PA system blared again. "Attention on deck! Attention on deck!" Nothing further until the murmur of conversation went silent and the only sound was the dull hum of the ship's engines. And then, "This is your Commanding Officer. Men, you already know we sail to our destiny. The Italian people have spoken. Mussolini has been ousted. Today, Italy has switched sides and joined the Allies. But the Germans still occupy the country, and it's our job to drive them out. The Italians are on *our* side now. Together, we *will* succeed. Together, we *will* defeat the Nazi menace. You've trained. You're prepared. God go with you. That is all."

It seemed as if the roar of the cheering must have been audible all the way to the shore. But it soon went quiet as the portent of those words sank in. Frank's thoughts drifted to his birth mother and father, who were forced to flee Italy. This wasn't how he'd wanted to come to their homeland. But now he was here, and he was determined to take pride in being part of the liberation.

•    •    •

The vibration of the engines became almost indiscernible as the ship slowly came to a halt offshore. And then the activity began in earnest.

Destroyers and PT boats in the surrounding water began laying smoke screens around the transports. Orders came fast and furious over the PA. Sailors to lower the LCTs into the water. Designed to carry tanks, the LCTs would ferry the assault forces to the beaches first before returning for the vehicles. Soldiers from this unit or that ordered over the side to scramble down the ropes and into the LCTs. Loaded LCTs circling around the transport ships, waiting to form assault groups before heading to the beach. The same orders, the same actions repeated on dozens of ships up and down the beach from Maiori to Paestum, the British in the north, US forces concentrated on Paestum.

They'd trained for this, but now it was real. Men packed shoulder to shoulder in the LCTs, Frank and Ray side by side. A deathly quiet hanging over the boat. Fears that could no longer be pushed aside. Every man on his own, with only his buddies to protect him. Who would die on the beach? And would their families ever know what happened to them? The sound of the water lapping against the sides of the LCT did nothing but heighten the fear.

And suddenly, they were in the middle of hell. The ship-to-shore bombardment began, pounding the beaches in an effort to clear the landing zone. The brilliant flames of thousands of rockets launched toward the shore.

The enemy lost no time answering. First came the Luftwaffe, strafing the LCTs and dropping heavier payloads among the ships. Antiaircraft guns from the ships came alive, sending some of the planes into the water and exploding others in the air above. And still the rockets fired, clearing the beaches. The noise was deafening.

Then the LCTs began moving toward the shore. This was it. The machine gun squads and four mortar squads lined up closest to the ramp – getting some firepower onto the beach was the first priority. Frank saw Jack and his cronies in the row after that, real fear in Jack's eyes instead of the bravado he'd shown earlier. Frank could hear his own heart pounding.

It had been hammered into them time and again in practice drills. Nineteen seconds to unload once the ramp went down. Get as far up the beach as you can to leave room for the next wave to unload. Stay low. Run like hell. Fire at anything that's firing at you. Use your grenades for machine gun nests. Get off the beach and into cover as fast as you can. They'd done it over and over in the Algerian desert, but no one was firing back at them then. Now it was literally a matter of life and death.

As they neared the shore, Frank reached for the chain around his neck to make sure it was still safe inside his shirt. He'd carried his father's cross with him all his life – a talisman of sorts. He nodded at a soldier with a chaplain's patch and clerical collar and wondered if he should go over and ask for a blessing and forgiveness for his sins.

Too late. Heavy machine gun and mortar fire raked the craft next to theirs in an ear-splitting blast, and now bullets and shrapnel begin pinging off the front of the ramp and the helmets of some of the men. Any sense of organization vanished as most of the men massed as close to the ramp as they could in an effort find some protection from the enemy fire. Frank grabbed Ray's arm and pulled him into a crouch in the shelter of the side of the LCT. No sense getting caught up in the mayhem that was sure to happen when the ramps went down.

Frank felt the adrenaline coursing through his body. He tapped his rifle nervously and noticed Ray was doing the same. All around him, men were praying aloud. Suddenly, someone screamed "Jesus, get me outta here" when a bullet hit the man next to him, splattering blood everywhere.

As the LCT slowed and the ramp began to go down, the boat commander shouted through his bullhorn, "Everybody move out! Keep your feet moving. Push forward!"

Frank had always believed his father's cross protected him. Now he was about to find out.

# CHAPTER 3

As soon as the ramp was down, everyone was exposed to the deadly fire from onshore. Men went down and their bodies became obstacles to others trying to get off the boat. The unloading seemed to be going in slow motion, and when Frank looked over the side of the ramp, he realized why. They'd lowered the ramps well off the beach to protect the LCTs, and men were having to jump off into the water. Everyone was getting bunched up and more men were going down – more bodies to trip over – more of a chance to fall victim to an enemy bullet.

Frank looked around for a way out of the mayhem. Lunging forward, he leaped over the side of the ramp, trying desperately to avoid the rain of bullets. The weight of his gear – seventy pounds more or less – dragged him under. It was almost impossible to get his bearings in the murky water churned up by so many boats, so many men, so much gunfire. Surface sounds were muffled by the water and the droning of the LCT engines, but it still seemed as if he could hear every bullet as its speed slowed with the resistance of the water. For a brief moment, time seemed suspended, and he was overcome by the same feeling of doom he remembered from the day he and his siblings had been left alone on the platform as the Orphan Train pulled away from the station. And then he heard Tony's voice in his head. "You can do it, brother. Save yourself. Push forward."

Somehow, he found the surface and started swimming. The weight of his backpack sapped his strength, and, more than once, he wanted to pause for a rest. But his training told him the best way to avoid the bullets was to keep moving. The sea was full of floating bodies, and when he crawled up onto the beach, he found it covered with more bloody corpses. The screams of the wounded and dying added to the din of artillery and rifle fire. Exhausted, he collapsed on his belly in the sand, breathing hard and hoping his pack would shield him from incoming rounds.

Catching his breath, he raised his head to look around. A barge full of jeeps and trucks and ammunition trailers was being offloaded to his left. To the right, about two hundred yards away, he saw a soldier step on a *Schützenmine* buried in the sand, tripping a canister of shrapnel that deployed about three feet above the ground, blowing the man to smithereens. Instinctively, Frank buried his head in the sand as some of the shrapnel landed close by, barely out of lethal range. Even if his rifle wasn't functional after being in the sea, he knew now it would at least be useful to prod the ground for mines and booby traps.

The surrounding mountains provided a stadium view for the Germans to aim down at the beach. Screaming 88s exploded in the sand, the blasts so loud and the concussion wave so strong it felt to Frank as if his eardrums were rupturing. And then the Luftwaffe turned their attention to the beach. Everywhere, men ran and fell and screamed and died, and Frank knew he had to get out of there.

Where was Ray? Had he made it to shore? Getting to his feet, Frank glanced over his shoulder and spotted his friend emerging from the water nearby. He got to his feet and waved both arms wildly, screaming at the top of his lungs, "Ray, over here! Come on." They zigzagged up the beach toward a collection of vehicles, most of them bombed and useless. "Behind that jeep," Frank yelled, making a beeline for one that looked more or less intact, Ray hot on his heels.

A dead soldier draped over the steering wheel and a leaking jerry can that had been knocked from its holder added to the smoke from the mortar fire and the smell of death from end to end of the beach – an overwhelming stench they couldn't escape. But at least the vehicle gave them enough cover to take stock of their situation.

Hundreds of bodies floated in the sea, so many men who never made it to shore. Blood, gore, bodies, and body parts covered the beach. Men flailed about in the water, desperately trying to save themselves. The barrage of gunfire and strafing by aircraft never let up.

"Look!" Ray pointed to the ancient tower Frank had spotted from the LCT. "Lots of the gunfire's coming from there. We're sitting ducks if we stay here."

"Damn! We need to get to the brushy area behind those rocks." Frank pointed into the bay. "If we wait for that next wave of LCTs to start unloading, the Germans will concentrate on them. That's gotta be our best shot."

"Hey, man, I don't know. What about the land mines? Might be better to take our chances here rather than risk getting blown to bits."

"You'd rather get blown to bits when a mortar shell lands here and all this fuel blows up? See all those body parts where guys stepped on a mine? If we follow those, we've got a clear path."

Just then, an LCT started to lower its ramp and the German gunners redirected fire toward the incoming boats. "Come on – let's go," said Frank.

Ray threw up his hands. "You're crazy, man. But we're gonna die if we don't get off this beach. Let's get the hell outta here."

Halfway to the rocks they were spotted, their final sprint punctuated by a hail of rifle fire. Diving behind the rocks, gasping for breath, they rolled onto their bellies, heads up to look around. "Holy shit!" Ray exclaimed. "I don't *ever* wanna do that again."

Frank tapped Ray on the shoulder and pointed back where they'd just come. Jack Watson was trying to follow them to safety. He'd made it past the first two bodies but was frozen in his tracks, staring down at a corpse lying face-up, eyes open, intestines hanging out, and legs missing.

Ray yelled, "Jack, run! Come on!"

"Jack, you're gonna die out there!" Frank shouted. "Run, you fool! Run!"

They kept yelling at him, but he didn't move – it was as if his legs no longer worked and he couldn't tear his eyes away from the dead body. The LCT had disgorged its load and was headed back out into the bay, so the German gunners focused back on the beach. Bullets flew. Soldiers ran for cover, some trying to randomly return fire into the hills.

Men fell. A mortar round hit the jeep they'd just abandoned, sending flames and jeep parts high into the air. And still, Jack didn't move.

Suddenly, he screamed and went down, blood spurting from a wound in his leg. Frank watched, flashbacks of Jack's bullying and name-calling swirling through his head. But he made his mind up quickly. Bully or not, Jack was lying on the beach dying. "Cover me, Ray. Fire in the direction of that machine gun." He pointed toward the tower. "I'll try to drag Jack over here."

"Have you lost your friggin' *mind*?"

"Come on, Ray, you know we can't leave him out there to die."

Ray shook his head, disbelief written all over his face, then grabbed his rifle and started firing toward the tower window. Frank dashed out onto the sand, grabbed Jack by the belt, and started dragging him toward their brushy cover. Jack's unconscious body was like a gunny sack full of bricks – dragging him was too slow, leaving both of them vulnerable. Frank bent down, threw Jack over his shoulder, and started for the rocks. Just as he thought he was safe, a bullet pinged his helmet. He heaved Jack behind the brush and then dove in himself.

Ray dropped his rifle and tugged at Jack's trousers, trying to locate the wound. "Damn, he's bleeding! How can we get him to the medics?"

Frank pulled off his belt and improvised a tourniquet on Jack's upper leg. "Gotta get that gunner in the tower first. No way I'm crossing that sand again with him still up there." He started rummaging in his pack. "You think grenades that have taken a swim still work?"

Ray reached into his own, much drier pack and came out with three grenades. "How about these?"

Frank grabbed the dry grenades and crouched behind the rock closest to the tower. "Blast everything you've got at that tower, Ray. Keep those bastards away from the window." He scrambled along behind the brush until he got to the very edge, then looked back at Ray and nodded.

Ray started firing and Frank dropped to all fours, crawling as fast as he could toward the side of the tower. He grabbed a grenade, pulled the pin with his teeth, counted to ten, and heaved the grenade into the air. Too low, it ricocheted off the side of the tower and exploded in the sand about fifty yards away. Frank flattened himself on the ground.

When his ears cleared from the blast, he could hear Ray still firing but had no idea how much ammunition his friend had left.

Then he heard Tony's voice in his head again. "It's the bottom of the ninth, Frank. Two outs and the count is three and two. Gotta get this one over the plate. You can do it."

Frank took two deep breaths, trying to calm himself. Then he grabbed a grenade, pushed himself to his knees, pulled the pin, and started counting. When he got to twenty, he stood, looked straight at the window of the tower, and lobbed his pitch, flattening himself immediately to the ground.

A deafening blast. Screams from inside the tower. Frank looked up to see smoke pouring from the window. He had one grenade left and tossed it in to finish the job, then sprinted as fast as he could back to the brush and rocks.

Ray had gotten Jack upright and was shouldering his rifle. When the smoke cleared, they could see the pillars of the ancient Greek temple at Paestum – the rendezvous point for their unit. Frank hoisted Jack in a fireman's lift, and Ray carried their rucksacks and rifles.

They stayed in the brush as long as they could but eventually had to emerge onto more open ground as they got nearer the temple. Luck was with them – they'd only walked a few yards in the open when a medic jeep pulled up beside them. "That guy alive?" asked the driver as he stopped the jeep.

"For the moment," Frank replied.

"Put him on the stretcher," said the medic, jumping out to help. He took one look at Jack's wound and the improvised tourniquet and grabbed his medic's bag from the back seat. "Looks like you saved this guy's life." He handed Frank back his belt then applied a proper tourniquet. "Lost a lot of blood, by the looks of it, but I think he'll make it."

Frank and Ray watched while the medic started an IV and applied a field dressing. "Hop in," said the medic. "I'll give you a lift to the rendezvous." He dropped them off just inside the perimeter before heading on with Jack to the impromptu field hospital that had somehow been set up amid all the chaos and carnage of the landing.

Frank and Ray sat beside a stone wall and watched as other battered and wounded men slowly made their way into the temple area. Somehow, they'd made it off the beach. They were safe for now. "Look at that," said Ray, pointing to the American flag flying over an improvised headquarters.

"Beautiful," said Frank.

"Hey, man, we survived round one." Ray pulled off his helmet and used his sleeve to wipe his face.

"Yeah. But this is just the beginning." Frank leaned back against the wall. He thought about Tony . . . about how proud he would be that his little brother had made it this far. As soon as Frank could write home, his first letter would be to Tony.

# CHAPTER 4

"Guess we can't sit here any longer," said Ray at long last.

"Too bad," said Frank. "Not sure I've got the energy to move."

Ray struggled to his feet, picked up the rifles and rucksacks, and reached a hand down to Frank. "Come on, buddy. Let's go find a bed and a latrine – not necessarily in that order." Frank let his friend pull him to his feet, and the two of them trudged off toward the American flag.

They hadn't gone far when they reached a line of men moving slowly forward into the inner precincts of the temple. As they approached the headquarters, the line split into two, a lieutenant with a clipboard on each side of the path processing the arrivals. By the time they reached the head of the line, they knew the drill – name and unit, each arrival duly checked off against the papers on the clipboards. Would the names not checked off be declared MIA or KIA? Frank didn't want to think about that – or about how close he'd come to not having that precious check mark beside his name.

"Moster, 143rd of the 36th," said Frank, as he listened to Ray echo "Haas, 143rd of the 36th" to the officer opposite.

"One-forty-third's over there," the lieutenant told Frank, pointing vaguely ahead. "Past the temple. Guys are bedding down in some empty buildings across the road. CO's called for muster at oh-nine-hundred."

The first building Frank and Ray came to was already filled with snoring soldiers. In the second, there was still some open space in the middle. They wandered in, dropped their gear, and sank to the floor.

With the stress of the day slowly subsiding, Frank realized he was thirstier than he ever remembered being in his life. He fished in his rucksack for his canteen and downed the contents without pausing for breath. From the glugging sounds to his left, he guessed Ray was doing the same.

"Looks like we better find some place to refill these," said Ray. "Gimme yours and I'll do the honors. You can stay here and guard our stuff and our spot."

Frank was too tired to argue. While Ray was gone, he looked around. Very few men he recognized. How many had been lost on the beach? There was no doubt now. The Germans had no intention of retreating. The liberation of Italy was going to be hard won, but won it had to be.

There was no field kitchen yet, so supper was hardtack and a can of beans from the rations in their rucksacks – washed down with another canteen-full of water. By the time Ray returned with the second refill, Frank had made a pillow of his rucksack and stretched out on the floor. He didn't expect to sleep. Exhaustion proved him wrong.

• • •

There was no reveille – just the sounds of men stirring shortly after daybreak. Frank was roused from a dreamless sleep by someone stumbling over him, headed for the door. He sat up and looked at his watch. Just past seven. Why did it feel like he could sleep for another twelve hours and still not be rested?

He nudged Ray. "Hey, man, you're so good at scavenging. Think you might find some coffee?"

"Who're you kidding, Frank?"

"Bet the officers have some."

"And they're going to give it to us. Fat chance," Ray snorted.

Frank stretched his aching muscles and got to his feet. "Gotta go find the latrine."

"Out the front door. Turn right. Follow your nose."

They breakfasted on crackers with a bit of jam spread on them, then gathered up their gear and headed outside to find a crowd had gathered around the flagpole. "Grab your mess cups, guys, and get your asses over there," shouted a soldier running back toward the building they'd just left. "There's coffee, and it ain't gonna last long."

"What'd I tell you?" Frank nudged Ray, and they took off at a trot.

The coffee was lousy, but still, it was like nectar from the gods. Tilting his head as far back as he could to drain the last drop from his cup, Frank sighed then looked at his watch. "Eight fifteen," he told Ray. "We've still got time. Let's go check on Jack."

They found the makeshift field hospital – a scene of barely managed chaos where doctors and medics had been working all night – and were surprised to find a familiar face from home. The face was familiar, at least, but nothing else about the man was. Normally meticulous about his appearance, Joe Bezner looked like he hadn't slept in days and his uniform was splattered in blood as he worked feverishly to dress an amputated limb. He barely glanced up when Frank and Ray stopped beside him. "Gotta finish this, guys. Whatcha need?"

Frank watched the care Joe was taking with his work, oblivious to everything else going on around him. "I need to know you'll be the medic if a Kraut bullet finds me."

"Sure, Frank, anything for you."

"We came to check on Jack," said Ray.

"He's alive." Joe finished tying off the dressing, yanked off his gloves, and tossed them in the bucket of bloody gauze and cotton at his feet. "He'll make it. We're shipping him back for surgery to remove the bullet. They told me about the belt tourniquet. Hell, Frank, you could be a medic yourself."

"No way, man. Couldn't deal with all this. I'd rather do the fighting."

"Not me. Shit, I was praying like never before when I unloaded from that LCT." A devout Catholic, Joe also wore a cross on his dog-tag chain. He and Frank had gone to mass together back home in Texas. "I crouched behind the cab as our truck plowed down the ramp and onto the beach. We tried to help the injured but couldn't save most of them. At one point, I had to belly-crawl through sand trenches and under barbed wire."

"We were just a half hour or so ahead of you," said Ray, "and it was fucking awful!"

"And those goddamn 88s," Frank added.

"Never saw such carnage." Joe shook his head as if trying to shake off the horror. "Hope I never do again."

Frank glanced at his watch for the third time that morning. "We gotta go, Joe. Muster in fifteen minutes. Watch your six, man."

The captain was new. Field promotion after all the carnage on the beach. Pointing at Frank and Ray, he said, "You two . . . I want you with A Company to protect the right flank as we push the Krauts out of the Tobacco Factory. G2 says they've got a strong foothold there, but we need it as a base for the advance to Rome. Command thinks they'll spread out as our main force advances and may even flee toward Altavilla to join up with forces there. That's why the right's so important. We'll give you a head start to get further out on the flank before the main body moves forward."

"What's the next rendezvous point?" Frank asked.

"Our first goal is to take the Tobacco Factory, set up base there and then try to control Altavilla. That town's built like a fort on a hill, so the Krauts will likely have protective forces all around the perimeter." The captain pointed to the map. "We control this road coming in and the south slope of Mount Soprano, but rest assured, the Krauts are lurking in these surrounding hills and farmlands."

Two battalions of field artillery along the eastern banks of La Calore stream were meant to protect the American advance. But the German *Panzergrenadier* Regiment 15 was waiting and, supported by German artillery, they split the US forces, and the tanks turned to follow as the 142nd pulled back. That left a gap for the 143rd to start climbing the slopes of Hill 424. If they could take this hill, they could go on to capture Altavilla and trap the Germans between the 142nd and the 143rd.

Out on the right flank, Frank and Ray started the strenuous climb through woods and brush. "This gear on my back's killing me," said Ray. "Think I'm getting blisters under my arms from the straps."

"I'm right behind you. Just keep movin'," said Frank. "We may need all that ammo."

Two miles up the hill, they came to an opening in the trees. Frank extended his arm to the side. "Ray, stop here." Within seconds, artillery fire pounded the men who'd walked on into the clearing.

"Get down!" Ray shouted. "Find some cover. I see where the firing's coming from. We gotta radio back for support."

"Give me the coordinates."

Suddenly, a mortar shell landed right in front of them and then another just to the left. The rest of the company scrambled back for cover, set up their machine guns, and started returning fire. Frank finally got the radio out and reported their position. "We're taking fire from the woods. Six men down – all dead. No way we can advance."

"Hold your position," was the only reply.

The exchange of fire continued. Twice, the radio squawked static, but nothing else. Frank tried to raise someone on the other end and got no answer.

By midafternoon, it was clear they were in a stalemate, neither side intending to budge from their position. Three more men had taken hits – two with shoulder wounds, one dead. At the sound of rustling in the brush behind them, Frank pivoted, rifle at the ready. A lieutenant burst through the trees, arms held high, gasping for breath as if he'd just run all the way up the hill. Frank lowered his rifle, and the man rushed over and crouched behind a big rock. He waved to those nearest to gather round.

"New orders," he said. "Can't afford to run out of ammo going nowhere here. So we've gotta get in behind them. First squad stays here and keeps their attention. Second, you're with me, back down the hill then around the side toward Altavilla. You guys," he pointed to the corporal who was leader of the first squad, "try to make 'em think there's more of you than there really are. Buy us some time, you got it? The rest of you, get your asses down the hill now."

One squad against a whole company of Krauts, thought Frank as he watched men scramble away into the brush. Not the best odds. He fingered the cross on the chain beneath his shirt then turned to Ray. "I'll take the machine gun. You just keep the ammo rolling, okay?"

"Roger that."

They kept up the gunfire, pausing occasionally to shift positions, hoping to confuse the enemy. The sun was starting to sink over the top of the hill when a mortar round landed close enough that the blast wave sent Ray flying backward and knocked the gun off its tripod.

Frank scampered back to find Ray lying on his back, struggling to get up. "Ray . . . hey, man . . . you all right?"

Ray looked dazed and pointed at his ears, "I can't hear you." They took cover behind a rocky outcrop, Ray shaking his head, trying to clear his ears. Finally, he said, "I'm okay. The blast just knocked my hearing out for a minute. Let's get our asses over with the rest of the squad."

"I think we're done here," Frank told the corporal. "Sun's going down, and we'll be sitting ducks once it's dark. We need more ammunition and men to keep this up."

"Yeah," came the reply, "but we can't get back to HQ." The corporal spread out a map, studied it briefly, then pointed to a spot. "We should be safe for the night here by La Cosa creek. Moster, you and Haas take point and find a good defensive position. Everybody else follows in groups of two. We set up a line along the creek."

By dark, they'd settled in beside the creek and set up a watch rotation. Sometime around midnight, Ray nudged Frank from a deep sleep and whispered, "Listen. Hear that humming in the distance?"

"Sounds like a bomber."

Within minutes the mountainside lit up as exploding bombs started fires in the brush and trees. Tracer rounds arced through the sky, and naval artillery pounded the enemy positions. German defenders began to scatter like termites crawling out of burning woodwork.

There was enough moonlight to see movement on the hillside. "Frank, look – Krauts coming down the mountain." Ray got his rifle into position.

"You get those two bastards running across the field, and I'll take out the three on the hillside by that big tree."

The Germans took cover and returned fire, setting off exchanges all along the American line.

Before dawn, the Germans had regrouped and were coming in with tanks. Despite some difficulty with the sloping terrain, they were bearing down on the Americans.

"Ray, look. That tank is turning right at us!" Frank yelled as he heard the unmistakable sound of a turret in motion.

"Run! Jesus Christ! Run!" Ray screamed.

They scuttled along the creek and over the ridge, escaping with only their rifles and a pair of binoculars. The tank fired and the explosion in the creek showered them as they raced for their lives. They could hear the loud creaking of the tank treads advancing toward the creek.

"We can't outrun a fucking tank on foot," Ray screamed.

"Keep zigzagging. He's having trouble with this terrain," Frank replied, gasping for breath.

An explosion shook the ground under their feet. And then another, causing them to glance back over their shoulders. A rocket had hit the tank, setting off explosions of the ammunition inside. German soldiers screamed as they climbed all over each other trying to escape the burning tank, some of them with their clothes on fire.

Frank and Ray just ran. Separated from the rest of their company, with no idea if anyone else had survived, they were on their own, exhausted, covered in dirt, and hungry, with nothing to do but keep running to try to find safety.

# CHAPTER 5

They ran until exhaustion overtook them. By then, the sounds of fighting were faint in the distance. "What now?" Ray asked between gasps for breath.

Frank bent over, hands on his knees, taking in huge gulps of air. He couldn't remember when he'd ever run so far. At night, over rough terrain, they were lucky one of them hadn't taken a fall and broken something. "We're never going to find our unit in the dark in these hills. Hell, I don't even know what direction we've been running in."

"Roger that. It's quiet here. Let's just hunker down 'til daybreak."

As dawn broke, they began to reassess their situation. "The rendezvous point was west of our positions last night," Frank rubbed his forehead and looked around at the landscape, "so I guess we go that way." He pointed away from the rising sun.

Ray slung his rifle over his shoulder. "Guess we better start walking."

It wasn't long before they chanced on what seemed like a farm compound – house and barns at the top of a hill, vineyards cascading down the slopes, and pastures with a notable absence of grazing animals. Even at this distance, they could detect movement near the farm house. Instinctively, they dropped to their bellies and crawled to the cover of some bushes on the bank of the nearby creek. Peering through the binoculars, Frank whispered, "Krauts. Loading up their vehicles." Handing the binoculars to Ray, he added, "Looks like they're in a hurry to get out of there."

"Yeah. I wonder what's in those satchels? And are those baskets full of food?" Ray handed the binoculars back to Frank.

"Could be. Any idea what they might have been doing there?"

"Hilltop position. Could be an observation post of some sort. Watching our movements . . . directing artillery . . . maybe just radioing positions."

"Yeah, that's what I was thinking." They watched the German vehicles head down the lane and turn right on the main road. "You think maybe we ought to check it out?"

"Let's lay low and see if there's any more activity." They watched from the safety of the brush for another two hours. Nothing stirred around the house or barns. No vehicles arrived. No unusual sounds disturbed the pastoral scene.

"I'm hungry," said Ray. "You think they took all the food with them?"

"I guess there's only one way to find out."

The big barn was between the creek and the house. Frank made a dash for it as Ray covered him. Standing just inside the barn door, Frank held his own rifle at the ready while Ray ran across the open ground. Frank put his finger to his lips, then pointed upward toward the hay loft. "Noises," he mouthed. "Someone's hiding." They took cover behind a half wall.

"*C'é qualcuno qui?*" Frank called out. Anyone here? He waited for a reply, hoping against hope he wouldn't need to resort to German. Nothing.

"*Buon giorno. Mi chiamo Francesco. Sono Americano.*" Hello. My name is Francesco. I'm American.

Now there was more rustling above, a male voice, barely audible, and what Frank could only describe as a whimper. He stepped out into the open area of the barn, saying, "*Siamo americani. Vogliamo aiutarli.*" We want to help you.

To his surprise, seven sets of wide eyes peered over the hayloft edge like swallows looking out of their nest. A middle-aged man and woman, four young children covered in sprigs of hay, and a beautiful girl about Frank's age, all tightly gripping the loft rail and looking as if they'd seen a ghost.

The man reached back into the loft, and Frank and Ray were immediately on alert, their rifles at the ready. The children screamed as the man pushed them out of sight behind a stack of hay. The girl hid behind a post.

Frank said, "Stop. Hold it right there."

The man quickly raised his hands in surrender, dropping something, while the woman made the sign of the cross. Ray yelled, "Keep your hands up."

"What was that you dropped?" Frank asked.

"Br . . . bread basket," the man stuttered. "This is my farm. This is my family. This is our last loaf of bread. You can have it. Just don't shoot."

Frank motioned to the man, who came slowly down the rickety wooden ladder holding his basket out to the side. Ray kept an eye on the loft while Frank inspected the basket, discovering nothing more threatening than a stale loaf of bread. "*Come si chiama?*" Frank asked. What's your name?

"Ernesto Perna. And this is my wife," he pointed up to the loft where the children had re-emerged from behind the hay bales, "and our children. We have been hiding here in the barn since the Germans came. Three days ago, they shot my neighbor – threw his body off the hill like an animal. They ate everything from our garden and slaughtered our last cow. Only a few chickens remain."

Frank and Ray had seen the devastation wreaked by the Germans as they'd walked from their last hideout. Mounds of rich soil in disarrayed piles around huge craters created by mortar blasts. Destroyed fences that could no longer contain the cattle. The stinky carcass of a dead water buffalo. Frank had farmed in Texas and knew what crops and livestock meant to the survival of a farm family.

"How long have you been hiding here, Mr. Perna?" he asked. "What have you been eating?"

"A few days." Ernesto still seemed unsure about trusting these two soldiers who'd appeared from out of nowhere.

"More than a week, Papa," the beautiful girl seemed unafraid of correcting her father.

"Do you know what happened two days ago?" Frank asked.

Ernesto looked at Frank, then Ray, then back to Frank, "I don't know what you're talking about."

"Italy joined the Allies. We're on the same side now," Frank said proudly.

"Then why are you bombing us?" the beautiful girl yelled from the loft. "I heard your planes."

"We're trying to push the Nazis out – trying to get them out of Altavilla and the hills around here. They know the territory; they know where to hide; and they don't negotiate. So we have to bomb them."

"Why should we trust you?" Ernesto said.

"We're here to give you your freedom back," Frank replied. "Would you rather trust the Germans?"

Finally, Ernesto smiled. A smile that told his family it was safe to come down. He introduced them as they descended the ladder, ending with, "My eldest daughter, Ida."

As Frank took Ida's hand to help her off the ladder, their eyes locked for a moment and he felt an inner trembling. She was stunning. Deep, piercing brown eyes and perfectly formed lips. But those eyes and lips betrayed her distrust as she sized up this new set of soldiers who'd invaded her home.

Ray did his best with a few words of broken Italian tinged with the bit of Spanish he knew from home. "Mr. Perna . . . uh . . . *bellissima famalia.*"

"*Grazie!*" Ernesto responded proudly.

Frank finally snapped out of his spell and returned to the conversation. With Frank providing the translation, he and Ray told them about the landings in Salerno Bay and how the British and Americans were here to help drive the Nazis out. As the adults talked, the younger children ran around the barn, enjoying the freedom they'd been denied since the arrival of the Germans.

Suddenly Carmela screamed. "*Ernesto! Dove è Beppe?*" She jerked her head all around, scanning the barn, looking for their youngest child. Pulling at her hair and shouting "*Beppe, dove sei?*" she ran around the barn peering behind hay bales and into milking stalls, desperate to find her baby. Frank glanced out the door and saw the child walking across the field toward the house. "*Signor Perna, eccolo.*" There he is. Frank pointed out the door. "Ray, stay here with Carmela and the children. We'll go after Beppe." They dashed out of the barn armed with nothing but Frank's rifle and a club-like piece of wood Ernesto grabbed as he ran out the door.

The child had quite a head start, so had almost reached the house. "We saw five Germans loading up their vehicles and leaving over two hours ago," Frank told Ernesto as they ran, ducking and dodging among the vines for cover, "but I've no idea if they left anyone behind." A noise from the direction of the barn caught his attention, and he looked back just as Ida ran out to follow them. Damn, Ray, he thought, how did she get away from you? Now he had to look out for Ida behind them and Beppe ahead and hope there was no one left in the house.

The rifle shot rang out before Frank could decide whether to wait for Ida or plunge ahead after Beppe. Ida screamed. Frank shouted "Take cover," and she scurried into the vines.

Frank scanned their surroundings, but the sniper was completely out of sight. From the sound, he guessed the shot came from inside the house. "Let's get to the cover of that smaller barn," he told Ernesto, "then we'll make a dash for it." When they looked around the corner of the barn, Beppe was nowhere to be seen. Had he just walked up onto the porch and inside?

Rifle at the ready and club in hand, Frank and Ernesto sprinted for the side of the house then froze in position, listening for any sound of voices or movement inside. Frank risked a quick peek in the window. A Nazi helmet on the bed, uniform jacket hanging on the door. The Germans had left at least one man behind. With short whispers and hand signals, Frank relayed his plan to Ernesto.

Seeing no one as they peeked around the corner of the house, they ran for the front door and stopped on opposite sides of it to listen once again. Frank used his fingers to count one . . . two . . . three . . . and they stormed the entrance. Not a soul in sight. No sign of the sniper. No sign of Beppe. Dear God, Frank thought, please don't let the Krauts have captured the child. Rifle at the ready, he began to search the rooms. The parlor, clear. Back into the hallway. He heard a sound from the next room, and Beppe wandered out toward the front door, his attention focused on the toy in his hands.

Suddenly, the back door slammed. Frank ran through the house and out the back, but the soldier – carrying a rifle but without his helmet – was behind a shed. Frank checked on Ernesto and Beppe to make sure they were safe and no other Germans were in the house. Then he turned his attention back to the Nazi soldier. As Frank got into position to see behind the shed, he saw the German soldier running over a hill, a bit too far for an accurate shot. Frank fired once anyway, just to make sure the man kept running toward the ridge and didn't circle back to the farm.

Back inside, he checked to make sure Ida was okay. She had caught up to them and was cradling Beppe in her arms. The sniper's shot had just barely grazed her arm, but Ernesto was hovering like a mother hen nonetheless.

"Ida, why didn't you stay in the barn like I asked?" Frank said.

She replied, "I watched what they did to my neighbor, and I wasn't going to let that happen to my baby brother."

"You were close to being killed yourself." He looked at her and saw the fight in her eyes. The compassion, the fearlessness to protect her family. Much as he felt for his own family.

With everyone safe for now, Frank decided to see what was over the ridge. He quickly found a vantage point where he could see below, and his jaw dropped at the sight. At least ten tanks plus support vehicles in the distance, a mile – maybe a bit more – away. Through his binoculars, he could make out the swastikas on the tanks. Troops were gathered in groups, receiving orders. Unquestionably, battle preparations underway. And the sniper was still running toward them, carrying the news that American soldiers were in the vicinity.

He wasted no time getting back. While he was gone, Ernesto had surveyed the house and now was ranting about all the damage the Germans had done and the valuable things they'd stolen. He was red-faced and angry, futilely punching his fists in the air at an enemy who would never feel his wrath. Ida, still reticent and unsmiling, murmured, "*Grazie per aver salvato il mio fratello.*" Thank you for saving my brother. But there was no time for niceties.

"Look, Ernesto," Frank interrupted the older man's ravings, "I'm sorry for your loss, but we have to get out of here. There's a German tank battalion just over the ridge, about to get underway. We have to get your family to safety. Come on, let's go. You can worry about things here once it's safe to return."

Back at the barn, Frank filled Ray in on the situation. "We've got to find my unit," he told the Pernas. "They were supposed to be taking Altavilla."

This was just what Ernesto needed. To be able to do something useful to protect his family. And now he had two American soldiers to help. "If the Americans have taken Altavilla, we can go there. It's not so far. I have this old truck." He led them to the back of the barn. "I've been working on it at night, hoping to get it to start. With any luck, there's enough gas to get us there."

While Frank told the family what was about to happen, Ernesto and Ray rolled the truck out of the barn, and Ernesto jumped into the driver's seat. When he hit the starter button on the floor, nothing happened but grinding and more grinding. He paused to fiddle with the choke.

And there it was . . . the roar of tanks and trucks in the distance. They had to get out of here now. Ray raised the hood of the truck and poked around at a few things, then signaled Ernesto to try again. Finally, the engine fired up with a huge puff of smoke out the tailpipe. Ray slammed the hood shut and everyone dashed to the old truck.

Frank helped Carmela and the children climb over the tailgate and then crawled in the back to look out for them. Ray jumped in the cab with Ernesto. It was a bumpy ride across the fields, but Ernesto knew a path that would get them on the road to Altavilla.

They turned left onto the road, which wasn't much smoother, suffering from the effects of heavy military traffic and repeated bombardments. Ernesto shifted gears leaving a plume of dust behind. Going uphill put a drag on the old engine with this load. At the top of the hill, Frank looked back down the road. The sight through his binoculars was anything but comforting – a column of German tanks headed in their direction. Ernesto had said the Nazis wouldn't relinquish Altavilla easily, and it looked like he was right.

"Holy cow!" Frank shouted "Signor Perna! Step on it, they're coming!" Frank yelled.

The old truck sputtered and jolted. Ernesto pressed on, pulling the choke to full throttle and pushing the accelerator to the floor, frantically holding on to the steering wheel as they bounced all over the road. Ida sighed and murmured, "Thank heavens the town is only a few kilometers ahead." She and Frank huddled over the bouncing children and tried to allay their fears by pretending they were riding a rollercoaster. But they both knew the danger was real. And Frank also knew he had to get to his commanders to tell them what was coming.

The terrain was quite hilly, so his view of the approaching column came and went as the truck pressed onward, but the sound never diminished. Just before they crested the last hill before the town, he got a really good look. Tanks in the lead. Canvas-covered troop trucks. Jeep-like vehicles with mounted weapons. More trucks carrying bazookas. Thankfully, the pace of the tanks was limiting the speed of the column's advance.

Just outside the town, they came to a checkpoint, US military vehicles barricading the road and soldiers with guns drawn and aimed at the approaching truck. Ray hung out the window and Frank stood up in the bed of the truck, both doing everything they could to make their US uniforms visible as Ernesto slowed the truck to a halt. The soldiers at the barricade finally took their weapons out of firing position and ran up to the vehicle. Frank and Ray gave a hurried update on their situation. "You need to get yourselves and these people to the command post," said the lieutenant in charge. "Back at a place called the Tobacco Factory."

Frank translated for Ernesto. "*Sì. Il Tabacchificio Fiocche,*" he replied. "I know the place – it's near Persano. Last I heard, the Germans had taken it over."

"We control it now," said the lieutenant. "Corporal," he beckoned to one of the men, "take a jeep and escort these people."

The two vehicles sped off in the direction of the Tobacco Factory. It wasn't long before they began to hear distant sounds of battle – explosions that said the Germans were intensifying their efforts to repel the American invaders. The children covered their ears and grimaced in fear at each blast. Ida held Beppe tightly. "*Non abbia pauro, bambino.*" Don't be afraid, baby. "Our new friends will look out for us."

# CHAPTER 6

The old Tobacco Factory was a scene of utter chaos: infantry teams setting up perimeter defenses, transport and logistics units trying to get vehicles and fuel organized, communications teams setting up radio stations, medics tending wounded soldiers, orders barked at the top of men's lungs, adjutants getting a makeshift headquarters organized, hungry soldiers downing C-rations whenever they could grab a minute between tasks, some soldiers grabbing a few minutes of much-needed sleep, others cleaning and readying their weapons for the next assault. Frank, Ray, and Ernesto piled out of the truck and headed toward what looked like a group of senior officers studying maps at a small field table.

When waiting for someone to notice them got no results, Frank cleared his throat and said, "Excuse me, sirs."

A captain rounded on them, looking thoroughly irritated at the interruption. "Not now, soldier. Can't you see we're busy here?" And then, as an afterthought, he added, "How'd you get through here anyway?"

"We're just in from the field, sir. And we have some intelligence you'll want."

"Go find your lieutenant and tell *him* whatever it is you think's so important. And get that civilian out of here." He seemed to have only just noticed Ernesto. "Could be a spy, for all you know."

"Sir, we just need five minutes of your time."

"You have your orders, soldier. Now follow them."

A major in the group who'd been watching the exchange appeared to notice Frank's reluctance to leave. "Not so fast, Captain. Let's find out what the man knows."

Frank and Ray explained how they'd gotten separated from their unit and stumbled onto the Perna farm and what they'd seen on their escape. "When we left the checkpoint, sir, the German column was advancing on Altavilla in force. I'm sure that checkpoint's been overrun by now."

"Damn." The major shook his head in frustration and looked back at the map. "I thought we had that town secured."

"If our troops are anywhere near there, sir, they're probably in the midst of a raging battle even as we speak. Sir, with respect, I think you should listen to what Signor Perna here has to say about the German movements. He's been watching them, and he knows the terrain and their hideouts."

"He speak English?" asked the captain, unwilling to completely let go of his irritation.

"Just let the man speak, Captain," said the major.

Ernesto walked toward the map. "Here and here and there." He pointed as Frank translated. "Those are the best places for the Krauts to go to ground and either prepare an ambush or regroup for an all-out assault on your positions. They started from this location when they first took Altavilla. From the top floor, I can point out some landmarks they'll use." They all trooped upstairs. "You can see from up here, sir, how they controlled the roads from this spot. Once they get Altavilla back, my guess is that they'll come after your positions here next. They won't retreat easily."

"Damn," the major said again, surveying the scene. "We expected resistance but not an all-out counterattack. Captain, get back downstairs and rework those plans." Thoroughly chastised, the captain couldn't retreat down the stairway fast enough. The major descended more slowly, continuing the conversation with Frank and Ernesto.

"Get Mr. Perna some food, Sergeant, then bunk here for the night. The 143rd's up in the hills. Just find a squad to hook up with for now."

"Sir, we've got the whole Perna family out in the truck – five children in all. This is no place for them."

"You're right about that. Most of the locals have evacuated to churches that aren't in the path of the fighting. I'll show you on the map. Haas, you stay here. We need every man we can get. Moster, your orders are to get that family to safety and guard the church overnight. Load up with some more ammo before you leave. We'll pick you up in the morning."

"Sir, I've no idea how much gas is in that truck – if it will even get us to that church."

"Corporal!" the major shouted at a soldier running past. "Get a jerry can and fill up this man's truck."

Frank saluted the major and was about to leave. "One more thing, Sergeant. We've had reports of some sniper fire from the hills around here. Keep everyone low in the back of that truck and don't waste time on the roads."

"Yes, sir!" Frank saluted again. "And thank you, sir."

Frank found the improvised quartermaster location and loaded up on ammo, ration packs, and chocolate bars for the children. By the time he got back to the truck, the gas had been poured in and Ernesto was ready to go. Frank climbed into the back with Ida and the children and handed a chocolate bar to Massimo. The boy's face lit up as he unwrapped it and took a bite. Finally, Ida smiled – first at the children as she divided the rest of the bar among them and then at Frank.

"Your Italian is very good."

"My parents were from Italy. We spoke Italian at home until . . ." His voiced quivered and he looked away.

"I'm sorry. I didn't mean to upset you," Ida said.

"It's okay. I just miss my family."

"Do you have brothers and sisters?"

Frank hesitated, unsure if he was ready to reveal the heartbreak of his past to a girl who was still very much a stranger. Instead, he boomeranged the question back to Ida. "Why don't you tell me about Italy and your wonderful family?"

"My father was born here and has farmed this land all his life. From childhood, he knew he wanted to marry my mother, and as soon as her parents would let them, Papa asked his father for land to start a family and a life of his own. Papa promised to keep up the family tradition of working the land, so Grandpa carved off a large section of the family estate and gave it to them for a wedding present. My parents always wanted a big family, and Papa likes to brag about us. 'Boys,' he says, 'to inherit the farm and girls as beautiful as their mother.'" Ida dropped her eyes in embarrassment.

"Go on," Frank encouraged her. "Tell me about your life on the farm."

"We grow vegetables and a few olives and some fruit. And you saw the vineyards. We had livestock, of course . . . a few cows and pigs and chickens . . . and a whole herd of water buffalo that my parents built up from the three they bought soon after they married. The buffalo pulled the plows, but their milk also makes the most delicious cheese.

"Papa didn't just work the farm, though. He was leader of the local land improvement cooperative that built and maintained irrigation systems for the farms. Massimo and I loved to ride around with him in this old truck when he went to check the water levels." She paused. The wistfulness in her voice tore at Frank's heartstrings.

"I wish you could see Altavilla – or at least the Altavilla we knew before the war. It sits atop two ridges with sloping terraces all around. Some say the site was where the final battle of Spartacus occurred. From there, you can see the Gulf of Salerno and the rivers that flow into it. When all this is over, I want to go back to Salerno and along the Amalfi coast and over to Capri. It's so beautiful – I've read it's one of the most beautiful coasts in the entire world.

"You know," she retreated from her dreams to the tale of her family, "the south of Italy is not so rich, but we had a good life. We all pitched in. Even Massimo started helping Papa in the fields when he was just a boy. We had enough from the farm to feed ourselves and live comfortably. And sometimes enough to sell in the markets so Papa and Mama could put a little extra money back for the future. But that all changed when the Nazis came."

She stroked Beppe's hair and kissed his forehead as the truck slowed. They'd arrived at the church. Ernesto parked the truck close by – they could only hope it would be safe on the streets – there was no place to put it under shelter. A number of families had already taken refuge in the sanctuary. The priests had gathered as many pillows and blankets as they could find in the town, and there were still a few that hadn't been claimed. Ernesto found an unoccupied side chapel where the family could bed down together.

The next morning, Frank produced the rations he'd collected at the Tobacco Factory. "It tastes pretty dreadful," he said, "but at least it's food." The younger children took one bite and pushed the rations away.

"You have to eat," Carmela scolded them. "It's not polite to refuse when your friend gives you something to eat." The children grimaced and reluctantly reached for the rations, but they just poked at the unsavory food. So Frank made a game of it, scrunching up his face and holding his nose with every bite. It didn't take long before the kids were laughing and mimicking him, and before long, all the ration packs were empty. Carmela and the girls did what they could to fix their hair and freshen up. Then they all sat down in the chapel to wait.

"What now?" asked Ernesto.

"I'm afraid it will be a bit of a waiting game," Frank replied. "The captain asked me to make sure you were safe here at the church and keep watch over you for now, so I'm here for the day and maybe longer. They'll scout the area around your farm, and if the Germans have moved away, as we suspect, you'll be able to return tomorrow."

"Well, yesterday I told you about my family," said Ida. "You said yours was from Italy, but where in Italy?"

"My mother was from Salerno, but my father came from Corleone, in Sicily."

"Corleone – that's a dangerous place," said Ernesto.

"Exactly. That's why they left. But things didn't get much better from there."

"What happened?" asked Ida.

"It's a long story."

"Well, looks like we're here for a while with nothing but time on our hands. Maybe your storytelling will keep the children entertained." She gathered Beppe in her lap, and Frank began his tale.

"I was really young when our family lived in New York," Frank began. "So young I'm not sure how much I actually remember and how much is from the stories my older brother Tony told me. Either way, it's the story of my life so it feels like real memories."

# CHAPTER 7

*New York City, 1919*

Pasquale and Catherine Peccaro came to America like so many Italians in 1912 – looking for opportunity and to escape the poverty and the Mafia control in Sicily. They came with nothing but their clothes, but Pasquale was industrious and determined to make a better life for his family. The immigrant neighborhood where they lived was like so many in New York – five-story tenements blending one into the next, creating a seemingly endless brick palisade as far as the eye could see. The only thing that broke the monotony was the balconies. Some were empty or in poor repair – just metal hanging from the brick wall. Others were more cheerful, filled with pots of colorful flowers. Many served a more practical purpose. For Catherine, it was a place to hang clothes to dry. For the Peccaro children, it was a place to watch the outside world and to access the fire-escape ladders they loved to climb.

The main entrance to their building was an old, creaking wooden door that was never locked and that opened into a small entryway with a winding staircase that gave access to all five floors. The apartments were small – just two rooms and a tiny kitchen – with sparse furnishings. The bedroom had nothing more than a couple of mattresses on the floor, a small wooden dresser for the four children, and a chest for the adults.

But it was down below, at street level, where the neighborhood came to life. Colorful awnings for the storefronts and canvas canopies on the sidewalk for the street peddlers created a continuous, perpetual market on both sides of the street. There were pushcarts offering fresh vegetables, fish, meats, and sausages. Bins outside the green grocers overflowed with all manner of fruits and vegetables. Clothing and dry goods hung in shop windows or filled the tables of the sidewalk vendors. Others sold spices, cheeses, salamis, dried meats. The street was alive with the sights, sounds, and smells of a bustling community.

Pasquale had a small shop where he sold fruits and vegetables and goods from Italy that he bought from incoming ships. Tony sometimes helped his father, bringing boxes up from the basement or helping the more affluent customers load purchases into their cars. Pasquale managed to make enough money to pay the rent and feed his family, but with four children, there wasn't much left over for extras. Their clothes were worn, and Tony was growing so fast that his knee-pants barely reached the tops of his boots, which were also getting too small for him. But that didn't stop him being cheerful and clever and helpful with his younger siblings.

Despite the hardships, life in New York was still an improvement over what it had been in Sicily. And in 1919, it looked like things were about to take a turn for the better. As Tony loaded twelve cases of heavy bottles into a Model T, he watched as his father counted several large bills and shook hands with the customer. No sooner had the Model T pulled away than its place was taken by a shiny new Packard Twin Six with large curving fenders covering metal-spoked wheels and white-sidewall tires. Two bug-eyed headlights sat on either side of the front grille, and top was down, revealing the luxurious leather of the interior.

The man who got out of the car was obviously rich. He wore a fancy suit and fine leather shoes that looked like they'd just been shined. He had a long, thick scar on one cheek and dark, bushy eyebrows and towered over Pasquale. "Inside, Peccaro," he ordered. Tony started to follow, thinking he'd be needed to help load this car too, but his father signaled him to stay on the sidewalk. Tony couldn't make out what they were saying, but it was obvious they were arguing. The rich man kept shaking his finger in Pasquale's face, and Pasquale looked agitated. When the rich man came back out on the sidewalk, he said, "You know what you have to do, Peccaro." Then he walked off down the street, stopping at other merchants, helping himself to whatever he wanted from the tables or bins. No one challenged him. No one asked him to pay. And a few of the vendors quietly handed him an envelope or a small package.

When the Packard finally drove away, Tony asked his father, "Who was that man?"

"His name's Petrillo, but you don't need to worry about him."

"What did he mean when he said you know what you have to do?"

"It's complicated, Tony, but nothing I can't take care of."

That night, Tony lay awake thinking about the baseball he'd gotten for his birthday and puzzling over his father's anxiety about the visit from Petrillo. His mother was asleep on the other mattress. Pasquale was still in the sitting room. It was late, and he wondered why his father hadn't come to bed. Then he heard the creaking of the front door to the building being opened followed by footsteps coming up the stairs. There was a knock on the apartment door, and Tony heard his father cross the room to answer it.

The wallpaper in the bedroom was peeling off in places, and there was a spot on the wall that adjoined the sitting room where an opening in the wooden lath was exposed. Tony peered through. His father was arguing with someone. Then he got a good look at the man – it was Petrillo. But Petrillo wasn't the only stranger in the room. The other one was a huge man with dark brown hair and a thick mustache with a five-day stubble on his face. He wore a black suit and a pullover wool cap on his head. All three spoke the Sicilian dialect, and the threatening tone of the visitors alarmed Tony.

"Pasquale, you're selling your alcohol in *our* territory. You know we own this neighborhood," said Petrillo.

The thug added, "Yeah. Whodaya think you are?!"

Petrillo ignored him. "You pay the *pizzo* or suffer the consequences. It's very simple. Just a small percentage, *capisce*? Our piece."

Tony knew what *pizzo* meant – a payoff, your protection payment. His father had told him how the *mafiosi* controlled everything in Sicily and how he'd come to America to escape them. Now it seemed he was face to face with what he'd hoped to escape.

Tony looked at his father, a man in his early thirties with a strapping physique. He could be aggressive and courageous, especially when it came to defending his family. But Petrillo towered over him, and the thug looked like he wouldn't hesitate to beat up anyone whenever his boss gave the word.

"And if you don't pay up," Petrillo continued, "either you move your moonshine business out of our territory, or we'll move you and your family out of here. Your wife will find your body in a barrel. Do you want that to happen?"

Pasquale stuck to his guns. "This is America. I have as much right to live here and sell here as you do."

"Tell him about America, Rocco," Petrillo told the thug.

"Yeah, this is America. So this is the American Cosa Nostra, *capisce*? You wanna do business in this neighborhood, you show us your loyalty. You pay da protection. First payment tonight. Then we decide how much you pay and what you and your family can do for us."

Pasquale said nothing, just folded his arms over his chest.

"We seen you collecting money today. Now where is it?" Still Pasquale said nothing. Tony knew his father kept his money in a coffee can near the woodpile by the stove. He hoped his father wasn't going to give them the fifty dollars he'd been saving or the money he'd gotten from today's sale. They needed it for groceries and rent.

Petrillo started wandering around, picking up odds and ends. He picked up the coffee can. Pasquale tried to grab it, but Petrillo had a solid grip on it and jerked it back.

Rocco pulled a pistol out of his jacket. As Tony watched through the slit, Pasquale grabbed a large, heavy log from the woodpile and hurled it at Rocco, hitting him in the head and knocking the pistol out of his hand. Rocco lurched toward Pasquale. Pasquale threw two punches, one a blow to the abdomen that forced Rocco to bend over, grab his gut, and stumble. As Rocco and Pasquale fought, Petrillo picked up the pistol and fired. Pasquale fell to the floor and the two men ran out the door. One turned around as Tony entered the room and said, "Boy, don't mess with us," then slammed the door and headed down the stairs.

The gunshot woke Catherine and the other children. Tony hurried over to his father's body, his mother right behind him. She screamed when she saw Pasquale on the floor in a pool of blood. He was gurgling as Catherine dropped to the floor beside him and propped his head in her lap. "Tony," he wheezed, "you're the man of the family now." And then he took his last breath. Tony ran to the balcony, saw the men on the street below, and climbed down the fire escape. By the time he made it to a first-floor balcony, they were driving away.

Back upstairs, Tony tried to comfort his mother, but she was inconsolable. His father's silver cross – the one he wore on a chain under his T-shirt – the only thing of any value that he owned – was dangling from his neck, covered in blood. Tony took it off and put it around his own neck. He was the man of the family now.

By then, all the children had wandered into the living room, Frank holding a small wooden soldier puppet from Italy that his father had given him. Tony knew Frank was too young to understand, so he gathered his little brother in his arms and rocked back and forth, trying, unsuccessfully, to hold back his tears. But through his tears, he kept repeating, "You'll pay for this, Petrillo. One day I'll find you and make you pay."

# CHAPTER 8

*September 1943*

Frank's story was interrupted by the arrival of a platoon of American soldiers. The leader, a second lieutenant, started barking orders. "All you people get your belongings together. You can't stay here. We're moving you out to some place safer." The man looked like he couldn't be more than eighteen or nineteen. Field promotions in the wake of the devastating loss of life on the beach were putting men in positions they were totally unprepared for, and this one seemed to think shouting made him sound more like he was in charge. When his words were met with blank stares, Frank stood up.

Before he could even get his hand up in a salute, the officer snapped at him. "Just what are you doing here, Sergeant? Trying to hide out with these civilians? My orders are to get them moved, and then I'll figure out what to do with you."

Frank stood his ground and completed his salute, hoping proper military protocol would convince this young upstart that he wasn't a deserter. "And my orders, sir, were to guard these civilians overnight. You must be the group I was told would pick me up here today."

"I don't know anything about that, but I'll figure out what to do with you later." And then he turned his attention back to the civilians. "Come on, people. Hop to it! We're moving out *now*!"

No one moved.

"Begging your pardon, sir," Frank said, "these people don't understand a word you're saying. I speak Italian. If you'll tell me what you want them to do and where you're taking them, I'll get everything organized for you."

The officer looked Frank up and down, apparently trying to decide if he could be trusted. In his peripheral vision, Frank noticed some of the other soldiers rolling their eyes and shaking their heads at the officiousness of their new commander. He'd heard stories about how hard it was to break in a newly minted second looey, and now he was seeing it with his own eyes.

"All right, Sergeant. There are trucks outside, and we're taking them to our headquarters in Altavilla. Get them organized and into the trucks. But we're pulling out of here in fifteen minutes and anyone not in the trucks gets left behind. Got it?"

"Got it, sir."

"And just remember I'm watching you. Don't get any ideas."

As soon as Frank explained what was happening, there was a mad scramble to gather up whatever people had brought with them. That was the cue for the other soldiers to pitch in and help – and a few of them even had Hershey bars for the children. The officer stood at the front door, glaring at the proceedings and trying to look important.

"Wait here," Frank told the Pernas, then walked up to the officer. "Sir, this family has their own truck. It's how we got here last night from the Tobacco Factory. Permission for them to join the convoy rather than leave their truck behind."

"Can they keep up?"

What Frank wanted to tell this bastard was, "They could lead you there better than you can find your own way – hell, better than you could find your own ass," but he bit his tongue. Making this guy angry wouldn't help the Pernas and might just get him assigned to KP for the rest of the war. "They can keep up, sir. We outran a German column yesterday afternoon." No need to mention, he thought, that what we outran was a bunch of tanks.

"All right. Tell them to get in the middle of the line. But if they slow things down, I'm leaving them behind. Got it?"

"Yes, sir."

"And you're riding with me. I don't want you getting any ideas."

"Yes, sir." Now, as he went back to help the Pernas, it was his turn to roll his eyes. Just hope there's someone where we're going, he thought, who can sort things out.

When they got to Altavilla, the civilians were routed to a separate area on the edge of the main camp so Frank didn't get a chance to say goodbye to the Pernas. The upstart officer, still determined that Frank was AWOL, dragged him to the command tent and was surprised to get a thorough dressing down from the CO of the 143rd. "Sergeant Moster's my best translator, Lieutenant. If he was with a group of civilians, then there's a damn good reason for it. So next time you take it upon yourself to drag someone in here for a court martial, you better be *damn sure* you've got your facts straight or you can kiss those gold bars good-bye. Now get your ass out of here and back to whatever you're supposed to be doing." The lieutenant couldn't salute and skedaddle fast enough.

The CO turned to Frank. "All right, Moster, find your squad. We're hunkering down here for a while to regroup and wait for reinforcements. There's a bridge to repair and the water supply to fix, and if we have time after that, I want to build some goodwill with the locals. Might need you for that."

"Yes, sir. Thank you, sir."

With help from some engineers dispatched from the Tobacco Factory, the men of the 143rd had the repairs completed in a matter of days, but the reinforcements had still not arrived, and new plans from Fifth Army command for the advance to Rome hadn't come down. So the next assignment was to help the locals, and Frank knew exactly who he wanted to help. He quickly discovered the Pernas had been allowed to return to their farm, the scouting reports having shown that the Germans had abandoned that area. Transportation was his problem. The master sergeant in charge of the motor pool wasn't about to let one of his precious jeeps be used for "a jaunt off to some God-forsaken farm," as he put it, so Frank had to improvise. Wandering through the town, he found a discarded bicycle that was in surprisingly good condition – good enough, at least, to get him to the farm and back.

When he knocked on the door, Ida answered. "Frank. What a surprise! Come in." She sounded genuinely happy to see him.

"Is everyone okay? I'm really glad you were able come home."

"Yes, we're happy to be back. But how did you get here?"

"I rode this from Altavilla." He pointed to the bike, where he'd leaned it against the porch. "Our orders while we wait for reinforcements are to help the locals, so I came to see if there's anything I can do here."

"You saw the damage to our farm when you were here last . . . lots of work ahead. I'm sure Papa would appreciate any help he can get. Where did you get that bike?"

"It was abandoned in a debris pile in town."

"Do you mind if I take it for a spin?" She flashed him a flirty smile.

"Sure. I'll go find your father and see what he needs done."

Ida took off on the bike.

•   •   •

What Ida hadn't mentioned to Frank was her intent to ride into Altavilla. She rode to an old store, hopped off the bike, and leaned it against the wall, hoping no one would take it. Frank wouldn't be happy if she lost it. Looking around to make sure no one was watching, she went quietly down the steps to the basement, not knowing if anyone had discovered this place. She knocked on the metal portion of the door – a double knock then a triple knock followed by an exact repetition of the sequence. A young man she knew peered through a peephole – he was a member of her biking club, their cover for their resistance efforts. She listened as he unlatched a series of locks then opened the door just enough for her to squeeze in and quickly shut it behind her. As her friend secured all the locks, Ida looked around the room. The printing equipment was still intact.

"Ida, I'm so glad to see you. Come in, have a seat. Sal . . . Marco . . . so many of us are missing." He sat down and continued to work. She watched as he carefully attached photographs on forged identification documents.

"I heard Sal was forced onto a train out of town, but I didn't know about the others. I hid Sal's brochures in our barn. My father was upset when he found them, so I had to destroy them."

"I still have a few. And we really need to get them to Battipaglia along with some maps. They contain coded information on locals that are on our side and the locations of German barracks and stations. But I've got my hands full here."

"I'll take them – is tomorrow okay?" Ida replied, eager to help despite the risk of incurring her father's anger yet again.

"You have to be very careful. There are barricades with German soldiers posted at the edges of Battipaglia and stationed in the city."

"Don't worry. I can handle it."

"I have an even bigger problem, but it involves a lot of risk," he said hesitantly.

"What's that?" Ida was always ready for an adventure.

"Well, I had hoped to send Sal since it's dangerous. If you get caught, you'd be subject to strict interrogation . . . possibly torture . . . even death. I don't think this is a job for a woman."

"What is it? You know I've completed other dangerous missions." She couldn't keep the indignance out of her voice. Why would he insult her by implying she wasn't fit for the job? She was one of the few women who really put her heart into this work. Was he still smarting because she'd beaten him in the last biking competition before everything fell apart? Or because she always did better than in him in school? His lack of trust in her ability was offensive.

"I don't have a lot of choice. We're short on manpower with all that's going on. You'd need to be extra careful and if you lose this, or get caught, you'd be putting us all in danger." He looked at her straight-on.

"What is it?" she persisted.

"Well, you know the forged identity documents require a special stamp. The stampers are difficult to copy, but I have one, and it needs to go to our people in Battipaglia. The Nazis know we're making these false documents, and they have the SS cracking down, trying to find our presses and stampers. If you get caught with this, there's no telling what might happen. They might just shoot you on the spot." He paused, holding the stamper in his hand, and waited for her to back out.

"I can do it." She took the stamper for a good look. It had a small cylindrical wooden handle with a circular stamp on the end of it.

"Looks easy to conceal," she said and put it in her pocket.

"Be careful and don't get caught. This isn't just an adventure. And there's more at stake than just your pride, Ida." He walked her to the door and locked it behind her.

The bike was where she'd left it. At least she wouldn't have to explain that to Frank. On the way back to the farm, she started making her plan. She'd need something to make her delivery legitimate. Food. No one would question that. Especially if she had more than one basketful. But in her enthusiasm to do something for the cause, she'd overlooked one small detail – her own bike was in serious need of repair. Could she wheedle Frank out of the use of this one for a day? How could she do that without him – or worse, her father – becoming suspicious? She'd have to figure something out. The one thing she was not going to do was go back to her friend and admit she couldn't fulfill the mission.

When she pedaled up to the house, Frank was waiting in the front yard. At least he was smiling. "So, you took a long ride on my bike. Off visiting a boyfriend?" he joked.

"No," she laughed. "I'm in a biking club, and after being cooped up in the barn and the church and your camp, I wanted to get my muscles back in shape. I can't afford to get flabby."

"That's great! You know, I was a rider at home in Texas. My brother and I loved biking. In fact, we rode eighty-three hundred miles across the United States a few years ago."

"Eighty-three hundred miles? That sounds impossible! But it explains those leg muscles!" she said.

He looked at her and winked, surprised that she'd noticed. "It was a trip I'll never forget. Tony and I left the farm in 1938 and rode eighty to a hundred miles a day to visit our parents' graves in New York."

"I'd love to hear about it."

"Maybe I'll tell you some day."

Suddenly she had an idea for her secret mission. "Hey, are you available for a ride tomorrow?"

"Why not?"

"It might be dangerous," she warned.

"Does this have something to do with your newsletter?"

"Papa told you about that, I suppose." She sounded just a little dejected. "Please don't tell him about this. It's really important, and it supports your cause. I need to get some pamphlets and maps to my associates in Battipaglia."

"You weren't thinking of riding there alone, were you? It's still controlled by the Nazis."

"Yes, I know. But this is what I've been doing for a while now, riding bikes under the guise of the local biking club. It was easy before. I'd just flirt with the soldiers . . . give them bread or fruit from my basket . . . and they never checked the underlining. Now that the invasion has started, they'll be suspicious of everything, including locals coming into Battipaglia. My cousin has a store in the town, and I think I can pull it off that I'm delivering goods to the store from our farm."

"Ida, that sounds risky. I'd hate for you to do that, especially alone."

"Well, big boy, come with me. These hills will tell me if you're a real rider!" she dared and then added, "And I could really use your help to make the delivery believable. You're Italian. I can get papers and clothes for you to pass for a civilian."

Frank thought about it, picturing in his mind a day of bike-riding with a beautiful Italian girl. What a contrast with the days of near-death on a beach landing! The thought that he still might die in this war convinced him he was entitled to at least one day of fun and risk. But more than anything, he didn't want her to go alone. "Okay, it's a deal. I have another day that I'm supposed to be helping the locals. I'm not sure this is quite what the CO meant, but why not? How are you going to smuggle those pamphlets through the checkpoint?"

"I'm still trying to work that out."

"I might have an idea for you. Let me see if we can hide them in the frame of the bike. I need some tools."

"Tools are in the barn. Come on."

Frank took apart the middle portion of the bike frame, where there was a large empty space. Ida put the maps and pamphlets there, and Frank reconnected the pieces of the frame. Unless someone totally dismantled the bike, they wouldn't find the documents.

"It's ingenious!" Ida beamed as she retrieved her own bike from a corner of the barn. The chain had slipped off, and it needed a new tire.

"And since you're so good with bikes, maybe you can help me fix mine," she said.

"I can probably find a tire – maybe a replacement wheel – somewhere in town," Frank said as he worked the chain back into place. "Then you'll be ready to ride."

"Great! Meet me here at dawn." She rummaged around in her father's toolbox and came up with a scrap of paper and a stubby pencil. Scribbling something on the paper, she handed it to Frank. "Now on your way home, stop by this address for your documents. You'll need to knock on the metal part of the door just like this . . ." She rapped on the wall of the barn and had him repeat the sequence until she was sure he had it right. "Give them my note. It's encoded but explains you can be trusted and why you're there. It won't take long."

After Frank left, Ida looked for a site to smuggle the stamper. She had to conceal it well, even from Frank. She rolled the stamper between her fingers and suddenly it occurred to her – the hollow handlebars. It would just fit.

# CHAPTER 9

The next morning, Frank left before sunrise and returned to the farm with the new tire and his false identification papers. Ida gave him civilian clothes, and they departed with baskets of grapes and fruit on their bikes. They pedaled on back roads through the hills, hoping to avoid any military action. But as soon as they rode into the German-occupied area, they were in real danger. They appeared innocent enough, but Frank knew if they were stopped, there would be questions about why he wasn't in the military. Ida had promised she'd have an explanation.

In just over an hour, they came to the outskirts of Battipaglia. Two German soldiers manned a barricade across the road into the city. There was enough space to ride a bicycle around the barricade, and Frank hoped they could just ride through quietly. Ida softly told him, "Just keep your cool."

"Halt! We must see your papers," the German guards shouted.

Frank felt sweat roll down the back of his shirt. He decided to let Ida talk; she obviously had done this before.

"We're making a delivery to our store in the city," Ida said.

"What store?" the soldier asked.

"*La Bottega*, in the center of town," Ida said.

"Get off your bikes." Ida's bike fell to the side as she was getting off. She reached for it quickly, her hand fumbling on the handgrip, but not before Frank heard a clanking noise in the handlebar. When she glanced at him, her expression had changed, and he noticed her lip quivering.

"Who is this man? Why is he not working or with his military unit?" the soldier barked.

"My brother. He's disabled. He can't hear well and he's slow. You know . . . mentally slow," Ida replied. "He helps me deliver fruit. Here . . . have an orange."

Frank felt the hair on the back of his neck stand up as the soldiers eyed him with their hands on their guns. He gazed off to the side with an empty look, his mouth hanging half open, pretending to be unfocused and clueless. The soldiers laughed and called him a poor imbecile, but seemed convinced, taking only a cursory look at identity papers before waving them through the checkpoint.

Once they were out of sight and out of earshot, Frank and Ida joked about his acting. Then he got serious. "What was the noise in the handlebar? I saw you grab the grip. Something you didn't tell me about?"

"We . . . uh . . . we're almost to the store."

"Look, you need to tell me. I want to know what I'm in for here," he said.

She pedaled faster, avoiding his question. Frank chased her as she led them to the store. By the time he caught up with her they were in front of *La Bottega* where several German soldiers were going inside.

They parked their bicycles, removed the baskets, and went in to look for her contact. It was quiet inside, but one of the soldiers kept eyeing them. When he finally turned away, Frank nudged Ida to look out the window. There were more soldiers outside, checking out their bikes. They looked at each other, and Frank could see the anxiety in Ida's face.

"Frank, follow me. Let's get the baskets to my uncle in the back of the store," Ida said. They dumped the fruit on the back counter and then went to return the baskets to the bracket on their bikes. As they walked out, two German officers were waiting.

"Are these your bikes?"

"Yes, sir."

"Show me your basket and your identification papers."

One officer took the baskets and tore the cloth linings to look inside while the other inspected their ID papers. Frank eavesdropped, hearing the younger officer address the older one as Einhart. Einhart was built like a tree with thick stocky arms bulging in the tailored Nazi uniform. His blonde hair, cut short, was barely visible under his helmet. All the wrinkles of his forehead crinkled together as he looked from Frank and Ida to their identification papers and back again.

Frank whispered to Ida, "They're suspicious of our delivery."

The soldiers found nothing in the baskets. The younger officer eyed the bikes, then took his knife and cut the beat-up leather of Ida's bicycle seat. He started to remove the seat.

Ida shouted, "Hey, I've got to ride that bike home."

"We will do as we please," Einhart shouted as the younger officer continued to inspect the bikes, pulling the seat off the frame. Frank's head pounded and his heart raced. Einhart ordered his junior to check the handlebars.

Frank's armpits filled with sweat, wondering what was in the handlebar. He glared at Ida with a look that could have turned her to stone. Her lip quivered again, and he could tell she was nervous.

The officer pulled the handgrips off and was about to look inside when a loud slam of the shop door drew everyone's attention to the oversized man bolting out with a bottle of wine in one hand and the other hand open. His palms were as beet red as his face, his hair graying, and his belly prominent.

"What's going on here, Einhart?" the man yelled.

"Do you know these people?" Einhart asked.

"Yes, my niece and nephew. They make deliveries. How the hell do you think I get all this fresh fruit your soldiers pilfer from my store?"

Einhart studied the ID documents awhile longer, then eyed Frank closely. Frank's heart was still pounding, and he could see beads of sweat on Ida's forehead although she managed to maintain her composure. "Well, if you can vouch for these two, I'll let them go. But we'll be on the watch for you." He shook his finger at Frank and Ida. "I better not see you after curfew or you're going straight to Gestapo headquarters." With a show of reluctance, he returned their papers.

"Einhart, come in. Have a drink." The Germans followed Ida's uncle into the store, but not before Einhart gave the two of them one last menacing look.

With the Germans off the street, Ida and Frank took the bikes back around to the alley where Ida's cousin was waiting. They quickly took Frank's bike apart and turned over the hidden documents. Ida pulled the handgrips off her bike and used a hook to pull the stamper out of the handlebar.

Frank's eyes went wide as he realized the extent of the danger.

Ida told her cousin, "You have to get the documents and the stamper to our safe house. Einhart will be suspicious if I go anywhere else."

"All right, but I have some documents to send back with you. They contain the latest locations of the German command here in the area. They've been moving around and sending reinforcements. Can you get these to the right people?"

"I know exactly where they need to go!" She looked at Frank and smiled.

While Frank hid the documents and put the bike back together, Ida's cousin produced a small bag. "Sandwiches and cheese for your trip back," he said.

"Thank you," Ida replied. "Now we've got to get out of town."

"You should have told me what you had in there," Frank admonished as they headed back toward the checkpoint.

"I thought the risk might keep you from coming."

"Maybe. But don't you think maybe next time I might not trust you?"

"What makes you think there'll be a next time?"

Frank was preparing his own retort when Ida pointed to the barricade ahead. "Look, Frank, the guards are leaving their post."

"Yeah. And quickly too. I'm not sure that's a good sign, but at least we don't have to play our act again," he laughed.

They pedaled fast to get out of town, and Ida chose a different route from the way they'd come. The hills were steep and Ida's pace made Frank sweat. She must have done this many times before, he thought, to do it so effortlessly.

Half an hour later, Ida asked, "How about we stop and take a break? I'm thirsty and a bit hungry. We have those sandwiches from the store. Let's get off the beaten path and find a picnic spot."

"Sounds good to me." Frank wanted a break from this pace. And besides, he was famished.

"There's a great scenic lookout point on the next hill, but we have to leave the main road. Follow me. We can follow the terraces. The zigzag makes the slope tolerable, but be careful. Stick close to the stone wall on this side of the path . . . the other side becomes a steep drop off. But it's worth it. At the top, you can see both sides of the hill and the valleys below. The view is incredible and if you can manage the path, it can be a shortcut over the mountain," Ida said as she took off.

It was a grueling trip up, but the reward at the top was indeed worth the effort. A spectacular view and a tree-shaded spot that was perfect for a picnic. They leaned the bikes against a tree and sat down to enjoy their sandwiches.

"You understood the guard," said Ida. "Where did you learn to speak German?"

"It's a long story. You remember I lost my parents in New York. After my father was murdered, my mom died from the flu in the 1919 epidemic. We had a rough time after that. Tony was scrounging for food, doing his best to feed us. My mother's friend, Giuseppe, tried to care for us in his apartment. I hate to tell you what we ate in those days, but in desperation, we went out at night and begged for scraps from the locals. Finally, Father Scott at our church hooked us up with the Children's Aid Society of New York. The rest of the story will answer your question. Do we have enough time?" She nodded yes.

# CHAPTER 10

*July 1920*

"There'll be food and clothes and people to take care of us," Tony told his siblings. "Father Scott thinks it's a good idea." Steve and Teresita didn't respond.

"I don't wanna to go," Frank whined. He was often inconsolable since the loss of both his parents.

"Frank, we can't continue this way, me and Steve sneaking out at night, trolling the streets. It's no place for kids."

"You said you would find that man and make him pay. I heard you say that. I want to stay!"

"Frank, there's nowhere for us *to* stay. We've worn out our welcome with Giuseppe. He has his own kids to take care of, so we only get scraps of food. Our clothes have holes in them. We don't have any more money for him."

"Can't the church help?" Teresita tried to comfort her younger brother.

"The parishioners have done all they can," Father Scott said. "There are just too many homeless kids. Like you, so many have lost their parents to the flu. The best we can do now is to get you to a family out west on the Orphan Train."

Frank ran to the bedroom and slammed the door behind him. "Don't worry, Father Scott," Tony said. "I'll have everyone ready to leave in the morning."

Tony went into the bedroom and found Frank playing with the soldier puppet his father had given him. Somehow, the simple act of using the sticks to control the puppet's hands and feet seemed to calm Frank when nothing else could. "You know we have to go," Tony told his little brother.

"But I want to stay here."

"Father Scott says this is our best chance to have a real family again. I'll look out for us, and I'll keep us all together. So is that okay?"

"You promise we'll come back and get the man that killed Papa?"

"Someday, Frank. Someday we'll come back," Tony promised.

The Children's Aid Society provided them with a set of clean clothes and some food for the trip. All their belongings fit in one satchel that Tony carried. Frank kept the soldier puppet in his pocket. And so they boarded the train headed south and west to their new lives.

It was a long journey, and the train was crowded – so many children all with the same plight. They met Ricardo and Jimmie, brothers from New York whose parents had also died from the flu. The fact that they all spoke Italian created an instant bond among the six orphans.

In Kansas City, all the children were taken off the train to stand on the station platform while local families decided who to adopt. It was heartbreaking to watch siblings being separated and taken to different families. The Peccaros clung together. "Don't forget, Tony," Frank whispered, "you said we'd stay together."

A family took Jimmie but not his brother. Ricardo swung his fists at the agency worker and the train attendant, who pushed Ricardo into a berth and locked him inside. Tony could hear the boy scream all night trying to get out.

The next stop was not far, Topeka. Once again, the children were paraded onto a platform – all except Ricardo.

"What happened to Ricardo?' Steve asked.

"I don't know, but they're not separating us like they did Jimmie and Ricardo," Tony said in a voice loud enough for his siblings to hear.

A man and woman spoke to the agent and pointed toward the young Peccaros. "Tony, can you bring your sister over here?" said the agent. "This lovely couple would like to talk to her."

Steve poked Tony. "We can't let her go."

Tony replied, "I told you, sir, we stay together."

"Look, we only have a few more stops. It'll be hard to find a family that can take all four of you." The agent walked over and took Teresita by the hand. "We're taking your sister to see this couple."

Teresita cried and tried to run back to her brothers. The agent grabbed her arm and pulled her along. She screamed and wailed, "No! No! Tony, Steve . . ."

The couple tried to talk to her, but she just kept crying, looking over her shoulder at her brothers. The couple asked the agent something and he held up four fingers. They shook their heads "no" and held up one finger as the woman took Teresita firmly in her grasp.

The train attendant rushed the rest of the Peccaro children back to the train – to the compartment where Ricardo was taken back in Kansas City. They heard the click and realized they were locked in – and Teresita wasn't with them. "You boys gonna have to spend the night here, now," the attendant said from the corridor, "seein's how you can't behave."

How were they going to get out? How were they going to find their sister? They tried to find a way out, but it was useless. They were stuck here. Surprisingly, the train didn't immediately leave the station. This was a loading stop for supplies, and it was two hours or more before the train started moving again. Once it did, the train attendant returned and unlocked the door. "All right, boys," he said, "you can go back to your berth now."

Tony was distraught. How were they going to get back to Teresita?

"The train's moving too fast to jump off," said Steve.

"I know," Tony replied. "We'll just have to think of something else."

They continued glumly back to their berth. One of the beds was in a bit of a mess, like somebody had been called away halfway through making it up. Tony started to straighten up the covers, then realized there was something underneath and threw them back. It was Teresita. "Shhhh," Tony admonished as the younger siblings started squealing and hugging each other. "How'd you get back here?" he asked his sister.

"I ran away."

"What happened?" asked Steve.

"They took me to their buggy and put me in the back seat. But I couldn't stop crying, and when I couldn't see the train any longer, I started screaming for Tony. The man turned around and slapped me in the face and said, 'You better shut up or that will be coming at you again.' He was really mad and he sounded mean.

"I tried to stop crying, but I kept looking back, trying to see how to get back to the train. It wasn't far to their house, and when we got there, the man and the lady both took hold of me and took me into a bedroom. 'This will be your room,' said the lady. 'But you must obey your new daddy. He has a temper. Now take a nap and rest, and I'll call you for supper.'

"I lay down on the bed and closed my eyes, and when she thought I was asleep, the lady left and locked the door. But I sneaked out the window and ran back to the station; and the train was still here, so I waited till no one was watching and got on and came here to hide."

"Good for you," said Tony.

"Don't let them take me away again, Tony," Teresita pleaded.

When they were far enough away from Topeka that the train was unlikely to stop and send Teresita back, the boys brought her to the dining car. The agents reacted by locking Tony back in the punishment compartment by himself, but the train continued southward.

At the next stop, they brought Tony back to his siblings. "I think we're getting to the end of the line," Tony said. "I don't know what happens if no one takes us. We need a plan."

After ten days on the train, they arrived in Gainesville, Texas. The land in Texas looked completely foreign to them – it was flat, and the sky looked colossal. The town had single-story buildings and wide streets filled with horse-drawn buggies, but very few automobiles – a far cry from the overcrowded city they knew. At the station, they marched onto the platform again. Several couples strolled by. One couple was just stepping out of their buggy. A tall, husky man accompanied by a small woman with pale skin. Frank held hands with his sister and put on a smile; Tony and Steve stood behind them; they were determined to look like a foursome.

The young couple walked straight to the agent who had taken up a position behind the Peccaro children to prevent any further mischief. "I am Leo Moster," said the man in a heavy German accent. "This is my wife Theresa. We're cotton farmers and want to adopt two children. We would prefer two boys. We can provide a fine home. Food. Shelter. We will raise them as Catholics."

Leo looked at Steve and Frank. "I'd like to speak to the two younger boys."

"Of course," said the agent. "They would be lucky to . . ."

"Sorry, sir," Tony blurted out, "but we have to stay together."

"They're siblings who've come all the way from New York." The agent at least tried to be helpful.

The Mosters looked at each other. The wife's eyes were soft and kind, but Mr. Moster shook his head. He spoke privately with his wife then waved at another couple nearby. The four adults stepped away to talk with the agent.

Tony began pacing the platform, overwrought at the thought they might have to split up, and Steve wasn't making it any easier. "Tony, you said we could stay together. These people speak funny. I think they're Germans."

World War I had caused a backlash against the German culture in the United States. Tony knew all about the anti-German sentiment in New York and how people tried to shed every vestige of their German heritage. But maybe things were different here. "Don't call people names," he told Steve. "We're Italians, you know. Show some respect, or we're never going to get off of this train."

The adults came back. "We have an agreement," said the agent. "This is Joe Sicking and his wife, Margaret. Their farm is close to the Moster farm. They want to adopt two children and don't mind if one of them is a girl. So, two boys would go with the Mosters, and one boy and a girl with the Sickings. And they'd make sure you children get to see each other from time to time."

Tony didn't say anything right away. He had to think about this. These people looked nice, but how could he be sure they'd keep their promise? After all, they could have cooked this story up with the agent just so the kids would go along. But then he remembered what Mr. Moster had said about raising them Catholic. "Do you promise to raise us all Catholic?" he asked.

"We're all active at Sacred Heart Parish," Mrs. Moster answered.

"And you too, Mrs. Sicking?" Tony wanted to be sure.

"Yes, son," Margaret replied.

"And you promise that we'll all see each other every Sunday at church?"

"Of course," said Mr. Sicking. "And during the week sometimes too."

Tony looked at his siblings. Steve nodded. Teresita held his hand. Frank was holding onto his soldier puppet.

"There's one other thing," said Tony.

"What's that?" asked Leo.

"I go with Teresita. I promised my mother on her death bed that I'd look after my sister, and I want to keep that promise."

"That's fine with us," said Leo. "Theresa and I were interested in the younger boys anyway. You okay with that, Joe?" Joe nodded in assent.

"All right," Tony sighed. "I guess it's the best we're going to be able to do."

Part of the Orphan Train protocol was that adoption papers were already drawn up, just waiting for the new parents to sign. It was only a few moments before the formalities were complete and the new families were ready to depart. As Tony and Teresita prepared to leave with the Sickings, it finally dawned on Frank that he wasn't going with Tony. He ran to his brother and clung to his leg, begging, "No, Tony, I want to go with you."

Tony knelt down and hugged his younger brother. "I won't be far away, and I'll see you every Sunday. And Steve will be with you, and he can look out for you too."

"But I want you, Tony." Frank was almost in tears.

"I'll tell you what." Tony reached inside his shirt and brought out his father's silver cross that he'd worn ever since the day Pasquale was shot. He unclasped the chain and fastened it around Frank's neck.

"There. Now you have me and Papa looking out for you all the time."
He stood up and tousled Frank's hair.

The younger boy took the cross in his hand and tucked it inside his shirt just like Tony had always done – just as Pasquale had always done – and walked back to where the Mosters waited for him. He reached up and took Theresa's hand as Tony called, "See you Sunday."

# CHAPTER 11

*September 1943*

"And did your new families stick to their agreement?" asked Ida when Frank finished.

"They did indeed. The four of us were together at church and in school and for birthdays and all the special occasions. Somehow it didn't feel like we were really separated at all – except for where we slept. And we've stayed close as adults. And that's how I learned German." Frank grinned.

"I love a happy ending. Maybe I'll have one when this war is over." She paused. "But now, we should get moving. The quicker we get these documents back to Altavilla, the quicker your division can use them." She started packing up their leftovers.

The beauty of the hillside had mesmerized Frank. Sloping terraces of vineyards and perfect rows of small grape vines. Rich soil for the vines and for the grass and foliage in uncultivated areas. A winding, graveled path that created a passage for vehicles through the hilly terrain.

Ida's voice brought him out of his daydream. "Look down in the valley – on the road coming up the hill. Are those military vehicles?"

Frank looked down the hillside. "That's a British military convoy . . . headed our way . . . and fast."

They grabbed the bikes and started down the opposite side of the hill. Another terraced trail – not as steep as the one they'd climbed, but with the same stone walls and steep drop-offs as it zigzagged through the terraces. Descending, they had a view of the entire trail and the valley below. Suddenly, Frank stopped short.

"What's wrong?" Ida asked.

"Look down there." Frank pointed to the bottom of the trail. "Germans coming this way."

"*Porca vacca*, Frank!" Holy cow! "We're caught in the middle!"

"I don't think we can turn back to Battipaglia. We can't pedal fast enough to outrun the Germans. And if they caught us out here in a battle zone, it's not likely they'd buy our story."

"You're right. They'd shoot first and not worry about asking questions." Ida's voice betrayed her fear. "What if we go back to the top of the hill and join the British?"

"I think the British are trying to make the battle happen on this side of the hill, so they have the high ground. And once they realize how close they are to each other, both sides will start spreading out into battle formations."

Ida kept looking back and forth between the top of the hill and the convoy below, the worry creases between her brows deepening. Suddenly, she broke into a smile. "I have an idea . . . follow me."

"What do you have in mind?"

"My brother and I have combed these hills for years. I know them like the back of my hand. We have some secret hideouts in the stone ruins in the ravine where we used to play and hide from each other."

Years of erosion from drainage off the hilltop had created gullies and streams on the slopes. Ida pointed to a break-off point from their path. Sliding on the dirt and rocks, they tried to carry their bikes down the side of the slope into a deep dry gully.

"I think we're going to need to ditch the bikes for now," Ida said. "Let's see if we can hide them in the fallen trees over there."

"Fine, but we'd better take the documents with us in case we aren't able to get back here." Frank quickly removed the documents, and they abandoned the bikes and covered them with plant debris.

As they walked deeper into the ravine, Ida pointed to stones jutting from the edge. They climbed up. "A great lookout, but not much of a hideout," said Frank.

"Not up here, but follow me."

Underneath the stone was a narrow gap. "Good thing you're slim, Frank. We have to squeeze through this crevice. It was easier when I was a child, but I think we can do it." Ida went first and then helped Frank into the cavern.

"Wow!" he exclaimed, looking around the dark hole. It was small but they could crouch over and both fit inside. Two stone walls of a small cave had collapsed, leaving an even smaller, dangerous cavern. The cave was created from a stream hundreds of years ago. Over the years the stream changed paths and dried up at this site. If the stones collapsed again, they would crush the space inside. "This is an amazing hideout."

"I know. My brother and I loved this place. These rocky hills probably contain lots of hidden ruins that haven't been discovered. No one has excavated here because there are much more exciting findings closer to the ocean. But we made up lots of great tales as children when we played up here."

Suddenly a loud boom reverberated through the valley. The ground under them vibrated. Ida jumped and turned to Frank.

"That was a mortar blast. And I hear gunfire in the background. The battle's starting," he said.

"One of those blasts near here could collapse this little cave."

"Well, from the sound of the last one, I think we're far enough away." Frank tried to calm her fears even though he knew a howitzer blast could destroy this spot easily. There wasn't anything they could do now but wait out the battle. At least there was a little light coming through the gap they'd slid through. "Come sit over here with me." He patted the ground beside him. When she slid over, he put his arm around her and said, "Don't worry . . . we'll get out of here." They huddled close as the mortar blasts continued. She covered her ears and closed her eyes against the noise and the constant vibrations of the earth.

The blasts were getting closer and the gunfire louder. "I'm going to look through the gap and see if I can tell who's advancing."

"No, Frank, I don't think that's a good idea. What if they see you?"

"I won't crawl out – I'm just going to see if I can see anything by sticking my head through the gap." He scraped some green moss off the side of the cavern and covered his face with it and found some mossy ferns to cover his head.

Ida laughed and Frank smiled back, glad he could take her mind off the danger. Then he proceeded to scoot to the gap. He looked through the opening and didn't see anyone, so he poked his head out. He could hear more than he could see. The Germans were behind them but close. The Brits had advanced from their previous position. The battle was closing in.

As he retreated into the cavern, the ground shook like an earthquake, and one of the stones shifted. Ida gasped. Frank reached for her hand and they huddled together listening to the shells and gunfire. The waiting was agony.

When the noise finally abated, they heard voices . . . German voices. Really close. Bootsteps. The clunk of something landing on the rock above them. And then the rat-a-tat-tat of continuous firing, so loud they were forced to cover their ears. It went on for what seemed like an eternity but must have been only ten minutes.

When the firing stopped, Frank heard one of the Germans say, "Hans, we need more ammunition. Quick, get it out."

"*Oberleutnant*, that's it. I have no more."

"Then get your rifle ready."

Frank couldn't tell Ida what he'd heard. Neither of them dared to speak. They hardly dared to breathe.

The sounds above changed. Rifle and pistol fire. Getting closer. Shots ricocheting off the rocks and trees.

Another shot, a scream from directly above them, and then a thud. A hand and arm fell into the gap. Time seemed to stand still.

"Hans! Hans! Are you okay?"

No answer.

Frank and Ida stared at the hand and the blood dripping from it. Ida shivered. Boots scampered above, the sound of a soldier running quickly, firing as he ran. Then another scream and the firing stopped.

They listened and waited. The hand hung in eternal stillness as the blood stopped dripping. Finally, all the firing ceased. It was near sundown when they decided to venture out. Frank pushed the arm aside and exited first. He dragged the dead soldier away from the stone and then helped Ida out of the small gap and onto the stones above. A German machine gun abandoned beside the rocks. Hans' bloody body next to the stone. Another body ten or fifteen yards up the ravine. Frank went over to inspect that body and found a Luger pistol and knife left on the belt of the dead German. He grabbed both the Luger and the knife and ran back to make a plan with Ida.

"It looks like the Brits ambushed the machine gunners over the ravine. If I had to guess, I'd say the Germans have retreated and the Brits have moved on to Battipaglia. We should be able to get back to Altavilla, but it's probably better to travel at night. Can you find your way in the dark?" Frank asked.

"I know these trails like the back of my hand. I can find our way to the farm."

"It's too risky to backtrack to the bikes. Since I have the documents, let's just move forward."

When dark fell, they set out on foot.

# CHAPTER 12

The landscape they walked through was a startling contrast to what they'd viewed from the vantage point of their picnic earlier in the day. The moonlight revealed blown-out craters and damaged, smoking groves, the rows now in shambles. Medics had cleared the bodies, but mangled equipment, empty shell casings, and battle debris were scattered all over the terraced hillside. Thick wine groves lay tangled and burnt from mortar blasts. With the documents tucked inside Frank's shirt, they walked and ran down the terraces and slid downhill on wet grass.

"My father is going to be worried sick and mad as a hornet," said Ida.

"I'll try to talk to him about it – tell him what a significant strategic advantage these maps will be to the Allies."

"He'll be so mad he won't care."

"I was thinking. Because your dad knows this area so well from his irrigation work, what if we let him present these maps to my CO and take the credit? Truth be told, it's not a good idea for me to turn them in. I could wind up in trouble for ending up behind enemy lines while I'm supposed to be helping the locals. Do you think your father would do it?"

"Well, maybe. Papa *has* wanted to help the Allies. He was too old to join the military, and he despises Hitler."

The noise of mortars and machine guns was gone. The only thing audible was the sound of burning debris. They moved carefully through the abandoned battlefield, stopping to take cover from time to time, just as a precaution. Between the groves of ancient grape vines, there were forested areas thick with trees and paths covered with broken branches.

"Be careful through the clearings," Frank warned. "Avoid stepping on unspent shells or burning debris. And let's steer clear of the open fields. There could still be snipers out there."

After half a mile of careful movement through the battlefield, Frank said, "I think we're out of the danger zone. We need to pick up the pace. Can you run with me?"

They darted between trees and rocks and over broken branches and fallen trees as they moved downhill through the brush. "Frank, did you hear that?" Ida asked.

He stopped running, "What?"

"I thought I heard moaning."

They listened but heard nothing. Frank resumed running and jumped across a large broken branch. Ida followed but didn't get enough height to clear the branch and landed on top of it, causing it to jerk out of position and stir up a pile of leaves and dead brush.

A loud moan came from the under the pile of brush. Frank had already turned around to help Ida up when a German soldier started to drag himself out of the debris. Blood from a leg wound covered his uniform and left a trail in his path as he tried to move away. He looked like a scrawny wounded bird trying to flee the nest.

Frank stepped in front of Ida to protect her, but the soldier didn't have a weapon. "Come on, Ida, let's keep moving."

But Ida stood stock still, unable to take her eyes off the wounded man. "He looks just about the same age as Sal's younger brother, Giovanni – fifteen, maybe sixteen. They were together when the Gestapo grabbed Sal. Giovanni took off running, but the Gestapo shot him. No one dared help him as he lay there, bleeding, in the street. The Gestapo just watched as he bled to death and then loaded Sal onto the train." She looked back at Frank. "What are we going to do?"

"We need to get *outta* here – back to your farm."

"We can't just leave him. Look how much blood he's lost," she pleaded.

"What would we do with him? How am I gonna explain a wounded enemy soldier to my lieutenant? Hell, how would we explain him to your father?"

Ida walked toward the soldier, who tried to back away, dragging his lower body and pushing back with his arms.

Frank tried one more time. "Ida, leave him. Your father's going to be furious enough as it is." When she didn't reply, he realized she was going to help the man whether it made sense or not. Sighing heavily, he followed her and called out to the soldier. "*Halt. Wir werden Ihnen helfen.*" Stop. We'll help you.

"Look . . . the blood's coming from his thigh. If we can get it to stop, maybe he would live." Ida looked desperately at Frank.

Frank assessed the situation. He tried to pull the soldier's shirt off, but the man resisted. Frank got up. "We can't help you if you don't let us."

Ida took the boy-soldier's hand as he screamed with pain from the struggle and another gush of blood poured out. "*Sie werden sterben wenn ich die Blutung nicht stoppen kann,*" Frank said. You'll die if I don't stop the bleeding.

The boy looked at all the blood and finally nodded his head. He lay back, the weakness of blood loss obviously setting in.

Frank ripped the trousers and looked at the wound. There was a bullet hole oozing blood. He tore the pant leg in half and began stuffing an edge into the bullet hole. He tried to make conversation with the boy to take his mind off the pain. "How did you wind up here, so far away from the battlefield?"

"I was on the far flank. And then we got out-flanked so I was caught in the middle and hit by a stray shot from one my own soldiers." He winced as Frank pushed on his wound. "I couldn't keep up when they ran so they left me behind and said they would come back, but no one came. I crawled as far as I could and then took cover in the brush."

Frank used the other half of the torn trouser to wrap around the leg above the wound. The bleeding ceased.

"Well, now what do we do?" he asked Ida.

"We have to get him to a hospital . . . or at least somewhere to get food and water. He'll die out here alone on this mountain."

"Damn. So you want me to carry him?"

"I'll try to help. We can put his arms around our shoulders and carry him together."

Frank thought about it then just heaved the boy onto his back and began walking. It was a long walk. They alternated the load – Frank would carry the boy for a while, then they'd carry him together. By the time they reached the Perna farm, they were exhausted. They stopped at the barn where Ida climbed up into the hay loft and came down with a folding cot. "I stashed it up there before the Germans came. Even if Papa wasn't making preparations, I thought I had to do something."

They laid the boy on the cot. He was pale and weakened by the blood loss but awake enough to talk.

"*Wie heissen Sie?*" Frank asked. What's your name?

"Alphonse. Name . . . Alphonse. Do you have any water?" His voice was shaky and raspy and his lips were dry and cracked.

Ida went back to the hay loft and found a cup left over from when the family had hidden out up there. She filled it from the pump, and Alphonse guzzled it down.

"Frank, we need to go talk to my father, but I don't know how he's going to feel about having a bloody Nazi soldier in his barn."

"Let's hide him in one of the stalls. We can come back later with some food and check his bandages. He's not going anywhere with this leg injury."

They dragged the cot with the boy on it into a stall.

"I didn't want to do it," the boy squeaked.

Frank and Ida looked at him. "Didn't want to do what?"

"I know what you're thinking – how could I fight for Hitler? I saw the same atrocities you have. Now I'm going to die," he whimpered as if apologizing or confessing.

Exhausted and frustrated from the journey, Frank couldn't help but raise his voice, "Why did you do it then?"

"Hitler Youth. It was expected. All fit, school-age boys required to participate. My father was a butcher in Munich. We barely scraped by. My father worked for a Jewish man who owned the store. When the SS arrested the Jewish man, my father became the boss – he already knew everything about the business. The Nazis gave him the keys to the store in exchange for providing the best cuts of meat to certain politicians and businessmen in the town. And of course, my brother and I were expected to participate and recruit for Hitler Youth."

"Sounds like a bribe," Frank said.

"Yes, but it was happening everywhere. I didn't like it. I lost my friend – the son of the Jewish store owner. They just disappeared. No one knew where they were taken, but truckloads of Jews were taken from their homes. My dad said the same would happen to us if we questioned the raids. We were told just go along with it and everything would be fine. I could hear my mom and dad argue about it at night when they thought we were asleep. But how could my father refuse? Now he would have enough food for us, and after all, he had worked in that store all his life. So maybe it was due to him."

"Did you find out what happened to your friend and his dad?"

"I never saw them again. These were common stories among the Hitler Youth; our fathers prospered from the movement. I obeyed my father and dutifully attended the camp. When word spread the Americans were getting involved and there was going to be an invasion, I was put on a train to Italy even though I was not the usual age to be sent to the front. I wanted to go back to my family, but punishment for insubordination is harsh. My father would have lost the store, and I would have been jailed . . . maybe flogged or shot. I had no choice."

Ida wiped the boy's brow with a cloth. He was feverish.

"Stay here in the barn," Frank told him. "We'll bring you some food and water. Try to keep quiet. If you're discovered here, we'll have a big problem."

The boy nodded and closed his eyes. Frank and Ida walked to the farmhouse. "Time to face the consequences," she said.

The entire family was in the kitchen. Ernesto began shouting as soon as Frank and Ida walked in. "It's after midnight, young lady. Where have you been? And *you*!" He pointed a shaking finger at Frank.

"Papa, I can explain," Ida began but Ernesto cut her off.

"You just disappeared. How can you do that to us? To your mother? She's been crying all evening thinking you were captured or shot by the Germans for dealing with those resistance friends of yours. And *you*!" He turned his full fury on Frank. "You should be *ashamed* of yourself!"

"Papa, it's *my* fault. I asked him to come with me."

"*Dio mio.* You think that's some kind of excuse? Where have you been? What have you been doing?"

"I *had* to go, Papa. The documents had to get to Battipaglia, and there was no one else. So I made a delivery to the store."

"My brother's store? Now you have *him* involved?"

"My contact met me there. Don't worry. Uncle is okay," she reassured her father.

"Signor Perna, your daughter has acquired information that will be extremely helpful to the Allied advance. Please, sir, it's terribly important to get this information to my commanding officer right away," Frank pleaded.

"Frank, you should go now." Ernesto was no longer shouting, but there was still smoldering anger in his voice. "I don't want my daughter involved in this danger any longer."

"Mr. Perna, will you take a look at these maps first?" Frank had pulled the documents out of his shirt. "Please, I need your help. You know this terrain. These maps are important, but we need to know the lay of the land. Your knowledge and experience would save us having to scout things on our own – it would help immeasurably."

Ernesto stared at Frank for a long time, then at the papers in Frank's hand, indecision written clearly on his face. Finally, he said, "All right. Show me what you've got there."

They went into the kitchen and Frank spread the maps on the table. Ida interpreted the codes on the descriptions. The scattered sites on the map appeared to flank the town of Battipaglia.

Ermesto studied them closely. "Yes, you will need to know about Mount Sammucro and the other hills the Germans are using for cover."

"No one could explain it to my CO better than you, sir. I saw how they listened to you back at the Tobacco Factory. Would you come with me?"

Ernesto's demeanor had changed. The import of Ida's information was beginning to overcome his anger that she'd risked her life to get it. It seemed as if he, too, recognized how crucially important these maps would be. "If it will help protect my family, I will help you," Ernesto said.

"It's the best way."

"Okay, let's go to your headquarters. We'll take my truck. Ida, you stay here with your mother. And promise me . . ." Ernesto's tone was once again stern. ". . . promise me this is the *end* of your shenanigans. No more disappearing. Your mother can't take it anymore."

"In that case, Papa, I need to tell you about the boy in the barn."

"What?! What are you talking about?"

Frank intervened, "Sir, we rescued an injured boy on our way back here. He has a leg injury, and we dressed his wound and carried him to the barn."

"Are you telling me there is an injured American soldier in our barn?"

"No, sir, there's an injured German soldier in your barn."

Ernesto grabbed his gun and stormed out. Frank and Ida ran to get ahead of him.

"Papa, you don't need a gun. He's weak and bleeding."

"What were you planning on doing with him?"

"I don't know. We hadn't gotten that far yet." Ida was anxious, uncertain what her father might do.

"Sir," Frank tried once again to calm the situation. "I think we should load him in the back of the truck and take him to the medics at our headquarters. He'll be a POW, but he'll get medical care."

Ernesto hesitated. Then he handed Ida the rifle and marched toward the barn, Frank hot on his heels.

# CHAPTER 13

Not a word passed between Frank and Ernesto as they headed toward Altavilla. Only the clamoring of the engine broke the stillness of the night. Frank was worried. Had he lost Ernesto's trust? And just at the time he'd gained Ida's? How could he make amends?

"Sir, I want to apologize for endangering your daughter." Frank finally broke the silence.

"Frank, I've been upset with her risky behavior for some time now. She has a mind of her own . . . believes her young friends have an answer and have better ideas to fight the Germans. Actually, I should thank you for bringing her home alive. If she'd been on that trip alone, she might not have returned."

"I recognized that stubbornness you refer to. In fact, that's why I helped her. It was pretty obvious she was going – alone or otherwise."

"It's hard for a father, Frank. I want to keep her safe. But what can I do? First Mussolini, then Hitler, now the Allies running roughshod over the country. The young people feel this is their battle. And who can blame them? All they've seen is poverty, poor economic conditions, and fighting. They want to change their future."

"That's why we're here, Ernesto."

"For the love of God, I hope so. We can't go on living like this. And I'll do anything to protect my children," Ernesto admitted.

"That's why I want you to be the one to give this information to my CO. You can explain these locations and how to control the terrain. Even better, I think, than Ida – and even she showed me caves and places to hide I would never have found on my own. We could really use your help."

The silence in the truck returned. Frank knew Ernesto was weighing the pros and cons of helping this new set of invaders. After so many years of war, these people must be exhausted. But there was nothing certain, yet, about who would end up on top of this fight and who they'd be answering to in the end.

Now it was Ernesto's turn to break the silence. "Okay, Frank, but you must promise me one thing. You must protect my daughter and make sure no harm comes to her. I know what the Nazis do to traitors and to the resistance fighters. It's not something you imagine for your child. So I'll help you to keep those things from happening to my family."

"For as long as I'm here, sir, you have my promise. I'll do whatever's in my power to protect Ida . . . and all your family." Frank knew it was likely his unit would eventually move on. But there was no need to remind Ernesto of that in the moment.

They stopped at the triage center long enough to turn Alphonse over to the medics then went straight to the command tent. Despite the late hour, both the CO of Frank's regiment and the major were there, poring over maps and reconnaissance reports.

"Rumor has it you just brought in a wounded German, Sergeant," said the CO. "Care to explain?"

Geez, thought Frank, how'd the word spread so fast? "We found him in the Pernas' barn, sir. Must have just wandered in, looking for somewhere to hide. Seemed like making him a POW was better than just leaving a kid to die. He can't be more than about fifteen or sixteen."

During this exchange, the major had been studying Ernesto's face. "I've seen you before," he finally said. "At the Tobacco Factory, wasn't it?" Frank translated.

"*Si, signor.*"

"And why are you here now?"

"Mr. Perna's come into possession of some documents he thinks may be important, sir," Frank supplied.

"All right," said the major, "let's see what you've got." Ernesto handed over the papers.

The major took a long time studying the maps before asking, "So what are these markings?" With Frank's help, Ernesto explained, pointing out camouflaged rocket launchers, bunkers in the foothills, machine gun nests, antitank guns buried in straw stacks.

The senior officers took the documents over to their own map table and began pointing to things, first on one and then the other, apparently comparing the two. Then the major turned and stared at Frank and Ernesto in silence for what felt like an eternity.

"Moster, can you vouch for the authenticity of this material?"

"As best I can tell, sir, I believe it to be reliable. I trust Mr. Perna."

"What's your estimate of the date of this information?"

"We think it's accurate as of one or two days ago. The man who brought these claims to have seen the Germans in these hills" – Frank walked over to the map table and pointed out the hill where he and Ida were trapped during the battle – "just yesterday."

The major and Frank's CO studied the documents again in silence.

"You were right to bring this to us, Sergeant," said the major. "It's priceless. Even our best reconnaissance hasn't been able to precisely locate the Germans in this area. But it's vital we gain control of Battipaglia. Securing that railroad junction and those two highways is the only way we can control troop and supply movement." The major looked back down at the maps, then added, "Time to update our battle plans."

"The British forces should be trying to hook up with us," said Frank's CO. "We'll have to bring them into the picture."

"I'd pinpoint the British forces to be right about here," Frank pointed to the map again.

"If that's correct, they must have strayed from course from our last communication with them. Our information suggests the enemy brought in tanks and two battalions of infantry and pushed the British out of town. If that's the case, we need to get some reinforcements to this location to help them. They had only a small battalion and limited communication ability."

"Major, I'd be happy to lead a reconnaissance team with Mr. Perna's assistance."

"I can't guarantee his safety, Moster, so if he comes, he'll have to volunteer. Get a team together and report back here in an hour for the attack plan. And don't forget to go by the medical tent and do the paperwork on that POW."

# CHAPTER 14

Ernesto didn't hesitate – he seemed now to be fully committed to helping the Allies – or at least to helping Frank. The plan, assembled in the wee hours of the night, called for a joint attack involving infantry and tanks combined with an air bombardment to clear the Sele-Calore corridor and take both Persano and Battipaglia.

"Frank, I have to tell my brother to get out of town. He's right there, on the main street in Battipaglia," said Ernesto.

"Ernesto, we can't tell anyone of the plan. The Germans might find out and run."

"I won't tell him any details . . . I'll just insist that he come to the farm."

Frank didn't reply. He would just have to ignore Ernesto's call because he knew it would be made no matter what anyone said . . . and Frank knew he would do the same if it were his family.

They rode along with Frank's infantry company, a radio operator in the jeep with them so they could keep command apprised of the operation and relay coordinates. The sound of planes overhead drew Frank's attention. "Fighters and bombers headed for our battle," he said quietly.

Ernesto's face was lined with worry. It must be terrible, thought Frank, to have a war playing out on your home soil, among people you know. Even in the short time he'd known the Pernas, he felt a kinship with them and worried for their safety.

"I understand, Ernesto," he said quietly. "I don't like the bombings either. But my Italian blood boils when I think about the Nazis trying to take over Italy. They have to be stopped."

"Mussolini was an oppressor, Frank, but these Nazis are just savages. I've heard stories of them lining up Italian soldiers and shooting them just because they're Italian. I know this has to be done. But it breaks my heart to know so many innocent victims will be in the line of fire."

As their jeep approached the front line, distant explosions and billowing clouds of smoke signaled that the bombings had begun targeting sites on the resistance maps. Resounding explosions that shook the earth for miles around marked successful strikes on ammunition dumps. Once the bombers took out the anti-tank gun positions, British and American tanks moved in.

For three days, the Allies pounded Battipaglia, destroying the railway yards and crippling the German supply route. By then, the major roads to the area were in control of the Allies. Nearby towns were reduced to rubble. Battipaglia was badly damaged . . . ancient buildings destroyed . . . stone debris cluttering and obstructing the streets.

Frank watched Ernesto as they drove through the town at the head of a convoy. Unabashed tears flowed down the older man's cheeks as he saw the destruction firsthand and the corpses lying in the rubble. The town was almost deserted; those still left were fleeing to safety. No time to collect belongings, preserve relics, or even grieve lost loved ones. On one street there were a few buildings still intact, and Frank thought he recognized it as the place he and Ida had come to.

"*Guarda*!" Look! Ernesto pointed excitedly. "My brother's store! There's nothing left!" Then he crossed himself. "*Dio mio*, I hope they got out before this happened." He crossed himself again.

Further on, a huge pile of rubble blocked the road and Frank slowed to a stop to figure out how to get around it. "Listen," said Ernesto. "I think I heard a cry coming from the rubble."

Frank cut the engine and signaled the truck behind them to do the same. For a moment there was nothing but silence. Then they heard it again. A shrill cry that was definitely coming from under the rubble. Frank and Ernesto ran to the pile and began clearing away stones as soldiers from the vehicles behind joined them. And the cry kept getting louder and louder.

"I see it," Frank shouted. "A baby covered in dirt . . . wedged between the stones."

They worked more carefully now. A large slab had fallen, making a sort of cave in the middle of the pile, protecting the baby from the falling stones. They cleared a narrow path to the squalling infant. Several soldiers held the slab in place so it wouldn't shift while Frank got the baby out. A little girl, in a pink blanket, covered in dirt and dust from the falling masonry. She was crying, but there were hardly any tears – a sure sign she was dehydrated. Frank instinctively cuddled her and cleared the dirt and dust from her face and eyes. Thin and malnourished, she was lucky to be alive. Ernesto said, "I'll get water from the jeep."

Men huddled around Frank and the baby. No doubt, some were thinking of their own little ones back home. The rest hurriedly cleared the road so their convoy could pass through. German snipers could be anywhere in what was left of the blown-out buildings, so it wasn't safe to loiter. Frank's CO, who was in charge of the operation, came to the front of the line to find out what was holding things up. "Find a place for the baby in Altavilla," he told Frank. "It's too dangerous here, and who knows where her relatives might be. We can worry about finding them after it's safe to return here."

Then he turned to Ernesto. "You're a brave man, Mr. Perna, risking your own life to help us. I'm grateful. I'm sorry you had to witness this horror, but without your help, so many more would have died. We're setting up a base here, but Frank's unit is assigned to Altavilla for now to help with reconstruction. They'll do everything they can to protect your family."

"It makes me sad to see my country destroyed," Ernesto lamented. But then he stood a little straighter, stiffening his resolve. "Push Hitler out of Italy, sir. Help us get our country back. And I will try to help my friends see that the destruction should not be blamed on you."

# CHAPTER 15

It had been quieter than usual in the Perna house for the past three days. Even the younger children could sense the anxiety. They played quietly and tried not to annoy the adults. Carmela busied herself in the kitchen, baking bread – the only way she knew to take her mind off the danger she knew her husband was in. In the living room, Ida passed the time talking with her friend Vincenza, whose own anxiety arose from the fact that her husband was in the Italian army. Soft-spoken, with sculpted cheekbones, perfect skin, and piercing eyes, Vincenza did her best to shield her son Tito from the realities of the war.

When Ernesto and Frank walked through the door, the atmosphere in the house changed instantly. "Papa! You're home!" Ida jumped up and embraced her father.

Carmela ran from the kitchen, gave Ernesto a quick hug, and then started scolding him. "What were you thinking, leaving us all to worry like this?! And for three days! And what if you hadn't come back? What if I was left alone with the children like Vincenza?"

"There, there," Ernesto soothed her. "I'm home and safe so you've no call to worry." He seemed to understand that Carmela's words were nothing more than an expression of her relief.

"And our cousins?" asked Clorinda, the elder of Ida's younger sisters. "Where are they? Did they get out before the battle?"

"We have to hope so," Ernesto tried to put a brave face on things – the children didn't need more things to have nightmares about. "Lots of people left. But I don't know where they are." While the younger children clambered around their father, Ida introduced Frank to Vincenza.

"Very nice to meet you, ma'am." Frank nodded his head in acknowledgment.

Vincenza's smile was only fleeting.

"Vincenza's had a difficult time," Ida explained. "We think her husband was imprisoned or killed by the Nazis. He was in the Italian army, and after the capture of Mussolini, he was taken to Rome. Then, when the government capitulated to the Allies, she got word that he's unaccounted for – maybe dead. No one can tell her anything – not what's happened or why."

The little boy sitting next to Vincenza moved even closer, clinging to her arm. "Tito . . . my son." She stroked his hair and patted his shoulder reassuringly. "My Fabio had so little time with him. He was here on leave several months ago and said he would be back in September, but that was the last time we saw him." Vincenza bit her lip, trying to hold back tears that came anyway.

"Vincenza's going to stay with us for a while," said Ida.

"All this fighting has given Tito nightmares," said Vincenza. "And the explosions . . . he cries at the least noise. Even ordinary noises wake him up now, and it's hard for him to go to sleep."

Frank smiled at the young boy. Tito smiled back and slowly let go of his mother's arm. Frank remembered the days when he had nightmares, after the death of his parents. He'd lie in bed at night, holding his soldier puppet and hoping they would come back.

Tito inched closer to Frank, studying his uniform. The child ran his fingers over the cloth badge on Frank's shoulder, fascinated with the sky blue arrowhead with a large T in the center, the identification of the 143rd – the T-Patchers. Frank picked the boy up and tossed him on his shoulder. They ran around the room, Frank bouncing him around and playing. The boy laughed and smiled at his mother, who was beginning to regain her composure. "It's the first time I've heard him laugh in days," she said, as she headed to the bathroom to dry her eyes.

"Did you get medical help for Alphonse?" Ida asked.

"The surgeon was looking at him when we left. He's a registered POW now, so he'll be properly taken care of." Frank paused for a moment. "You'd have been proud of your father, Ida. With your documents and his help, we seem to have the Germans on the run."

Just then, Ernesto returned to the living room. "Papa, tell us what you've been doing. Frank says you saved the day."

Ernesto just looked her in the eye and shook his head "no."

"Were you able to use the information we got from Battipaglia?" She couldn't contain her eagerness even though Ernesto seemed reticent. "Papa?"

"Ida, I'll tell you what happened, but I don't ever want to speak of it again. Many Italians lost their lives in the past few days. I don't like war. I don't want to be part of it. I just want my family safe and my country back."

"Papa, I'm not a child anymore. I've heard the bombings and seen the fighting. I want the same things you want. That's why I went to Battipaglia. I'm sorry I frightened you, but there are dangers everywhere, even on our farm."

"Ida, I know you're not a child. But the things I witnessed . . . no one should have to see that. The destruction, the death, the stench of dead bodies. It's beyond description. We rescued a baby from the debris and brought it to the convent orphanage. The nuns say they'll try to find her relatives, but it's likely they all perished in the bombing." He left out the worst of the details but gave her enough that she could grasp the true extent of the horror and devastation.

She sighed. "I'm sorry, Papa. And I'm glad you're home safe. Vincenza is staying and helping me cook tonight. Could we ask Frank to stay for dinner?"

"We don't have much, Ida, but he's welcome to share what we have," Ernesto replied.

"I brought some potatoes from my garden," Vincenza chimed in. "So we'll have more than you think, Mr. Perna."

Ida beamed. "Frank, will you stay?"

"My CO allowed me the evening off to bring Ernesto home, and I'd love a home-cooked meal," Frank replied. "We don't get that kind of food in the army."

"Do you mind keeping an eye on Tito while we cook?" asked Vincenza.

"No, ma'am. Happy to help." Frank grinned. Ernesto and the boys went outside. Ernesto sat on the porch, holding Tito on his lap, and watched while Massimo and his brother found a ball and began throwing it back and forth with Frank.

"Massimo, do you play baseball?" Frank asked.

"American baseball! I like Babe Ruth!"

His brother shouted, "I like Lou Gehrig. Can you teach us baseball, Frank?"

"Maybe, let's see if you're any good. Take this ball and step back and throw it to me right here."

Frank and Massimo threw the ball back and forth.

"Okay, do you have something we can use for a bat?"

Massimo ran down to the stack of wood outside the barn and brought back a club that resembled a bat. Frank said, "That'll work. I'm going to pitch a ball to you, and let's see how hard you can hit it."

Frank had played a lot with his brothers and was always ready for a pickup game of neighborhood baseball. He tossed the ball to Massimo. On the fifth pitch, Massimo knocked the ball out to the garden.

"Let me try! Let me try!" his brother shouted.

"Okay, your turn. And Massimo you stand out by the garden and try to catch it . . . that is, if your brother can hit the ball," Frank said as he threw a slow, underhand pitch to five-year-old Beppe.

After an hour of hitting, throwing, and running, the boys were worn out. They returned to the porch, and Massimo hopped on the swing with his father.

"Frank, have you seen a real baseball game, like with Babe Ruth and the Yankees?" Massimo asked.

"Well, as a matter of fact, I have. In 1938, I met the New York Yankees." Both boys had their eyes wide open as they turned all their attention to Frank. Just then Ida stuck her head out the door to say "Dinner's ready."

"But, Ida, Frank was about to tell us about the New York Yankees," Massimo whined.

"He can tell you after we eat. I want to hear about that trip too. Papa, did Frank tell you he toured the US on a bicycle? Eight thousand miles!"

"No, he didn't, but it sounds like the boys want to hear all about it. Let's eat dinner and then maybe Frank can take our minds off the war and tell us about his trip."

"Papa, did you see any planes today?"

"Yes, Massimo, I did."

"Did they blow anything up?"

Before Ernesto could react, Ida said, "That's enough, Massimo. Papa doesn't want to talk about that. Come on, everyone, let's eat."

The boys fidgeted all through dinner. At the end of the meal, Massimo and Beppe each grabbed one of Frank's hands and practically dragged him back into the living room, with Tito clinging to his leg. "Now you can tell us, Frank." Massimo could hardly contain himself.

"Not so fast," said Ida. "I want to hear the story, too, but we have to clean up first."

"Awwwwwww, I don't want to wait." Massimo lamented.

"Go," said Carmela. "If the boys will be quiet, I can hear from in here, and I'll join you as soon as I finish."

A hush settled over the living room as Frank began, "It all started on a dare, really."

# CHAPTER 16

It was June of 1938. After a long, hard day in the hay field, my brothers and I made a beeline for Gottlieb's Longhorn Saloon. The finest cold beer on tap – or so the sign proclaimed. A bunch of the local guys were at the bar, and it soon became apparent some of them had been there awhile.

"Well, look who just came in the door." Jack Watson's voice was just a little too loud, a sure sign he'd started his drinking much earlier in the afternoon. "Looks like the wops decided to have a drink with us, Dieter."

"All right, Jack, that's enough." John Gottlieb, the bar's owner, didn't have to raise his voice to make it clear he meant business. "I don't want any trouble here."

"I'm not causing trouble. Just wondering what brings the dagos to this fine German establishment."

We grabbed three stools at the opposite end of the bar, hoping to avoid a confrontation. "Three cold ones, John," Tony ordered for us.

"Comin' right up, Tony. And Dieter says he's buying."

When John slid our mugs across the bar, I raised mine in Dieter's direction. "Thanks, man."

"Least I can do for helping with the baling. Without you guys, Dad and me would've been out in this heat half the night. Couldn't take the chance of a sudden rain ruining the crop."

Jack just couldn't let it go. "Wouldn't you pansies rather be back in New York doin' some easy job?"

"Not really," I replied as Tony downed most of his beer in one gulp, a sure sign he was getting irritated with Jack.

"Take it easy, Tone," Steve said quietly. "You know what he's like when he's had one beer too many."

"What about all those stories about going back and getting revenge for your dad. Ya' know something? I bet you *never* go back!"

I glanced at Tony. The look in his eyes was one I hadn't seen in years. Sure, we'd talked about going back to avenge our father. I'd even made Tony promise me we would. But after years of a Catholic upbringing and a quiet life with our adopted families, the four of us – me, Tony, Steve, and Teresita – had made peace with the past. Or at least I thought we had.

Tony had always been the one to defend us from the bullying. Maybe now it was my turn. "Sure we'll go back, Jack." I kept my tone light. "One of these days."

"On what? A tractor?" That got a big laugh from the German guys.

"Maybe we'll go on our bicycles," I shot back.

"No way! You're crazy! I'll bet ten bucks you never do that."

Tony had had enough. He slammed his mug on the counter. "You're damn right we'll go back, Jack Watson. My bicycle gets me all over every road in this county, and it can damn well get me back to New York."

Steve gave me one of his "please do something" looks, but by then Tony was fired up. "Anyone else want to up the ante?"

"I've got another ten says you won't make it even if you *do* go," one of Jack's cronies chimed in.

And suddenly everyone in the saloon wanted in on the action. By the time they'd all put their bets on the bar, there was close to two hundred dollars in the pile.

I pulled Tony aside. "Are you nuts? Going to New York on bicycles? I was just kidding when I suggested that."

"Look, Frank," he replied. "Two hundred dollars is a lot of money. We planned to do this. The Depression's still on; there's still not enough work for everybody; and there's that craziness with Hitler in Europe, so you can bet there'll be another war before long. If we're ever gonna do it, now's the time. And two hundred dollars would go a long way."

"But bicycles, Tony? People will think we've lost our minds."

"Don't let other people tell you what's possible, Frank. We can do whatever we set our minds to."

I still thought it was a hare-brained scheme, but Tony's mind was made up. He'd saved our lives when we were orphaned and at risk of starving. Maybe I shouldn't deny him the chance to finally prove these bullies wrong. I let go of his arm and he marched back to the bar.

"You're on!" Tony announced to raucous cheers. "We'll do it and that money," he pointed to the pile, "will be ours."

"But you'll have to prove it," said Dieter. "Otherwise, we'll never know you really did it."

"I'll find a way."

"How 'bout you walk up to Lou Gehrig or Joe DiMaggio and ask them to autograph a home run ball for your buddies in Texas?" Jack sneered. "You won't never make it there on no damn bicycle."

"All right, that's enough," John intervened. "Now I'm going to put this in my safe." He gathered up the bills. "And when you boys get back with proof, the money's yours."

"Hey, we need to set a deadline," someone shouted from the table in the corner. "How about they have to do it by Christmas?"

"That okay with you boys?" John asked. Tony nodded; I felt sick to my stomach; Steve just looked sad.

"Then that's the bet," said John. "New York and back by Christmas. Otherwise, you owe these men two hundred dollars." Tony shook John's hand and we headed home.

And so it began. Breaking the news to our families was harder than standing up to the bullies in the bar, but Tony was determined. Despite the pleas of Theresa and Margaret for their husbands to talk some sense into us, Tony insisted we were men now and had a right to do what we wanted. We had the money from the hay harvest, and it was time to see some of the world and make peace with our parents.

The Mosters had known this day would come eventually, though they'd done everything in their power to forestall it. "Just don't do anything you'll regret, Frank," Leo told me. "Find out what happened . . . even find out what happened to the men who killed your father . . .

but stay out of trouble and come back here safe. Theresa would never forgive me if anything happened to you boys."

Teresita was stoic. She was always closer to Tony than to me, probably because they'd been adopted into the same family. But she and Steve had shared the experience of the Orphan Train with us, so they understood why we felt so compelled to know why our young lives had been so cruelly upended.

Florence, on the other hand, was distraught. The Mosters' natural child, she'd been born premature and was still small and skinny. I'd helped care for her when she was a baby, and my reward was the kind of devotion and big-brother hero-worship only a little sister can give.

"Frankie, who's going to read to me?" she wailed through her tears. "You said you'd teach me how do a puppet show, just like you."

"I know, Flo," I picked her up and gave her a hug, "I *will* teach you when we get back, I promise. And I'll bring you something special."

I worried about Florence. Even though I knew we'd be back, I also knew she'd fret the whole time we were gone.

Tony took charge just like he'd done when we were four young children in need of someone to take on the role of the parents we'd lost. "We need new bicycles if we're going to travel that far," he said. So we sold our old ones and bought new Hawthornes from Montgomery Ward. The frame was heavier than most bikes, but it seemed like that would be an advantage for the kind of trip we were planning. They had a fancy paint job and headlights and a speedometer so we could keep track of how far we rode each day. There was a carrier over the rear wheel with a built-in tail light, so we could attach our duffels, and white sidewall tires. We added a rear-view mirror, mounted on the handlebar. With more cars and trucks than ever on the roads, we knew we'd have to be on the lookout constantly in case the drivers didn't see us. The seats were covered in brown leather and mounted on heavy metal springs, but the springs didn't do much to help with comfort.

"I'm calling mine Baby Snooks," Tony declared as we worked out how to mount water canteens onto the front of the handlebars.

"Why do you want to name it after that annoying brat on the radio?" I asked.

"*Everybody* likes Baby Snooks," he replied. "Besides Baby Snooks is famous. And I'm betting once word gets around about what we're doing, we'll be famous too." His enthusiasm for what we were about to do was growing by the day. "So what're you naming yours?"

"I don't know. She sort of reminds me of old Aunt Betty Lou."

Tony laughed. "Betty Lou it is, then."

Then came the question of what we'd put in the duffels. We had to be careful of the weight. Yes, we were fit and strong from working on the farm, but we'd never make the distance Tony had planned each day if our gear was too heavy. So we got it down to a change of clothes for each of us, cooking utensils, a tent, food and supplies to hold us for several days, and a baseball and two gloves so we could relax at the end of each day. I threw in a small sack of soft wood pieces, a knife, a hunk of leather, and a ball of string.

Tony had our route all worked out too. He gathered the families together one evening to show them. "We'll head north . . . get away from the southern summer heat. Seventy miles a day," he said, pointing out where that would take us for each of the first three days. "A stop to visit our cousins in St. Joe then on to Chicago. Then we'll head east for New York."

"What are you going to do for money?" asked Leo. "I'm not sure it's safe for you to be carrying lots of cash all that way. What if someone decided to rob you? Then where would you be?"

"I've got that all worked out with Teresita," Tony beamed. "She's got a list of places and dates where she'll wire us money. So we'll never have more cash on us than what we need to buy supplies between those points." Leo nodded his approval.

"Tomorrow's the Fourth of July," said Tony. "We'll celebrate here with all of you. Then we'll be off the next morning. And the next time you see us, we'll be on our way to collect that big stack of money Gottlieb has in his safe."

Tony and I stepped out on the porch while everyone else was poring over the map, looking at all the places we'd be going. "I know you're excited about this, Tony, but we can't claim that money if we can't prove we got all the way to New York and back. How're we gonna do that?"

He reached into his pocket and handed me a small black book bound by delicate gold string and filled with blank pages. The hard cover said "Autographs" in gold cursive script. "Autographs?" I asked.

"Autographs. From mayors, governors, sports professionals . . . anyone and everyone who can prove we were actually in those places."

I smiled at my brother. He'd gotten us from New York to Texas. Why should I doubt he could get us back to New York again?

# CHAPTER 17

As the glowing yellow ball of sun rose through streaks of orange and purple clouds, we departed from the tiny Texas town of Muenster on the morning of July 5, 1938. Friends and family gathered to see us off. Even Jack Watson and his cronies showed up. As we pedaled past them, I heard Jack say, "How about a side bet, guys? Two bucks says they don't get any farther than Oklahoma City."

The July heat was brutal. Even before we reached the Arbuckle Mountains in southern Oklahoma, it felt like we'd been pedaling steadily uphill. By the time we got to Turner Falls, we were both drenched in sweat. "Ready to call it a day?" Tony asked. "Looks like we just clicked over our seventy miles."

"You'll get no argument from me. Let's find a good spot to camp."

Tony pitched the tent while I started a fire and roasted hotdogs. After we ate, we brought out the gloves and tossed the baseball back and forth to unwind. "Okay, how we gonna get these autographs along the way so Dieter will believe we really did this?" I asked.

"We're going through Oklahoma City tomorrow. We can swing by the capitol and see if we can get an autograph from the governor!"

"Fat chance, but we can try."

"And if he's not there surely we can find another official." Tony was certain this would work. I didn't share his confidence.

We put the ball and gloves away, and I grabbed my sack of soft wood. Choosing a piece, I sat down in front of the tent and began whittling, something I often did to relax.

Tony laughed, "What are you making?"

"You'll find out soon enough. Why don't you tell me a story while I whittle? I know you told me many times before, but tell me again about our real parents. I remember Papa's face but I don't recall as much as you."

Tony propped his feet up and put his hands behind his neck. "Well, it's been a long time . . ." he started reminiscing. "Papa was a stocky man – built like a tank – but what I remember most about him was his face. When he'd come home after working all day, the first thing he'd do was march straight to Mom and give her a big kiss. Then he'd go sit on the sofa, and we'd all run in and jump on his lap and he'd ask us how our day went. We didn't have much money, but enough to live on when Papa was working. Mom took care of us and she worked, too, watching other kids for our neighbors. Although some would call her bossy, because you could hear her yelling from the balcony to do our chores, she had a sweet smile and a warm personality, and I remember her beautiful face."

"I remember riding on Papa's shoulders. He would carry us around that small apartment. I wish he was still here." I looked up at the sky as if I could somehow connect with him again.

"I'll never forget the night he was murdered. I ran out to the living room and stood over Papa's lifeless body lying in a red sea. Then the man smiled and said, 'Boy, don't mess with us.' I can still hear the sound of Petrillo's voice even now, twenty years later." Tony's voice cracked.

"I want to find him and look him in the eye," Tony continued. "I want to see his face when we tell him who we are. I want him to feel the pain we've felt for years." This trip was about closing a door, a time we both wanted to forget but couldn't until we settled with the man who had destroyed our family.

"Mom was never the same after Papa died. She tried to stay strong for the four of us, but I heard her crying secretly in her bed. We didn't have much food, and she'd sacrifice her meals so we kids could have enough. I watched her waste away to a skeleton, her arms and legs skinny as toothpicks. Sometimes, when no one could see, I cried too over what was happening to her. When the flu came around in 1919, she had nothing left to fight with. It took her like the Grim Reaper in the night.

"And not just her. So many people. I'll never forget – when Steve and I would go out looking for food, there'd be bodies stacked up on porches or on the sidewalks waiting for the mortuary vans. You and Teresita were too young for it to matter, but for Steve and me, there wasn't even school – they'd all been closed.

"He never said so at the time, but I'm sure that was part of the reason Father Scott was so insistent about putting us on the Orphan Train. He knew it was the best way for us to stay alive."

"You know, Tony, this road . . . it's the same route as the Orphan Train. You can see the tracks just over there. And I remember these mountains."

"I remember sitting on that train thinking the ride would never end. And at every stop, when no one wanted us, I couldn't help but wonder if I'd done the wrong thing to let Father Scott send us away. I'll never forget standing on that platform and the look on Teresita's face when they separated us. God, Frank, what would have become of her if she hadn't gotten away? What if we'd never seen her again?" Even as an adult, Tony could still feel the enormity of the burden on his small shoulders to find a home for himself and his siblings.

"But she did get away . . . and you found a way to keep us together. I know now that we couldn't have survived on the streets of New York City. Just look what wonderful families we have. Living with my German family has been a great experience. Did you hear they had to stop teaching German in the school?"

"Why?" Tony asked.

"State mandate. Everyone's concerned about what Hitler's doing, and with so many Germans in Texas, I guess they're just worried about possible pro-Nazi sentiment there."

"Well, that was one of the hardest classes in high school, but we managed to pass. If I remember right, you always got As," Tony laughed.

Before the sun went down, we each took out our notebooks and wrote something about that day's journey. I remember exactly what I wrote that first day.

*After riding through the Arbuckles, I'm whipped—bad hills and bad wind. People are pretty nice and friendly here in Oklahoma.*

The next morning, I woke to the sorest legs I ever remember having in my entire life. I suppose I shouldn't have been surprised. I'd never ridden seventy miles in one day before, much less ridden in such hilly terrain. Tony was rubbing his calves as we struck the tent. When he caught me noticing, he said, "Yeah, I'm sore, but we can't slow down on the second day or we'll never get there. Besides, it'll get easier the more we do it." So we packed up and pedaled out, though you couldn't convince my legs that anything was getting easier.

We spent the next night just outside Oklahoma City and kept heading north. I recognized many of the town names as places the Orphan Train had stopped. When we paused for a water break on the third day, I took a quick look at the map where Tony had plotted out the entire trip. We were two hundred miles from home. "Here, give me that," he said and attached the map loosely to his handlebar. "It'll be fun to watch the landmarks on the map as we ride."

We checked and tightened our gear like we always did after a rest stop. "I don't think we'll cover as much ground today. I'm tired and hot." I told him as we climbed back on the bikes.

"Maybe," said Tony. "Let's just get back on the road."

Each pedal rotation caused my leg muscles to scream with pain. The reciprocating noise of the pump jacks in the oil fields was monotonous, but it turned out to be a good way to keep pedaling in rhythm and take our minds off the fatigue and aching. As we crossed the Cimarron River just north of Guthrie, the weather began to change. Ominous clouds were boiling up ahead of us. The air started to feel thick and soon took on the damp, earthy smell of rain. As the clouds closed in, obliterating the blue sky, the temperature dropped. Distant rumblings of thunder rolled across the prairie. "Let's get a move on and try to make it to the next town before this storm breaks." Tony picked up the pace and I followed, finding it easier to ignore my sore legs in the cool air.

A strange calm ensued. The clouds were roiling above, but there was no wind at ground level, which made our pedaling easier still. We'd covered several miles when the calm was suddenly replaced by a gusty wind that blew road dust and grime into our eyes. Loose debris blew away and trees in the fields on either side of the road bent away from the strong gusts.

A sudden, ear-splitting clap of thunder shook the ground beneath us just as a jagged bolt of lightning struck a huge oak tree, splitting it down the middle. The sky rumbled like an angry god and more lightning flashed around us.

"Looks like we better find cover," I yelled to Tony as raindrops began falling, though there was no obvious cover in sight. For a few minutes the rain felt good. Then a swirling vortex of wind yanked the map off Tony's handlebars and whisked it up into the sky. Tony stopped to look for it.

I passed him by while he was off his bike. "Keep going, Tony. It's gone."

"But all our contacts are written on it."

"I know, but we gotta get out of here. Look at those low, black clouds."

And then the rain started falling so hard it felt like pitchforks on our backs. "The supplies are getting soaked," Tony yelled.

The rain was now coming down in sheets. It felt like we were trying to ride through a wall of water. Gushing rivers of water filled the sides of the road, making it impossible to see the pavement. I turned to say something to Tony just as his tires slipped in the gravel and mud, toppling him off his bike and spilling the contents of his duffel. The cooking pan bounced a couple of times on the hard surface, and utensils and food supplies scattered all over the road. Our box of matches was quickly soaked.

The dark clouds made the day seem like night. Just then, a car came over the hill, its headlights illuminating Tony in the road. The driver honked and swerved as a startled Tony jumped out of the way, but the car didn't manage to avoid hitting Tony's bike and flattening the cooking pan. I jumped off my bike and ran back. "Tony, are you okay?" I asked, surveying the carnage.

"Just a few scratches on me," he replied, "but look at Baby Snooks!" He'd picked the bike up out of the road. "Pedals locked . . . the frame and stem bent. It's completely unusable. Our cooking pan ruined! No food, no matches." I'd never seen Tony this close to despair. There might have been tears in his eyes, but in that rain, there was no way to tell.

"You're bleeding, Tone. Your back is soaked." It was my turn to take charge now. "Look." I pointed. "That looks like a farm house up ahead with a light on the porch. If you can walk, I'll ride ahead and see if they can help us." By way of answer, Tony limped slowly to the side of the road and started pushing his warped bike.

The farmhouse door opened just as I was raising my hand to knock. "You need some help? We heard the car honk and then hit something," the farmer said.

"My brother's back there on the road. I think he's okay, but I wondered if I could get him out of the rain and check him for injuries?"

"Sure, come on up. You boys need to take cover. These low clouds and winds are dangerous. This is tornado weather here in Oklahoma." Frank ran back to help Tony and pushed his bike to the porch.

"Name's Redbone," said the farmer. "I didn't catch yours?"

"Frank. And that's my brother, Tony. We're on a bike trip from Texas."

"Well, you boys need to get out of this weather. I got a storm cellar you can hunker down in. It's dry down there, and there's a kerosene lamp and a cot you can fold out to sleep on." The farmer had a good look at Tony's ripped shirt and bleeding back. "You're gonna need some bandages for that. Now let me take you to the cellar, then I'll go see what I can find."

While Mr. Redbone was gone, we got Tony's shirt off so I could get a good look at his injuries. He was sunburned from riding without a shirt the day before. The burn was red and a few blisters had formed. All that was aggravated by scrapes and cuts from skidding on the pavement. He had a couple of small abrasions on his face as well. Using his wet shirt, I managed to clean off most of the blood. "Looks painful, but I think you're gonna live."

"Nothing's broken. I'll be fine." Dry and rescued from the storm, Tony was quickly recovering his usual confidence.

Mr. Redbone returned with the bandages and then bid us goodnight. We fetched the bikes and parked them by the cellar door, moving all our gear inside to sort out the damage. Tony opened the torn duffle bag, "Wish we had some food left. I'm starving." He held up a flattened loaf of soggy bread and the remains of a squashed package of hot dogs. "Can't eat this."

I finished unfolding the cot and turned to face my brother. "Maybe we should just turn around and go back home tomorrow. We've lost all our supplies, the cooking pan, and your map with the contacts. I'm soaked and exhausted. And you're injured. This just seems impossible."

Tony got that look on his face that said "I mean business." "Frank, I'm going to find that man who killed our father if it's the last thing I ever do."

I knew better than to argue with him when he was in one of his stubborn moods. But his bloody, sunburned back, the scrapes, and the bruises that were coming up on his chest and arms weren't very encouraging. I dressed his wounds and let him have the cot. He was asleep almost instantly. I tried to whittle for a bit to take my mind off what we'd have to face in the morning. But it wasn't long before I doused the kerosene lamp and fell asleep myself.

When I woke the next morning, the cot was empty and Tony was nowhere in sight. I remembered the mood he was in last night. Had he decided I didn't have the gumption to go through with this? Did he take our one good bike and set out on his own, leaving me to make my own way back home? I bolted out the door, terrified that the only thing I'd see was a single broken bike. And there was Tony, out in a field pounding a fence post into the ground. My heart retreated from my throat and resumed its normal beating. "Hey, Tone, whatcha doing?" I shouted. Tony waved and pointed to the post, like he wanted to finish the task.

Just then, Mr. Redbone wandered up carrying the bike stem and a pail covered with a kitchen towel. "Have a good night's rest?" he asked.

"Yes, sir, I did," I replied.

"Your brother offered to repair that damaged section of fence if I could try to fix his bicycle. Looks like he's got it all done." Tony was trotting across the field to join us.

"Here you go," said Redbone, handing Tony the stem.

Tony held the stem up to his eye and sighted down it. "Wow, you fixed it! Looks straight as an arrow."

"Managed to get that frame straightened out too. Now you boys gotta be hungry. Mrs. Redbone seen you out workin' on the fence and sent this over." He uncovered the pail to reveal two bowls of gravy and a dozen biscuits.

It was all I could do to get out a quick "Much obliged, sir" as we dived into the breakfast. Mr. Redbone picked up the bicycle stem and said, "You boys eat up while I go put that bike back together. When you've finished, gather up your things and come on up to the house. We'll re-bandage that back of yours and get you all packed up. Gonna be real nice weather today. Always is after a storm like last night."

"You sure you still want to keep going, Tony?" I asked as I swallowed the last of my third biscuit. I never knew biscuits and gravy could taste so good. "Your back still looks awful, and those bruises have to be sore." What I didn't say was that I couldn't believe he'd actually gotten up and put in half a day's work on the fence before I even woke up.

"Why not?" he answered. "Doesn't seem like it could get any worse than yesterday, so if we survived that, we can make it the rest of the way." I don't know where he got his determination, but in that moment, it inspired me. If this trip was that important to Tony, I sure wasn't going to let him continue on alone.

We finished breakfast and started taking stock of our gear. Surprisingly, much of what was in my duffel wasn't soaked through. "My autograph book survived the rain," I exclaimed, holding it up for Tony to see. "Look! Dry as a bone!" And for some reason I still can't explain, that dry book drew me fully into Tony's enthusiasm for getting autographs as a way to prove we'd made the trip. We'd missed a chance in Oklahoma City, unable to see any sign of a capitol dome anywhere in the city, but now I was eager to start filling up that book. "It'll be the best autograph book ever. Maybe we'll even get some baseball players."

Tony laughed. "Okay, now *you're* the one who's dreaming."

At the farmhouse, Mr. Redbone had Baby Snooks and Betty Lou all cleaned up and ready to go. "You take this wet towel here, Frank, and clean up your brother's back while I go find some more bandages," he said.

Tony winced more than once as I tended to his wounds. The bruises were an angry purple, but no new blisters had appeared on his sunburned back. Redbone returned. "Mrs. Redbone says you oughta put some of this salve on the worst cuts afore you bandage 'em. She says they'll heal faster that way."

While I patched Tony up, Redbone disappeared into the house again and came out with a package in one hand and a slightly battered cooking pot in the other. "Now if you boys got room for this, there's a couple of cans of pork and beans and a dozen biscuits in here and a couple of Mrs. Redbone's fried pies. That should tide you over 'til you get some place you can replenish those supplies that got run over. And I filled up those canteens, so you're all set for water."

"I don't know how to thank you, sir," I said as Tony loaded the food and cook pot into his duffel.

"Least I could do for helpin' me fix that fence. I'd've been all day gettin' it mended. Where you boys headed on those bikes?"

"New York," Tony replied.

"*New York*! You got a long way to go!"

"Yes, sir. We're just getting started," said Tony, "but we have a plan. Well, we did have a map and a plan. Lost it in the storm yesterday. Any idea where we could get a new one?"

"Well, there's a gas station about ten miles ahead. Don't know if they'll have what you're lookin' for, but you can prob'ly find it in Wichita. Just keep going north on seventy-seven and it'll take you straight there."

Redbone waved goodbye as we started down his driveway toward the highway. Back on the bike, I realized I was actually excited about continuing the trip. Suddenly, it felt like the adventure of a lifetime. And I realized something else. There was a really big grin on my face as we reached the highway and pointed our bicycles north.

# CHAPTER 18

The sun was out after the big rain. The humidity was stifling, but each downhill stretch of road was welcome. We'd work up a sweat on the inclines but then build up speed and cool off as we rode downhill. Next stop: Wichita, Kansas.

"Frank, I got a problem. My high-speed gear's not working. I think it was damaged in the spill yesterday – and it feels like my wheel's warped too."

"We're not too far out of Wichita. Keep pedaling, and maybe we can find a shop there."

But no matter how hard he tried, Tony couldn't keep up, and fighting the wheel and gear problem was sapping his energy. "You wanna switch bikes for a while?" I asked him. He refused, but I could tell that the farther we rode, the pain from his back and the bouncing from the warped wheel were wearing him down.

When we came upon a roadside park, I said, "We need a break," so we stopped for lunch, and I took the opportunity to check Tony's injuries again. His skin looked like leather, the abrasions were starting to scab over, and his bruises all looked purple and painful. It would be foolish for him to try to go on to Wichita on a crippled bike.

"Let's figure out what parts you need and I'll ride into Wichita and get them while you rest here," I told him. Tony tried to protest, but I insisted. "Do we need anything more than a new wheel and a gear cable?"

"It doesn't look like it," he replied, giving Baby Snooks a careful once-over.

The guy at the first gas station on the outskirts of Wichita was able to give me directions to a bike shop, which saved an enormous amount of time. And luck was with us when they had the parts in stock. Those days, with the Depression still weighing on everyone, shops and stores often let their inventory get sparse.

Back at the roadside park, I found Tony napping on the big cement table. At least he'd had the sense to set the tent up as an umbrella to protect himself from the sun. Even after repairing the bike, there was still enough daylight to make it into town, so we packed up and pedaled on.

The parts for Tony's bike had used up most of our money, but the next day's destination was Newton, where we have relatives. It was also the first place on Teresita's list to wire us money. The two days with our cousins were a welcome break. Church on Sunday and wandering around Buffalo Bill's old stomping grounds looking for arrowheads on Monday gave our legs a much-needed rest. When we said goodbye, we had clean clothes, fresh supplies, and enough money to make it to the next stop on Teresita's list.

We biked through the Smoky Hills, with a stop in Salina for ice cream, and just kept going. The next few days took us through Junction City, Fort Riley, and Manhattan on the way to Topeka, where we arrived around noon.

"Let's go try to get the governor's autograph," Tony said.

"Shouldn't we figure out where we're gonna camp for the night?"

"Heck, we've got all afternoon for that. Come on!"

He was right – and it was hard to argue with his enthusiasm.

We parked our bikes on the capitol grounds and found a public restroom inside where we could make ourselves more presentable before taking the elevator up to the dome. Afterward, we wandered around the corridors until we found the governor's office.

"Look, Frank, there it is." Tony nudged my shoulder. "Just go ahead and go in."

"Okay." I opened the door slowly and saw a secretary talking on the telephone. She glanced up at the interruption. From her expression, it occurred to me that we must look like fish out of water in our cowboy boots and clothes with creases from being packed in our duffels.

"How can I help you young men?" she asked, finally hanging up the phone.

"We're here to see the governor," Tony said.

"Do you have an appointment?"

"No, ma'am," I replied. "We're from Texas and we're biking across the country and would just like to see if he'd sign our book." I held the black autograph book out for her to see.

She glanced at it before looking down to study the calendar on her desk, taking her time, clearly trying to make up her mind what to do with us. "I'm sorry, gentlemen," she finally looked back up at us, "but the governor has an appointment in five minutes, so he really has no time to see you." We must have looked pretty downcast; I could feel my shoulders sag in disappointment. Maybe our plan to get autographs was just too ambitious. She must have taken pity on us, because she rose from her chair, said "Wait here," and disappeared into the closed double doors behind her desk.

In a few minutes the doors swung wide open and a thin man of average height with gray hair and kind eyes came rushing through with a briefcase in one hand and his secretary trailing behind. "I'm Walter Huxman, gentlemen." He reached out with his free hand to shake each of ours. "I'm headed to another damn meeting, but hop on the elevator with me, and I'll sign your books on the way down." The elevator doors opened just as he finished signing Tony's book. "You know," he paused as he turned toward a long corridor, "I'm a cyclist, too, and I'd sure rather be taking off on bikes with you boys right now rather than rushing to another argument with cranky senators." And with that he was gone.

Tony had a big grin on his face. "See? That wasn't so difficult!" He was right, and just like that, I knew we'd be able to get all the proof we needed to claim that two hundred dollars waiting in Gottlieb's safe.

# CHAPTER 19

There were more hills as we made our way through Lawrence, Tonganoxie, and Kansas City, where we turned north toward St. Joseph, Missouri, another stop where we had relatives and where we expected Western Union to have our next wire from Teresita. One of our relatives had told a local newspaperman about our trip, so he was there for an interview when we arrived.

The best part of our break was getting caught up on the major league baseball season. Baseball had managed to survive the hardships of the Depression and was rapidly becoming the Great American pastime. We may have been Texans, but the Yankees were our team, and it was a real treat to listen to a game on the radio.

The weekly newspaper was published while we were there, and the reporter's story sent dozens of kids to our cousins' house hoping to get our autographs. Tony and I had a good chuckle over that. "Looks like the tables are turned on us," Tony said when the last group of young boys left the house. "Who thought anyone would want *our* autographs?"

But we had to keep going or we'd never get to New York and back before Christmas. From St. Joe, we went to Rulo in Nebraska. We had a friend who'd moved there and he'd made us promise to visit if we were ever within fifty miles. "My wife makes the best fried chicken and apple pie in the entire state," Johnny had written us shortly after the move, and we weren't about to turn down a home-cooked meal. "Don't get me wrong, man. I like your fireside-grill cooking on the side of the road, but I've been thinking about that fried chicken ever since we left home!" Tony laughed.

The quickest route to Chicago, where we'd planned to turn east, would have been to head north out of Rulo. But over supper, Johnny and his wife had told us about the unusual Nebraska capitol building. "It's got a dome all right," Johnny said, "but the dome's on top of a thirty-two-story tower right in the middle of the building. I never saw anything like it. And the governor's office is at the top of the tower."

That's all it took to convince us to take a detour, especially since it was only a little over a hundred miles away. We could cover most of the distance in a day. We were starting to get into a routine. Our legs were stronger, even if they still got sore on really hilly days, and with the long summer days, we sometimes managed eighty miles or more in a day. When we'd stop for a rest or lunch or to make camp in the evening, people would want to talk to us. Maybe we were just lucky, but we never felt threatened. Folks were just curious about what we were doing and wanted to talk.

Every evening, I'd do a little more whittling, adding more and more detail. "I still don't know what it is," Tony said one night. "Looks like arms and legs on a ball of wood right now."

"Just wait," I told him. "You'll see."

And every night, we wrote something in our journals – even if it was nothing more than how far we rode and where we camped that night. But most days, there was something interesting to record – a special site we'd seen, some of the people we met, and, of course, our short visits with important people as we collected our autographs.

They must have read the St. Joe newspaper in Falls City because people all waved at us as we rode into town. When we stopped at the drug store to refill our canteens, another reporter showed up, this one with a photographer in tow.

By the time we parked our bikes on the capitol grounds in Lincoln, people had already heard of us. "The drugstore cowboys from Texas" is what the Nebraska newspapers were calling us. That was enough to get us a ride up the private elevator to the governor's office. The view out the windows was spectacular, but so was the office itself. The marble fireplace with gold trimmings was something to behold. I wished we had brought the camera up to take pictures of that room. Beautiful silk draperies adorned the walls. On the wall above the governor's chair hung paintings of the four seasons. And when we left, we'd added Roy Cochran's signature to our autograph book.

"Another success, Tony," I said as we gathered up our bikes.

"I've been thinking, Frank. Let's spend the rest of the day here – go see the museum and zoo – then tomorrow, we can make it a short day and see Father Flanagan's Boys Town."

As we left Omaha on the 26th of July – just three weeks after we'd set out from Muenster – our odometers showed close to 1000 miles. By the end of that day, we'd covered eighty-two miles and were well into Iowa. The level terrain had made it an easy day, but it also made it easy for us to see the heavy clouds up ahead. At the first sound of thunder, we made camp and got everything under the tarp, out of the rain.

The morning brought sunshine and another nice, level stretch of road into Des Moines. It was easy to pick out the capitol dome, so we didn't need directions. As we got closer, two armored cars sped past. Something was up.

"Maybe we shouldn't go rushing into whatever's going on," I suggested.

"Let's just take a look," Tony replied. "We'll keep out of trouble."

At the capitol, there was a huge crowd carrying signs that read "Maytag Unfair" and "No Pay Cuts" and "We Have to Feed Our Kids." Men and women paraded up and down the front lawn chanting "You don't pay; we don't work" over and over. Opposite them, armed soldiers stood ready to intervene at the first sign of trouble.

Tony hopped off his bike and I followed suit. "I think we should get outta here, Tony."

"Oh, come on, let's just park the bikes and go inside." He started toward the bike racks near the capitol steps, which were full of men holding notepads or cameras. One guy with a camera was hanging around on the lawn near the soldiers. "You with the press?" Tony asked.

"Not the regular press," came the reply. "All the newspaper and radio guys are up there." He gestured toward the steps. "I just try to get the pictures they miss and sell 'em to whoever'll pay."

"So what's happening?"

"Maytag declared a ten percent pay cut for all their workers, so the workers went on strike. Coupla guys got beat up trying to cross the picket lines at the factory, so the governor called out the National Guard. Now both sides want him to intervene."

Glancing up, I saw more soldiers on the roof of the building with rifles pointed toward the crowd. This could get dangerous without warning. "I'm going back to the road, Tony. No autograph's worth getting ourselves hurt or killed for."

As I pushed my bike over the lawn, I suddenly realized the crowd was milling around, closing in on me. The chanting changed to "Scabs are Scum," over and over again. I looked back and saw Tony, apparently shouting to me, but couldn't hear him over the din. Why did the crowd think I had anything to do with the strike? We should've stayed away from this in the first place. I had no idea how I was going to get out of my predicament, and it was getting scary. Just as a burly guy with a heavy black beard tried to yank my bike away from me, half a dozen guardsmen pushed through the crowd shouting, "Enough! Break it up! Move back! This guy's got nothing to do with you!"

They escorted me to the capitol steps where Tony was waiting, and I realized I was shaking from my close call. The press had been taking it all in, snapping pictures from time to time. Suddenly, one of them pointed at our feet. "Hey, you're wearing cowboy boots. You the Texas guys biking to New York?"

Tony pushed me up the steps and toward the entry door, calling back over his shoulder. "Yep, we are." We were inside before the reporters could regroup to question us.

In the governor's office, the secretary was hardly welcoming. "Can't you tell the governor's a little busy right now?" she snapped. To her surprise, the inner door opened almost immediately.

"Is there a problem here?" asked the man who emerged.

"Just two farm boys wanting the governor's autograph, sir. Nothing I can't handle."

The man appraised us from head to toe, his gaze lingering on our boots. "The Texas bikers?" he asked.

By now, I'd recovered from my ordeal and replied, "Yes, sir. We had no idea what was going on when we planned to come here. We don't want to be a bother."

"I'm the lieutenant governor, John Valentine, gentlemen. Come inside. There's someone who wants to meet you. And maybe you'll let me sign your book as well."

"We've been watching out the window," said the governor, shaking our hands. "What possessed you to try to make your way through that mob?"

"It didn't have anything to do with us, sir," Tony said. "I never thought they'd turn on us like that."

Autographs in hand, we said our thank-yous and were making for the door when the governor spoke again. "Maybe you boys can do me a favor."

"Sir?" I asked.

"All those reporters down there. They're half the reason this whole business has gotten out of hand. The strikers want the attention and the press wants a story. They're feeding off each other. You think you could talk to the newsies? Distract them from the picketers for a while? That might be just the thing we need to calm this whole situation down."

"It's the least we can do, sir," I replied with a big smile.

When we emerged from the building, we were mobbed by reporters with questions. "You boys the Texas bikers?" "Is it true you actually saw the governor?" "You two really think you're gonna make it all the way to New York?"

"Hang on, guys," Tony raised his hands. "One question at a time." We sat on the steps, answered questions, and posed for pictures for about half an hour. The reporters wanted to see our autographs.

*Best Wishes, Lieutenant Governor John K Valentine*
*Nelson G. Kraschel, Governor of Iowa*

As the reporters began leaving to file their stories, I noticed that the picketers were also beginning to quietly disperse. We grabbed our bikes and went on our way. We passed the thousand mile odometer reading before we reached our next destination—Chicago.

# CHAPTER 20

We were getting close to the Illinois state line – about halfway to Chicago – when the rain started. We'd ridden through a couple of summer showers before. They never lasted long, and they actually helped cool us off on those hot summer days. But this was different. Water poured from the sky, and the wind was so strong we could barely make any headway. I couldn't see any sign of a place to shelter along the highway, but Tony must have spied something. When he turned down a dirt road, I followed, and we eventually came to an empty shed.

"Might as well sit down and relax," said Tony. "Looks like we'll be here awhile." He pulled out his shaving kit and a towel. I took out my bag of wood and string. "What kind of puppet are you making?" Tony asked. "I see the body parts coming together now."

"You'll see." I fiddled with the string connections while he scraped a razor over his face. "Tony, I've been thinking. How are we gonna find this Petrillo guy when we get to New York?"

"Don't worry. Creeps like that leave a trail. I'm sure the Mafia's still going strong there, and if we can find the right people, we can find him."

"Sounds dangerous. We don't have a gun or any kind of protection."

"We'll worry about that when we get there and check out the situation. I can't wait to look that scoundrel in the eye."

"I don't know, Tony. I'm worried about this plan. What are we going to do to this guy? I know what he did to our father, and we both carry a lot of anger about that. But, I . . . I don't think I could beat up or kill someone. And all these journalists writing about us and our ride to New York . . . How's it gonna look when they report we're on a Mafia revenge mission?" I fiddled with the strings in silence for a while. "Besides, what good would it do? It's not going to bring Dad back." I paused. Tony didn't answer. "You know, Bonnie and Clyde – they didn't make it out alive."

"Let's find him first. Then we'll see how you feel about it. Now let's pack up. Looks like the rain has stopped." Tony jammed his shaving kit back in his bag. I wasn't sure if he was angry at me or at Petrillo. Maybe both, because he wouldn't look at me as we loaded up our gear and got back on the bikes.

Before we got back to the highway, we hit a spot where mud from the fields had completely covered the road. Tony managed to get through, but by the time I'd gone another thirty yards, Betty Lou just wouldn't go. The tires were packed with mud so thick it clogged the space between the tire and fender. I shoved the bike down in the grass. This felt like the last straw.

"*Now* what are we going to do, Tony? I'm tired of this. Sure, it's fun when we get to meet someone important or when the reporters fawn over us. But we can't find a vacation cabin to sleep in, and we're running out of money so we couldn't afford to stay in a cabin even if we found one. How are we going to fix these bikes on our budget? I'm ready to turn back and hitch a ride home."

Tony got off his bike and picked mine up. "Look, Frank, this guy murdered our father in cold blood and got away with it. I'm going back. I'm going to find that bastard and challenge him. You can either stay here and pout or come along with me." He shoved Betty Lou into my hands then started pushing Baby Snooks toward the highway.

I stood there looking from my bike to Tony's retreating back. There wasn't much choice. I couldn't even thumb a ride out here in the middle of the fields. I pulled out a screwdriver and scraped enough mud out of the fender that the wheels would turn again then caught up to Tony.

We pedaled in silence for several hours as the rain came and went. Eventually, it cleaned most of the mud off the bikes, but the dirt and water had affected the chain and sprockets, which was starting to cause problems with shifting gears. Was this trip, in a similar way, affecting the close bonds Tony and I had always shared?

Things didn't get any better that night. Unable to find a vacation cabin near Moline, we had to settle for pitching our tent on the porch of a schoolhouse. At least we'd be dry if it rained again during the night. We bedded down at dusk. And then the mosquitoes came. Swarms of them, in their thousands. Buzzing around our ears. Biting, even through our clothes. Swat one and another took its place immediately. I tried pulling a blanket over my head as protection and that worked long enough to doze off, but then I'd wake up hot and sweating with no choice but to throw the blanket off. And the mosquitoes were right there, hovering, waiting. We gave up around 4:30 in the morning, had a quick breakfast, and got back on the road. At least when we were moving, there was enough movement of air to keep the pesky things away.

Halfway across Illinois, Tony's odometer stopped working. The leather ticker had worn out. He packed it with a rag and managed to get it working long enough to get to Chicago.

Chicago. We knew it was big, but we hadn't imagined the size of the highways and the number of cars. It took thirty minutes just to find a break in the traffic to get across the big highway we had to cross to get into the city. Fourteen lanes if you counted both directions.

Tony found the post office, where we picked up mail and our next wire of money. Now we could afford a room at a YMCA hotel and found one with a view of the Chicago skyline and a Catholic church across the street. A shower, a decent meal, and a good night's sleep were really welcome.

The next morning, we had to see about repairs for the bikes. The man at the front desk of the Y told us where we could find a Montgomery Ward nearby. The estimate was fifteen dollars for parts and labor – a huge chunk of our money for the next leg of the journey. But we didn't have a choice if we were going to continue. The repairs would be finished around noon, so we went to Mass while we waited.

"The bill is $14.25," said the cashier when we returned to collect the bikes. Tony reached for his wallet. "Wait a minute," she added.

"There's a note here that says 'No charge.' And you're supposed to go back into the shop. Come on, follow me."

She led us through a swinging double door behind the counter and into a big room where all the staff and a man in a suit were standing around Baby Snooks and Betty Lou. The bikes were clean and shiny and looked like new.

"Art Smith," the man in the suit introduced himself as he shook our hands. "I figured out who you boys are. You're the two from Texas we've been reading about in the paper, right? Those cowboy boots gave you away," he added with a smile.

I looked down at my feet and Tony grinned. "I didn't know we were in the news in the Windy City," he said. "But you don't have to do this, sir. We can pay for the repairs."

"I'm sure you can," said Smith, "but Montgomery Ward wants to thank you for the publicity the bikes are getting. With you showing up here, we've got some good information on how they hold up under hard use. And we really want to know more about the tires and overall wear and tear over a lot of miles. I'd be grateful if we could contact you at the end of your trip to get all that information?"

We exchanged contact information with Mr. Smith and took a quick test ride around the block before going on our way.

At City Hall, the mayor's secretary was willing to take our autograph books in for a signature, but she wouldn't let us meet him. "When he says he doesn't want to be disturbed, he means it," she said. Edward J. Kelly signed our autograph book and wrote "The Friendly City" even though he did not seem very friendly!

"I've been thinking," said Tony as we left the mayor's office. "It's been a frustrating couple of days. Whaddaya say we take in a baseball game? The White Sox are playing a double-header against the Phillies."

"Here, in Comiskey Park?"

"You bet! With the money we saved not having to pay for the repairs, we can afford it."

We took the streetcar to and from the ballpark. The Phillies won both games, notching up a total of seven home runs. A great day topped off by a dinner of hog-liver and French-fried potatoes. By the time we got back to the Y and started writing our journals, my enthusiasm for the trip had returned. I still wasn't sure I was happy about Tony's plan for confronting Petrillo but had decided not to think about that for the moment. After all, we'd have to find him first.

The next day, we checked out of the Y, paid the two dollars for our room, and headed south on Lake Shore Drive. There were sunbathers on the beach, carefully segregated into white groups and black ones. But we were going the wrong way for Chicago's big event that day. There were hundreds of cars on the other side of the road, heading into the city to see "Wrong Way" Corrigan, the aviator who wanted to imitate Lindbergh by flying from New York to Ireland nonstop. He couldn't get permission from the authorities, so he'd filed a flight plan to return to California. When he took off from Bennett Field in Brooklyn, he disappeared into the clouds and the next time anyone heard from him, he was landing in Dublin. He claimed his compass was broken, but everyone suspected that was just a ruse. He'd already had one ticker-tape parade in New York, and Chicago was honoring him that day. But we couldn't afford to stay if we were going to make it home by Christmas to win our bet.

We crossed another massive highway then skirted the south end of Lake Michigan, watching the smoke of the steamers as they sailed across the blue water. Then we turned inland toward Kalamazoo and Lansing, where we added Governor Murphy's signature to our collection.

In Detroit, another group of reporters wanted to interview us. "How far have you guys gone so far?" one of them asked.

"Over fifteen hundred miles," Tony replied.

"And how far you think the whole trip's going to be – all the way to New York?"

"Pretty close to twenty-one hundred," I replied.

"Damn!" the reporter said. "That's about a hundred times farther than *I've* ever ridden on a bicycle." That got him a laugh from everybody in the room.

"So, where're you guys headed from here?" someone else asked.

"Well, we went up to the Ambassador Bridge earlier." Tony was our usual spokesman. "Can you believe they charge twenty cents just to look around?" Another laugh from the room. "Anyway, that got us thinking. Since Canada's just over the river, why not go around the north side of

Lake Erie and add another country to our trip? We can cross back at Niagara Falls and continue on to New York City."

"Long as you're going to Canada," the first reporter said, "you planning to see the Dionne quints?"

"Hadn't thought about it."

"There's this place up near North Bay where they keep the girls and put 'em on display to the public a couple of times a day. Long as you guys are in the country, it'd be a shame not to see 'em."

"Maybe we will," Tony replied.

After the photographers snapped some pictures, we went back to the boarding house where we'd rented a room for the night for twenty-five cents, stopping at a gas station on the way to get a Canadian map. "So whaddaya think, Frank?" Tony asked. "Should we try to see the quints?"

"Seems a shame to pass up the chance, since they're so famous."

Tony had the map spread out on the floor. "It'll take us a long way out of the way, and I don't know if our money will hold out."

"What if we send a wire to Teresita before we leave here and tell her where to send enough to tide us over?"

"Yeah, I guess we could do that. Like you say, seems a shame to pass up the chance. And it's not even the middle of August yet, so it won't put our timetable in jeopardy."

So the next day, we joined the swarm of traffic that made the Ambassador Bridge the busiest border crossing in North America. People had read the short article about us in the *Detroit Free Press* that morning, so we were greeted by reporters and photographers and lots of well-wishers the moment pedaled into Windsor, Ontario. Everyone wanted a good look at our cowboy boots. "Not something we see in these parts," said one of the reporters.

"Hey, I hear you guys collect autographs," said another one. "How 'bout we take you over to the Town Hall?" The mayor was just as enthusiastic as everyone else in the town and actually came out to see our bikes and have his picture taken.

With Mayor E. S. Wigle's signature in hand, we pedaled on. Some local bikers rode with us through the hills around London, Ontario. When cars passed us on the highway, it wasn't unusual to see girls hanging out the windows waving at us. Every town seemed to have a local newspaper that wanted to interview us, and one of them even had a movie camera and asked to take a moving picture of us on the bikes.

And then, as always, we were brought back down to earth. Quite literally, in my case. I hit some loose dirt on the road and the bike just slid out from under me. It was a nasty spill, and I was lucky to end up with no more than a few scrapes and scratches. Betty Lou wasn't so lucky. With a broken handlebar stem, the bike was un-rideable. Fortunately, a compassionate soul in a truck gave us a lift to the next town, where our luck returned. There was a bike shop and they had the right part. But the repair took a bite out of our funds.

# CHAPTER 21

As night fell, the moon created a spectacular reflection over the water. Clouds floated past the moon like transparent cotton puffs. We'd found Sunshine Cabins on the shores of Lake Ontario and rented a beachfront cabin for the night. At $1.50 per night, it was expensive. "But worth it," said Tony, "after riding through the Hamilton mountains today. Can you believe we're actually in Canada?"

The sound of the waves lapping on the beach was soothing. "I don't care how much it cost," I chuckled, "after all that uphill grind today. This bed's so comfortable, I think I could sleep for days." We were doing our nightly journal entries.

"About seventy-five miles today," Tony commented, "but I'm exhausted."

"How's our money holding up? I spent six cents for the milk, eighteen cents for eggs, and another dollar for bread, butter, and jelly. Then there was $1.25 to repair the bike today! Do you think we could afford to see a Yankees game when we get to New York? I just know this is going to be another World Series year for them; three in a row. Sure would love to see a game!"

"I don't know; everything is so expensive. Let's see what we get from Teresita when we get to Callander."

By morning, we'd both recuperated and were ready to push onward. We turned north, going through Mt. Pleasant, Orillia, Bracebridge, and Huntsville before arriving in Callander on the afternoon of the third day. As we rode into town, we couldn't believe our eyes. Every corner and storefront had a billboard or a poster with pictures of the quintuplets advertising a museum or a product. A billboard advertising Karo Syrup showed the sisters sitting around a pumpkin with the Karo Syrup can in the background. Madam Legros had her own billboard: *Aunt and Midwife of the famous quintuplets*. Everyone seemed to be profiting or exploiting these children, selling their photos, souvenirs, memorabilia, charging to see their baby basket or whatever could be put on display! Then we came to the biggest sign of all that said simply **QUINTLAND**.

"This must be the place that reporter in Detroit was talking about," Tony said.

"Looks more like an amusement park. Look at all those cars in the parking lot! There's . . . what? . . . a couple hundred at least."

"Maybe more. After the government took custody of the babies, they were given into the care of a doctor who built a nursery and playground for them. But that reporter said they're on display to the public as well."

We rode closer to the grounds. A thick grove of trees behind the property prevented cars from getting to the back side of the buildings but looked like a safe place for us to leave the bikes.

"Let's see if we can get a peek at what's going on," said Tony.

We trudged through a swampy creek and came to a fence surrounding a playground. It wasn't long before a short man in a white lab coat came out of one of the buildings. He spotted us and hurried over. The coat had his name embroidered above the breast pocket: Dr. Allan Roy Dafoe. He had shifty eyes, and his eyebrows were thin with a spiky, inverted-V appearance and one raised higher than the other. "You there," he shouted. "You're not supposed to be here. Who are you?"

"I'm Frank; my brother here is Tony. We were riding bikes through the country and just stopped to see what all the cars are doing here."

The quirky doctor said, "This is the playground where the Dionne sisters play. Everyone wants to see them. After all, they're the first known surviving identical quintuplets in the world!"

"And you charge twenty-five cents to see them? Seems strange to have them on display for money."

The doctor looked as if he couldn't believe we were questioning him and his integrity. "I started on this journey when I delivered those babies in 1934. I never thought all five would survive. When they did, I was truly amazed and began researching and studying genetics." He rambled on and on about wanting to learn how this happened, why the girls survived, and could they live a normal childhood medically, sounding more like a mad scientist the more he talked. He swore he was devoted to the children and that the money was purely for their welfare. "I built this compound for them. Who are you to be questioning me?"

"Just a couple of guys on a long bike ride from Texas," I replied.

"Wait a minute. I read about you guys in the paper. You made the headlines when you crossed the Canadian border."

"I don't know why all these reporters are stopping us. It's kind of a nuisance," I said.

"Well, I got the same problem here with reporters, always wanting a story about the quints. Come on in. I'll introduce you to Papa Dionne and the girls." Somehow we'd found common ground over a mutual problem with the press. He bonded with us over that and signed our autograph books.

The girls were in a courtyard playing like girls that age always did. Two of them were on a seesaw; the other three were squabbling over something. The sisters were charming – identically clad in a blue sailor-suit dress with a white bow atop a head full of beautiful, flowing curls. They certainly didn't look like they should be in a sideshow.

Papa Dionne was a likeable fellow, if somewhat sheepish, but he seemed to like talking about his children. "We already had five when the quints were born, and I couldn't afford to take care of ten children. I was offered money by the Chicago World's Fair exhibition to bring the girls there, but at the last minute, I didn't take it. I didn't really know what to do. Then the government stepped in and took custody of them – declared us unfit parents, if you can believe that. But it meant there was money for Dr. Dafoe to build this place and help us care for them. I didn't really have a choice. At least they have shelter, plenty of food, clothes, and nurses to care for them."

"Sounds like a tough spot," Tony said, "but surely there's a better way than putting them on display to the public for money."

Papa Dionne looked a little sad. "All that money goes to the government. They say it's in trust for the girls so they'll have an income all their lives, but we don't see much. And the girls have a strict regimen. They eat, sleep, and play on the same schedule every day; and they're herded out to the playground for thirty minutes two or three times a day while spectators gawk at them through one-way glass. Every action, response, emotion the kids have is recorded, analyzed, and shared with the press."

And then he brightened a little. "But you know, nearly six thousand people a day crowd these roads to see the nursery. Every hotel in the North Bay area is fully occupied, and the tourism has given people jobs and gotten them off the relief rolls. My wife has a little souvenir shop across the street selling postcards of the girls and rocks from the property. People buy them as fertility stones – can you believe that? Heck, even land values around here have risen. So maybe it isn't all so bad."

While he was talking, I was thinking about what it was like to have your childhood disrupted. My brothers and sister and I had been lucky. We'd had a really rough patch, but we'd found families who took us in and gave us loving homes. These girls weren't even growing up in a home-like atmosphere. It was like they were nothing more than lab specimens. I couldn't hold back. "You know, Mr. Dionne, your daughters aren't growing up as children should. What's going to happen to them as adults? They're going to be scarred for life."

"Well, boys, I thank you for the advice. I know you've ridden a long way on those bikes and learned a lot along the way. I just don't see any way out of this. I got no money or means to take them away, and even if I did, they're wards of the Crown now."

As we pedaled away, my thoughts kept going back to those little girls. "You know, Tony," I said, "I can't work out what's worse – being locked up because of your religious preference or skin color, like they do in some places, or being put on display like freaks. Why can't people see we're all just people? Seems to me like there should be more respect for each other." Tony didn't answer, but then I didn't really expect him to have one.

# CHAPTER 22

We headed south in a heavy wind and over tiring hills back to Toronto. On Sunday, we found a church and went to Mass before moving on. The wind didn't let up, and we were stuck in a drizzly rain when we faced a brute of a hill. We learned later that no cyclist had ever climbed that hill before. Maybe it was a good thing we didn't know that in advance.

In Toronto, people were exceedingly friendly. My arm actually got sore from waving back at all the girls in the cars that went by. One carful of girls that drove past stopped and waited for us at the next rest stop. We signed autographs and flirted with the girls, who told us they had some Italian friends and invited us to meet them for dinner.

We found another beachfront cabin, this one at Sunshine Cabins on Long Branch and just a dollar for the night. Tony was eager to take the girls up on their invitation. I was really tired, but I let him twist my arm. The welcome was warm, the feast sumptuous, the girls good-looking, and we talked until nearly midnight.

Back at the cabin, I was almost asleep when Tony's voice came out of the darkness. "Frank, what kinda girl do you think you'll marry?"

"A beautiful Italian girl with big brown eyes and soft olive skin," I replied. "Just waiting for the right one."

"That's what I dream about every night."

After the hard ride back to Toronto, we took it easy going to Niagara Falls. The roar of all that water pouring over the falls was unlike anything else in the world. After taking photos of the falls and the whirlpools, we crossed the bridge back into the US and headed toward Buffalo. Biking through Buffalo required paying close attention to all the traffic, but we made it to city hall and were rewarded not only with Mayor Holling's autograph but the city seal in our book as well.

We decided to camp that night at the edge of a farm. There was a small house and barn set back away from the road, but we figured the folks who lived there wouldn't mind so long as we didn't bother them. A tractor on the far side of the field was making a lot of noise but going nowhere, so we trotted over to offer come help. "Hey," Tony yelled when the engine noise quieted down for a minute. "Let us help you get out of this mud hole!"

The farmer – a stocky, middle-aged fellow – looked surprised as he turned toward us. "Thank you, kindly. I'm in a jam and could sure use some muscle here!"

"I've been in this position on our farm many a time," said Tony. "How about you stay up there and work the throttle and we'll push from the back. We oughta be able to get you outta here."

It took a lot of pushing and tugging, with the big tractor tires spinning and slinging mud every which way, but they finally managed to get some forward momentum. "Now, give her some gas slowly," Tony yelled. One final heave from both of us and the tractor finally got a purchase on solid ground and drove out of the quagmire.

The farmer stopped his machine and raised his hands skyward, shouting, "Thank you, Lord!" Then he turned to look at us and we all burst out laughing. We looked like we'd been rolling in a pigsty – there wasn't an inch of us that wasn't covered in mud.

The farmer climbed down from the tractor and held out his hand to shake ours. "My name is John Robertson. Happy to meet you fellas. I don't think I would've gotten ole Bertha out of here without you!"

"I'm Frank Moster and this is my brother Tony. We've been on a bit of a long bike ride and saw you struggling."

"Then grab your bikes and let's get over to the barn where I can spray you down and get all that mud washed off."

While we cleaned up, John went over to where a woman was taking some laundry down from the line and came back with a couple of towels. "How about I thank you for your help with a hot supper and a couple of cots for the night. Betty's cooking meatloaf and potatoes, if you're interested."

"A hot meal sounds great, sir," I answered for both of us.

Betty was setting two extra places at the table when we walked into the kitchen with John. Her skin was darker than ours – lighter than most colored folks we knew, but her hair and features betrayed her heritage.

As we sat down to eat, Tony said, "Thank you, Mrs. Robertson, this sure looks good."

"Not Mrs. Robertson, son," said John. "Just Betty. Sure wish she *could* be Mrs. Robertson, but folks around here wouldn't take too kindly to that. It's been hard enough for them to see me and Betty as a couple, and they sure don't approve of the notion of us marrying. Heck, there's a group of men who parade around with white sheets over their faces who'd just as soon string me up. So, we moved out here in the country and stay to ourselves as much as we can. Grow our own crops. Milk our own cows. And we're just crazy about each other."

Through this whole explanation, Betty just looked at her plate and nibbled her food. But at John's last remark, a smile lit up her face. And when John turned the conversation to our trip, she joined in eagerly. At the end of the meal, Tony declared it was "the best meatloaf this side of the Mississippi," which earned him another of Betty's radiant smiles.

"Those cots I told you about are out in the barn," said John, handing me a paper bag full of something. "Eggs and ham for your breakfast in the morning and some extra to take on the road with you. Now you boys get a good night's rest there."

"Thank you kindly, Mr. Robertson," I replied. "And for whatever it's worth, we'd both be happy to stand up at your wedding someday."

John looked from me to Tony. "Maybe someday," he said wistfully. Then, with a hopeful smile, he added, "I sure hope it will come someday."

We found the cots and settled into our usual routine. I got out my whittling and started to work carving indentations on the smaller of two wooden circles. "How do you have the patience to work on that tiny stuff?" Tony asked.

"I don't know. It just relaxes me."

"So is it a puppet man holding a ball?"

"Just be patient. You'll see."

Getting through the Finger Lakes region meant lots of hills, but the mountain air was crisp and cool. We stopped at Lake Canandaigua for dinner, then rode onto a big three-lane highway passing through the finger lakes districts by Lake Canandaigua and Lake Seneca. The next camping spot was near Waterloo. That evening we discovered the first real tragedy of the trip. Somewhere along the way, Kid Wolf – my faithful carving knife – had disappeared.

We were getting close to our destination now. It was starting to feel like we'd actually make it. Our journal entries started to reflect a growing excitement.

*August 25: Another milestone on the odometer, so we splurged for supper at a restaurant. Liver, onions, potatoes, fried peppers, tomatoes, bread, and an orange drink for thirty-two cents.*

*August 26: Tony cooked flapjacks for breakfast with good ole Rajah syrup and Maxwell House coffee. Lots of wind and hills but we made it past Syracuse.*

*August 27: More mountains early, but easy sailing through Utica. Sent post cards home from Herkimer and camped by the Mohawk River.*

*August 29: Albany. Mail from home! And another addition to the autograph book. Governor Lehman, who's from the famous New York banking family. Stopped for the night in Clermont.*

There was a lot to see in this part of New York State: the Roosevelt Estate at Hyde Park, the site of the siege of Yorkton, which was an early defeat for the British in the Revolutionary War, the Mid-Hudson bridge near where we camped in Poughkeepsie. From Poughkeepsie, we took Highway 202 to Mt. Kisco, a fourteen-mile climb that left our legs feeling like lead weights, so we decided to splurge on a tourist room for $1.50 for a good shower and a good night's sleep. Tomorrow we'd be in New York City.

"Tony, I can't wait to see if there's anything I remember," I said as we settled down for the night.

"There will be, but there'll be plenty I *don't* want to remember too."

"How are we going to find this Petrillo guy?

"I think we should start at the church. It should still be there and maybe the priest can help us. I'd also like to see our parents' graves, in the cemetery there by the church."

When we got to the city, we rented a room at the YMCA near what had been our old neighborhood years ago. That first morning, as we rode around, Tony started recognizing things, and we finally found the cemetery with our father's grave. The lettering on the marker was badly weathered, but we could make out the last name and the date. We sat there for a long time in silence, each of us communing with our own thoughts, remembering when Papa was alive and the horrible night he was killed. And in that moment, I began to understand why Tony was so hell-bent on finding Petrillo. We spent the rest of the day trying to find our mother's grave, with no success. So many had died during the influenza epidemic, she might not even have a proper grave.

The next morning, we decided to spend the money for haircuts – fifty cents each – before heading to the church. Even after all those years, Father Scott was still there and was overjoyed to see us.

"Of course I remember you." He embraced both of us warmly. "My contacts at the Children's Aid Society told me you were placed with a Catholic family in Texas. I even read about you in the papers, but I had no idea they were talking about the same boys I put on that train twenty years ago. Sit down and tell me all about it." We talked for what seemed like ages.

Finally, Tony asked about our mother's grave. "I'm sure she's here, my son. Let's go check the parish records and find out just where."

As it turned out, her grave was just thirty feet away from our father's, but the marker was crumbling, and it was impossible to make out a name. "I guess no one cared enough at the time to put the graves next to each other," said Tony.

"Don't be so quick to judge, my son," said Father Scott. "It was a terrible time, with so many people dying. Sometimes the best we could do was find any empty spot we could to lay them to rest. At least she's in hallowed ground and not one of those mass graves that are so sad – rows and rows of nothing but plain white crosses with just a date and maybe a name – but so often just 'Unknown.'"

"You're right, Father. I'm sorry. But I want their markers repaired. That's money worth spending, don't you think, Frank?"

I nodded assent.

"You think it could be done before we leave, Father?" asked Tony. "I don't know when we'll be back, and I'd really like to see they've been properly taken care of."

"I'll see what I can do, but that one's in such bad shape, you may have to buy a new marker," replied the priest.

"Whatever it takes, Father."

•   •   •

It was getting late. Beppe had fallen asleep in his mother's lap, and even Massimo looked like he was fighting to stay awake. "Enough for tonight," said Ernesto. "Time for bed, Massimo."

"But I want to hear the rest of the story," Massimo whined.

"Frank can finish it the next time he comes. Now up to bed."

"Come on, Massimo." Carmela stood up with Beppe in her arms and held out her hand. Clorinda and Maria followed their mother and brothers upstairs, leaving Frank, Ida, and her father alone in the living room.

"So you made it to New York," said Ernesto. "And even managed to find the priest. That's pretty remarkable after . . . what . . . nearly twenty years?"

"Eighteen years almost exactly from when he put us on the train," Frank replied.

"I cycle with my friends all the time around here," said Ida, "but I can't imagine going that many miles from home. With all that happened at the beginning, I think I probably would have given up."

"We might have, too, if Tony hadn't been so determined to find Petrillo."

"Did you ever find him?"

"That's another long story . . . and some of it might not be suitable for the younger children. Besides, I really need to get back to the barracks tonight."

"Then we'll save it for another time you're here," said Ernesto. "After the children are in bed."

# CHAPTER 23

As it turned out, Frank's unit remained in Altavilla for several weeks to forestall any attempt by the Germans to retake it. The CO continued to assign men to help the locals as they tried to take the first steps on the road to rebuilding their lives. And that gave Frank the opportunity to return often to the Perna farm.

Vincenza was another frequent visitor. With her husband still missing, she depended on Ida to help with Tito while she searched for Fabio.

One day Frank brought a small box that he handed to Tito. The child took it shyly, not quite knowing what he was supposed to do. "Open it," said Frank.

"What is it?" he asked when he took off the lid.

"Here . . ." Frank helped him remove the object from the box and held it up for him. "A soldier puppet . . . as much like the one I had as I could make it." Tito was still unsure what to do. "Look," said Frank, working the sticks to make the puppet walk. "Let me show you how to do it." He gave Tito the sticks then held the boy's hands to show him how to move them. It didn't take long for Tito to figure it out.

Ida had been watching and sat down next to Frank as Tito ran off to show the other children what he could do. "You've made him very happy," she said. "*Grazie.*"

After supper, they gathered in the living room as always. Tito was already becoming quite adept at manipulating his puppet and wanted to show everyone. "He's very talented, Vincenza," said Frank. "It took me much longer to learn how to work the strings that smoothly." Tito grinned from ear to ear, his shyness disappearing with his newfound pleasure.

"Now," said Frank, "story time. Ida's told me hers, and you've all heard a lot of mine. How about you, Vincenza?"

Vincenza put her son on her lap and said, "Well, Ida and I have known each other for a long time. We've had a lot of good times in school and here on the farm. She knew Fabio well too. We were all in Catholic school together. But it was always Ida who was outspoken and getting us into trouble – even before the Nazis came to town." She smiled at her friend. Ernesto harrumphed.

"But when they did," Vincenza continued, "they came to our school to present topics on the Aryan nation and the perfect race. Ida never paid attention. One day, she got caught sneaking off for a bike ride during one of those lectures. The teacher made her write a paper on Mussolini, Hitler, and the Aryan supremacy."

Everyone laughed.

Ida said, "Maybe that's when I got disgusted with the situation."

Ernesto, still looking grim, left the room, no doubt thinking that was probably when his daughter started down her path with the resistance group. No matter how much he'd wanted to protect his children from the crazy politics of the times, he couldn't shelter them from it. Nazism was everywhere—in the school, in the streets, on the radio, in their politicians. And now, it seemed, he didn't want to hear anyone talk about it anymore.

"Well, Vincenza," Ida's voice brought Frank back to the conversation, "don't forget the time you and Fabio slipped off after curfew and were caught kissing in the street. If it wasn't for me asking that soldier not to punish the two of you, you would probably have ended up in jail!"

Tito was sound asleep on Vincenza's lap, his small hand holding hers as he slept, his innocent face so peaceful. Vincenza just smiled.

"But, Frank, it hasn't always been like this," Ida continued. "We used to have wine festivals and big Italian feasts with lively music. People were happy. We just want that back again – our own way of life back. I hope someday you can experience the country your parents and grandparents lived in. You would be very proud. When this war is over, Vincenza and I will take you to all the beautiful places here."

"I'd like that," said Frank. "I've always wanted to come here." Her piercing eyes looking deep into his went straight to his heart.

He decided he'd better break the spell. "So, Vincenza, you and Fabio got married and had Tito and . . ."

"And then Fabio had to go to the army. After he didn't come home for the leave he'd been promised in September, we started hearing stories about the Nazis rounding up Italian soldiers in reprisal for Italy switching sides. And that's when I got scared.

"I spent every spare moment looking for him, but there were so many places to look . . . US evacuation hospitals, convalescent hospitals, army field hospitals, mobile surgical units, the local hospitals, if they were still operational like the one in Altavilla. And it wasn't a matter of just looking once. Wounded soldiers were quickly moved from one place to another, depending on the nature of their injuries.

"In some of the hospitals, they told me they'd started seeing more Italian soldiers who told harrowing tales of brutal beatings at the hands of the Germans. That just made me even more desperate to find him. It all seemed so overwhelming, but I couldn't give up." There was a catch of emotion in her voice, and she paused to stroke Tito's hair.

Ida helped out. "That's when we found out about the clinic at the villa. One of the wealthy farmers in the hills closer to Altavilla . . . he'd lost a son in the war . . . anyway, he turned his villa into a nursing and rehabilitation center for Italian soldiers. We decided it would be easier for her to concentrate her search there. Maybe Fabio would be among the new arrivals who came every day. Or maybe someone would come in who knew him or knew where he was."

Vincenza had recovered her composure by then and picked up the story. "I went every day. Ida and Carmela would watch Tito for me so I could be sure to stay until all the new patients had arrived. One day, the charge nurse asked to see me. 'I've been watching you with the men as you ask after your husband,' she said. 'You have a kind way about you and they seem to respond. I need some help with simple things . . . changing dressings, helping the wounded soldiers who are just getting ambulatory. Do you think you could do that?'

"I didn't really know what to say, so I told her I'm not a nurse and she'd have to teach me. She just smiled and said, 'We can do that. Now I think I heard you say you have a son?' I told her yes, I do have a son, and we're having to depend on friends right now who don't have much either. Then she said, 'Well, I can't pay you much, but it might help a little.'

"So I asked if I could still talk to all the men to try to find out about Fabio. And she said, 'Of course, dear. And if I see anything about him in any of the reports, I'll make sure you know.'

"So I took the job. She was right – the stipend isn't much. By the time I buy food for us, there's not much left to give to the Pernas for watching Tito or to help with the meals we have here when I pick Tito up. But I give them all I can, and they've been a lifeline while I try to find my husband. I haven't had any luck so far, but I haven't given up hope."

"Well," said Frank, "I have a friend who's a medic. Next time I see him, I'll ask him to keep an ear to the ground for any news about Italian soldiers coming through our hospitals."

•   •   •

The Pernas were feeling the pinch too. Two days later, as he was clearing the table after another supper there, Frank overheard Ernesto talking to Ida in the kitchen. "Ida, your mother won't say anything, but I will. Those were the last potatoes out of the garden. The pantry is bare, and we're using up our reserves in the cellar. We can't continue to feed Vincenza and Tito and Frank and all of our own family."

"Papa, what am I to do? Vincenza has no money except that small stipend from the hospital, and she already gives us some of that."

"I know it's tough, but I have to provide for my own family first."

Frank walked in with dishes in hand, interrupting. Father and daughter both looked unhappy. Ernesto left the room.

Frank tried to lighten the mood as he and Ida started washing the dishes. "That was a wonderful dinner. Hope I didn't bore you with my biking story the other night. Your brothers seemed to enjoy it."

"I enjoyed hearing it too," she replied, though her expression hadn't changed. "It was so much more exciting than *my* life."

"I doubt that very much. Look at everything you've survived!"

"But that's just it. Survived. Not enjoyed. Not since the Germans came. Our farm was almost destroyed. We don't have much food now. There is nothing I can say to Vincenza to console her. They've imprisoned her husband or worse." Ida's eyes filled with tears. "And my father wants me to tell her we can't feed her or Tito anymore."

Her sadness broke Frank's heart as he wiped the tears that were now streaming down her cheeks. "I heard the end of the conversation with your father, and I have an idea." He wrapped her in his arms. "Try not to worry. I have to get back to the barracks. Early roll call in the morning. We have a bridge to repair."

They found Ernesto and Carmela on the front porch. "Mr. Perna," said Frank, "I know things are tight, and it isn't easy for you to feed all of us."

"I've been working the garden, Frank, trying to scrape up what I can."

"I'd like to repay you, and I have some ideas, if you don't mind."

Ernesto didn't reply.

"Ernesto, the cellar is almost empty," said Carmela. "We should be grateful for his help." Her husband just nodded.

The next day Ray came along with Frank. They brought two rabbits they'd shot in the woods, some wild onions, and a ten-pound bag of flour that they'd wheedled out of the KP sergeant. They'd had to agree to peel potatoes for two days. "Come on, Ray," Frank had cajoled when his friend seemed reluctant to go along. "It's just two days, and we're not gonna starve like these people might if they don't get some supplies."

After a lunch of Carmela's rabbit stew, baseball was the order of the afternoon. Apparently, word had spread among the neighbor boys that the tall American soldier had seen the Yankees play, so they all put in an appearance at more or less the same time, ensuring there were enough for two teams and a regular game. Frank played on one team and Ray on the other.

Ida and Vincenza sat on the edge of the porch to watch. Tito hopped up and down, watching the ball as the boys swung at it with the bat

Frank had improvised by carving up one of the small logs from the woodpile in the barn. Now and then, one of the boys sent the ball sailing. Ernesto and Carmelo watched from the porch swing.

"Ida," Frank called. "Come on over. Let's see if you can hit a ball."

"It looks like fun, but I'm enjoying watching."

After some coaxing, she decided to give it a try. She swung the bat, but her timing was off. He put his arms around her to show her how to hold the bat. She didn't shrink away, instead leaning into his embrace. When she missed the next pitch, he took the bat and showed her how to grip it, then told Massimo to throw his fastest ball. Ida stood back. Frank swung at the ball as Massimo threw a perfect pitch into the strike zone. The ball went flying over the fence into their garden.

Baseball games became a regular thing whenever Frank could get away from the barracks. Ida joined in – Clorinda and Maria too. Tito became a helpful foul-ball chaser. Baseball seemed to bring a little normalcy into a world of war-stricken chaos. After every game, Frank threw a few slow balls to Tito. He could barely swing the bat, but he had the biggest smile on his face whenever he made even the slightest contact with a slow pitch.

Over those same weeks, Frank and Ray began taking Massimo into the woods, teaching him to hunt as a way to put more food on the Perna table. They used the Luger pistol Frank had lifted from the dead German soldier in the hills to shoot rabbits, squirrels, and birds. Frank also brought his rifle, and on one lucky day, they shot a deer, and Frank taught Massimo how to gut the deer quickly to keep the meat from spoiling.

"I wish I had a knife so I could do this," Massimo lamented.

"Next squirrel we get, Massimo, if you show me you can clean it yourself, I'll give you the knife I took from the dead German," Frank replied.

Massimo jumped up and smiled. "For real?"

"If it's all right with your father."

The next trip Massimo cleaned the squirrel perfectly, and Frank made good on his promise. Massimo beamed with excitement as he handled the knife, pulling it out of the scabbard touching the blade, then tying it to his belt using the suspension rings on the scabbard. Frank also taught him how to make a homemade bow using a flexible branch from a tree, then tightly tying twine to both ends to curve the bow. They found long straight sticks and sharpened the edges for arrows. He set up a target site for Massimo to practice.

It was difficult to come by fresh vegetables and fruit from the army base but Frank brought what he could. Now that Massimo was able to hunt on his own, he started bringing home pigeons to eat. Despite Carmela's aversion, she cooked them because the alternative was killing one of the chickens. And they needed the chickens for eggs.

One evening over dinner, Massimo asked, "Signor Frank, you promised to finish telling us about meeting the New York Yankees. Beppe and I want to hear it. How about tonight?"

It was Ernesto who answered. "If you promise you'll go to bed right after."

"We will, Papa, won't we, Beppe?" The younger boy nodded enthusiastically as he kept on eating.

While Carmela and the younger girls did the dishes, Ida joined the men and boys the front porch. "So just before it was time for us to leave New York," Frank began, "Father Scott had a little surprise for us. He remembered how much we liked baseball and had gotten tickets to a Yankees game. I'm not sure who was more excited about the chance to see the Bronx Bombers in person – me or Tony."

"Bronx Bombers?" asked Massimo.

"That's a nickname people in New York call the team. See, their playing field is in a part of New York City called the Bronx. And Bombers is because they hit so many home runs."

"The next day, we met Father Scott after lunch and walked to Yankee Stadium. In the ticket area, we talked with a troop of mounted police who autographed our books. We had bleacher-seat tickets near the Yankees bullpen. As we made our way to our seats, we stopped an officer working inside and asked him how to get player autographs. 'Meet me right here after the game,' said the officer, whose name was Alfred, 'and I'll see if we can get DiMaggio's autograph for you.'

"The Yankees were playing the Washington Senators that day. Gordon got two homers and two doubles, and Crossetti made three double plays. Joe DiMaggio knocked a home run into right field that hit the fence and rolled so that Al Simmons couldn't field it. And he was so fast around the bases. He made it look so easy. And man, those Yankees could hit! Lou Gehrig had a great day, too, and the Yankees beat the Senators 7 to 4.

"We found Alfred and, with his help, got to meet and get autographs from three pitchers, two catchers, and Lou Gehrig. Alfred was fascinated by our autograph books, so we walked over to Sixty-Third Street to have a soda and let him take a closer look. That earned us an invitation to supper, and we stayed up until midnight talking with Alfred and his friends.

"On Monday, we headed back to Yankee Stadium, to try again for DiMaggio's autograph, but the crowds were too thick. The Yankees played a double header against Philadelphia and won both games. We'd witnessed one of the greatest Yankees teams ever—a team that would go on to win the 1938 World Series—the first team ever to win three consecutive World Series championships. Lou Gehrig's career ended the next year. We were lucky to have seen him play."

"Will you show us your Yankees autographs sometime, Frank?" asked Massimo.

"Well, I don't have them with me right now. But maybe when this war's over and life gets back to normal . . . maybe I could come back and visit and bring them for you to see." Even in the dark, Massimo's big grin was visible to everyone.

Carmela appeared at the front door. "All right, off to bed now. You promised your father." This time, Massimo didn't complain. He jumped up, took Beppe's hand, and followed his mother inside.

"I still want to hear about Petrillo," said Ernesto.

"Should we wait for Carmela?"

"She'll be right back," said Ida. "Beppe will be in bed in no time and the others can take care of themselves."

"All right," said Frank. "I think I left off after we'd found our parents' graves."

# CHAPTER 24

Once the arrangements for the new headstones were settled, I could tell Tony was ready to move on to the other business that had brought us here. I hoped he wouldn't just blurt it out to the priest, so I was pleased when he turned the conversation to other families we had known. Father Scott told us what he knew – some were still around, some had moved on.

"There was a bar in the neighborhood back then," Tony broached the real subject of interest. "Petrillo's or something like that?

"I don't think it's still around, but someone in the neighborhood might know if it's moved."

We wandered around and found a few old friends of our parents, but no one wanted to talk about what had happened to them. Everyone preferred to forget what they called the Mafia wars.

A couple of days later, we stopped into a little saloon for a beer. The man behind the bar gave us the once over a couple of times before looking around warily. Then he leaned over the bar and spoke in hushed tones. "You the guys been asking about Petrillo?"

I nodded.

"What's your names?"

"Peccaro," Tony replied.

"If you know what's good for you, you'll stop asking. Just give it up." He looked around the room again, making sure we were still alone. "See, Petrillo, he's *capo* of the Italians now and nobody dares cross him.

He put the word out years ago, ain't nobody supposed to ever say nothin' about Pasquale Peccaro. Mum's the word, see."

"You know about Pasquale?" Tony asked.

Again, the furtive glance around the room. "There was some kind of argument. Pasquale called Petrillo out. That's all I know. Petrillo ever finds out I talked to you boys, I'm a dead man. So youse best keep your mouths shut, understand?"

We both nodded.

"And keep your questions to yourselves if you don't want folks 'round here gettin' a visit from one of Petrillo's goons." And with that, he walked to the other end of the bar and started polishing glasses.

On Saturday, we went exploring. First, we rode the bikes right into midtown Manhattan, then through the dark, muddy streets of Harlem, and finally to Lower Manhattan and City Hall Park. It was a big disappointment that the mayor was out of town, but there was nothing we could do about it. At the end of the afternoon, we went back to our room, cleaned up, and set out to explore on the subway – destination, Jack Dempsey's Restaurant across from Madison Square Garden.

Walking through the big revolving door, we were immediately accosted by a man in a tuxedo who said softly, "Gentlemen, I'm sorry, but you can't come in here."

"Why not?" I asked.

"You must have proper attire to come in here to eat."

I couldn't believe we were going to be turned away. "Look, we came all the way from Texas on bicycles. We're big fans of Jack's and want to see him. People say he's here every night." In my indignation, my voice was a bit louder than I'd intended.

The maître d' put a finger to his lips in a shushing gesture. "Not tonight," he said, spreading his arms as if to herd us away. "Please step outside the door."

"Not so fast, André," said a gruff voice from the crowd. "Let those cowboys in!" And suddenly, there – right in front of us – was Jack Dempsey himself. He was a big man who towered over us both, but friendly and easy to talk to. "The nicest table you've got, André," he ordered the maître d' then walked with us to where André was already holding out a chair and brushing off the tablecloth. "Mind if I chat with you boys for a minute?"

"Of course not, sir," I replied. "Would you mind giving us an autograph?"

"Find me a pen, André, and see these gentlemen have whatever they want on the house."

All the commotion had drawn the attention of everyone in the restaurant, so when Jack left our table, his seat was immediately taken by a man identifying himself as a journalist and begging for a story. "I tell you what," said Tony. "You let us eat our meal in peace and then we'll talk outside, okay?"

The young man couldn't agree fast enough. We could tell he thought he had a scoop and wasn't going to do anything to jeopardize it.

When he met us outside the restaurant, Tony spoke up first. "We've gotten used to the reporters. And we'll give you your story, but there's something I want in return."

"Name it," the reporter said eagerly.

"There's a man named Petrillo." The reporter seemed to go pale. "And I want to know how to find him."

"You do the interview first, and I'll tell you what I know."

"That seems fair."

We answered all his questions there on the sidewalk and let him snap a picture of us at the entrance to Dempsey's. Then he beckoned us over to the edge of the sidewalk and looked around warily. That same furtive look we'd seen from the saloon keeper.

"You didn't hear this from me, right?"

We nodded.

"There's this bar in Little Italy." He told us how to find it. "Word in the newsroom is that gangsters hang out there all the time. That's all I know . . . all I can tell you . . . except, watch your backs. People have been known to end up dead after messing with Petrillo." Yeah, we knew all about that.

And then he dashed off, ostensibly to file his story, but from the way he looked all around as he hurried up the street, it seemed like he was pretty sure he didn't want to be seen anywhere near us.

We wandered over to Times Square, which was bustling with people on a Saturday night. We found a souvenir shop and bought a few things to take back to our families. I was surprised they had a small folding knife that was exactly what I needed to finish the puppet I was working on. Then we headed back to our room. The knife worked even better than I thought it would. I spent that evening cutting small pieces of leather to attach the feet to the legs and the hands to the arms. That created movable joints so that strings placed at strategic points above or below the joint could make the body part move. It was a tedious job but it took my mind off Petrillo.

The next evening, we headed for Little Italy. Open door markets hung sausages and meats from the ceilings. The inside counters were lined with cheeses and different types of fresh pasta. The smell of garlic and pasta seeped from restaurant doors, so enticing we had to stop and have a plate of pasta and meat sauce.

"That's damn near the best thing I've ever tasted in my life," I declared.

"It reminds me of Mama's cooking," said Tony. "I miss her and Papa so much. Let's go find the man responsible for his death."

We found the bar the journalist had mentioned, sat down at the counter, and ordered beer. It wasn't as sleazy a joint as I'd expected, but a few of the characters in the back booths looked like someone you wouldn't want to meet in a dark alley. The bartender was a voluble sort, all too happy to engage in conversation . . . until Tony asked if Petrillo was still around. Then he clammed up and walked away. Before we finished our beers, though, he was back, asking some pretty personal questions. We paid our bill and went back to our rented room.

The next night, Tony wanted to go back. "It's the best lead we've got," he said. "The only one, really."

"Tony, I don't know. Maybe we should check on the repairs to the graves and enjoy ourselves. Wouldn't you love to see the Yankees play?"

"I didn't bike all this way to give up. I want to find this guy." He was determined to go, and I wasn't going to let him go alone.

The same bartender was there, and he disappeared when he saw us walk in. In a few minutes, he came back with beers in hand.

"How you doin' tonight? Still looking for Petrillo?"

"Yes, we are," Tony replied. "Got any ideas?"

The bartender looked just to our left and gave a slight nod. Before we realized anything was happening, two goons appeared, one on each side of us.

"We hear you lookin' for Petrillo," the one on our left snarled. "What business you got with him?"

"Who are you and why is it any business of yours?" Tony asked.

"The boss don't got no reason to see you. Maybe you oughtta just get lost."

Without looking at him, Tony said, "Peccaro. Just give him that name – Peccaro."

The goons left. "What are you doing, Tony?" I asked. "Trying to get us killed?"

"No, but we aren't getting anywhere. I thought he'd at least have enough pride to answer us."

Within the hour, the goons were back. "Come with us," Lefty said as he pushed the muzzle of a pistol into Tony's back. Oh my God, was all I could think. Maybe Tony really was trying to get us killed after all.

# CHAPTER 25

I had no idea where we were headed, but we were forced at gunpoint to follow instructions. We were pushed into the back seat of a car with Lefty while the other guy drove. It was a nice Model T, the interior all black pleated leather. The steering wheel was attached to the chassis by a long black cylinder. Three pedals protruded out of the black floorboard. No one had said a word since we left the bar, not even Tony who was usually quick to ask questions. I guess he figured we'd find out soon enough.

The car had two gears, and, once we got out of the city and headed northeast along the coast, I figured we were doing a top speed of about fifty miles an hour. Finally, Lefty started talking. "You guys wanted to see the Boss? You're gonna see the Boss. But you ain't gonna see how we get there." He took out a long black scarf and tied it around Tony's eyes, then handed me a similar scarf. "Tie it on. And make sure you do it right. The Boss don't let nobody figure out how to find where he lives." Well, nobody but his goons, I thought as I tied on the blindfold.

We drove for a couple of hours or more before anyone spoke again. "Almost there, Lefty." The driver's voice came from in front of us. "Wanna take off their blindfolds?"

"Sure, Luigi, why not?" Lefty replied.

The countryside was unlike anything around New York City. Green vegetation everywhere, tall trees reaching for the sky, and outcroppings of rock here and there. It was sparsely populated. The few homes that were visible appeared to be farms, but now and then, we got a glimpse of a sprawling estate. We turned onto a lane with dense forest on both sides. The situation was starting to feel ominous, and I got a real sinking sensation in my gut. What had we gotten ourselves into? Whatever it was, we'd just have to figure it out. We'd survived difficult situations before.

The lane, as it turned out, was a long driveway that ended at an enormous Victorian home with a large porch overlooking the front yard and a three-story carriage house behind. A horse-drawn buggy stood outside the carriage house, to the side of the double-panel wooden door that must have been ten feet tall.

"Good to be back in Connecticut. I hate the City," Lefty mumbled as he got out of the car. He swung open both sides of the door, and Luigi drove in and parked beside a magnificent Packard convertible with a Twin 6 plaque on the front grill – the most gorgeous car I'd ever seen. How much, I wondered, does something like that cost?

Luigi opened the car door and we got out while Lefty secured the carriage house doors. I was still ogling the Packard when Lefty nudged me and said, "That way," pointing to a wide hallway with horse stalls on either side. Apparently, the carriage house served as a stable as well – a smart arrangement that allowed all the work of hitching up to be done indoors without having to brave the New England winter weather. Each stall had thick iron hooks mounted chest-high for tack and harnesses. Strangely, though, there were heavy steel bars on top of the partitions between the stalls and sturdy padlocks on the doors. I began to suspect the occupants weren't always horses. The floor was made of heavy wooden planks, a few of which seemed loose. Was that just from years of wear and tear under horses' hooves, or for some more sinister purpose? The sound of a train nearby interrupted my musings. It slowed, as if negotiating a switch or a crossing, and then sped away.

A voice came from upstairs. "Come on up."

They went through a small door and up a creaky flight of stairs to a stunning room. Its high ceilings were outlined in ornate copper molding that also trimmed out large squares in the ceiling. There were elaborate wooden doors that seemed to be other entrances to the room, and one wall boasted large windows that provided a view of some kind of manufacturing plant across a road. On another wall, a brick fireplace was topped by an immense wooden mantle on which there were two ornate glass vases that looked like they'd been brought from Italy. A third wall was home to a carved wood shelf with a glass cover that displayed colorful boxes of cigars from different countries. In the center of the room was a grandiose wooden table and chairs. Scattered elsewhere were seating areas with couches or club chairs and ashtray stands. The occupants of the room were an older man, obviously of Italian descent, dressed in a smart black suit, crisp white shirt, and tie, and several children of various ages. The man took a long draw on the cigar in his hand and blew the smoke out slowly before turning to the children. "Off with you now. Back in the house to play. I have visitors." The children scurried off with no objection, as if they'd learned long ago to obey without question. Then he turned toward us.

"Mr. Delvecchio, sir," said Lefty. "These're the boys that was askin' questions about the Boss."

"Welcome to the cigar room, gentlemen."

Tony had heard the name years ago, but we didn't know much about him – only that he was known as Danny D on the streets and that somehow, he and Petrillo were connected. We learned later that he came over from Italy around 1900, got started with petty crimes and small-time stuff, and performed well enough to work his way up the ranks of the mob to become a driver for some of their more audacious crimes. He moved from that into bootlegging and extortion, and he and Petrillo became serious players in the Mafia. They eventually made enough money to purchase homes outside the city and start families well away from where they did their business. Petrillo moved several hours north of the city and opened a bar; Delvecchio moved to Connecticut; but they maintained their connection.

Delvecchio always had a keen interest in automobiles, had the money to acquire some nice ones, and set up the manufacturing operation to build and repair parts as a way to launder the profits from his illegal activities, particularly the vast sums he made from alcohol sales during Prohibition.

By the time we stood in his cigar room, he was spending all his time in the country, letting his men handle the dirty business in the city. But occasionally he got involved, especially if there was a threat to the business or some other significant concern.

Delvecchio offered us each our choice of a cigar and then invited us to sit at the table. "My name, as you heard, is Delvecchio. And I believe yours is Peccaro." He spoke directly to Tony. The Mafia code of addressing the senior person present. "May I offer you a taste of my favorite whiskey?"

Tony was not a whiskey drinker. He had only drunk an occasional beer in Muenster. But, under the circumstances, he politely said, "Thank you." Delvecchio poured three glasses. Apparently, Lefty and Luigi weren't entitled to drink on the job. Sipping his own whiskey, Delvecchio continued. "My informants tell me you're from Texas – that you're the cowboys on bicycles who've been in the news of late."

Tony said, "We are," and took a sip from his own glass. I could see him struggle not to grimace as the whiskey burned his throat on the way down.

"And they also tell me you were born near Corleone?"

"Yes," Tony replied.

"And your father was Pasquale Peccaro."

It was more of a statement than a question. There was no need to reply.

"My father was a laborer in the fields outside Corleone, like your father and grandfather. I knew them both in the old country," Delvecchio went on. "I remember your father's bootlegging operation here. He created a high-quality product. Unfortunately, it got in the way of Petrillo's sales." He paused. Tony glared at him. Another train sped past on the nearby tracks, the vibration causing the glass vases on the mantle to rattle ever so slightly.

"My father was murdered in cold blood by that swine." Tony's voice was dark, almost threatening.

"Your father was offered a business deal for his fine wine. Petrillo offered him protection and business."

Tony took another swallow of whiskey, this time not flinching at the taste or sensation. His eyes never left Delvecchio's face. "Our father didn't want to work for the Mafia."

"Maybe you boys are smarter than your father."

"What do you mean by that?"

Delvecchio took a long puff from his cigar, then answered, "We've been wanting to expand our business to other locations, especially in the South. You look like you both could hold your own. That bike ride was a pretty impressive show of strength and determination. I'm looking for some men who are smart, tough, and driven. I thought you boys might want to start a little business with us. Looking for work? Why else would you be coming back here?"

"We're looking for Petrillo. We have a score to settle with him," Tony said.

"You're just looking for trouble," Delvecchio said.

"Look, Mr. Delvecchio, We appreciate the offer and the drink – but we just want to see Petrillo. We don't want your job. We're not here to compete with you. Can you tell us where Petrillo is?" Tony asked.

Delvecchio finished his drink and looked at us as if he were sizing up our thoughts. "I'll let him know you're here, but I don't think he's going to be happy to see you. He never liked your father, obviously," Delvecchio chuckled.

"Lefty, take these men to their quarters – the carriage house quarters. Maybe the manure will help them change their mind," he ordered.

Lefty pulled his gun out of his jacket and motioned us to move to the stairs as Delvecchio poured himself another glass of whiskey. Lefty tied our hands behind our backs with rope and then began to march us down the stairs.

I started to think about how we could escape. Should I try to squeeze Lefty against the wall, knock the gun away, and make a run for it? But then where would we go, especially with our hands tied? Except for the last mile or so, we had no idea where we were or how we got here. I needed time to make a plan with Tony.

"Turn right," Lefty said as we reached the bottom of the stairs. As we walked past the horse stalls, Lefty suddenly lunged and pushed us into one, quickly slamming the door as we stumbled and fell, and locking the stall. We could hear him laughing on his way back up the stairs.

We looked around the stall. The bars were too high and too close together to squeeze through. There was nothing in the stall other than a horse trough and a bit of hay on the floor. The thick wooden stall door was solid and the bars went completely to the ceiling. There were a couple of hooks on the wall and spattered blood on the floor below the hooks.

"Is that horse blood, Tony?"

"I don't know, Frank. How the hell would I know what horse blood looks like?" Tony snorted.

"How the hell did I let you wheedle me into this?" I snapped back. Then I remembered something. I turned sideways toward Tony. "Reach in my pocket and get my whittling knife out."

"You have it with you?!" Tony exclaimed.

"Yes, just reach in this pocket."

After a bit of fumbling, Tony finally got hold of the knife and got it open. He cut my hands free and then I did the same for him. Angry and frustrated, Tony pulled at the bars but soon realized they weren't budging. An hour went by as we tried to come up with a plan. Everything we thought of seemed impossible.

Then we heard the big carriage house doors opening. Footsteps slowly moved toward us. A plank squeaked . . . then another one . . . and then, through the bars, face-to-face with us, was Petrillo!

In a tailored dark suit, he loomed larger than life. He had a huge body with a long black mustache that matched his slicked-back dark hair. A scar and a shiny gold front tooth marred his otherwise perfect face. Tony recognized the scar. The man laughed out loud as we glared at him.

"I heard you boys were looking for me," Petrillo taunted.

Tony moved right up to the bars, his eyes never leaving Petrillo. Tony remembered the last time he saw Petrillo, so many years ago. The sickening events of the day Petrillo killed our father came swirling through his head. He puckered up his mouth and spat right between Petrillo's eyes.

The grin on Petrillo's face quickly turned into a glower as the saliva dripped down from the bridge of his nose. He took out a handkerchief and wiped it away. "Oh, you will pay for that, you little shit," he snarled as he turned and went up the stairs.

When the door slammed on the floor above, I asked, "Do you think that was a good move, Tony, with us behind these bars? How are we gonna get out of this one?"

"I had to. That bastard was laughing in our face. That was *him*! *He* is the reason we came back." Tony's voice was full of venom.

I looked around the stall, trying to imagine any possible way out. We could hear Delvecchio and Petrillo laughing and talking in the room above and slamming their glasses down on the table, but we couldn't make out anything they were saying. Cigar smoked seeped from the door and filtered down into the stalls.

Suddenly, the upstairs door opened and footsteps hurried down the stairs. In an instant, Lefty and Luigi appeared in front of the stall – two huge goons, each twice the size of Tony. They unlocked the door, and Luigi pointed a gun at me as Lefty slugged Tony with his brass knuckles. Tony fell to the ground.

I jumped forward, but Luigi cocked his pistol and pointed it at my head. Tony got up and threw a punch back at Lefty and Lefty back at him. There was nothing I could do. I thought about reaching for the knife, but the gun would win over a knife any day.

With the upstairs door still open, we could hear Petrillo laugh from time to time and knew he was listening to the fight. Tony yelled, "You bastard, Petrillo. Too chicken-shit to fight your own fight?"

Lefty slugged Tony again. Tony knew how to throw a punch – we'd sparred from time to time back home. He kept getting up, throwing punches, trying to defend himself. But Lefty was built like a rock and shrugged off Tony's fists. Tony, on the other hand, was suffering a severe battering from Lefty's brass knuckles.

Petrillo finally came back down the stairs to watch. "You know, you do resemble your father quite a bit – even more now that I see your face all bloodied."

That sent Tony into a rage. With sweat and blood rolling down his face and his eyes bulging, he screamed, "You son of a bitch, Petrillo! We lost our parents because of you." Tony swung as hard as he could, throwing Lefty against the bars then shoving him aside, trying to get at

Petrillo. Lefty got back up and stunned Tony with a chop from behind to the back of his neck. Then he picked Tony up like a rag doll and hung him by his belt on the big hook in the stall.

"Maybe you'll be a little more polite to Mr. Petrillo next time you see him," Lefty said in Tony's face.

With whatever energy Tony could muster, he picked his legs up and kicked Lefty in the balls causing him to fall backward holding his crotch.

"You stupid jackass, I'm going to . . ." Lefty said, reaching for his gun, but he was interrupted by Petrillo.

"Lefty, *NO*! Don't kill him yet. I'm not finished with him." Turning to me, Petrillo said, "And *you*, younger brother, try to learn something from this." With Lefty holding Tony against the wall on the hook, Petrillo slugged Tony with a couple of punches to the head.

They stepped out and locked the stall, then went back upstairs. The door slammed shut behind them.

I lifted Tony off the hook and wiped the blood from his face. "Tony, are you okay? Can you hear me?"

"Yes, I'm alive." He spat out a bloody tooth. "I just wish I was a little bigger – I'd have showed that guy."

"Well, we gotta get out of here. Just rest here for a minute and let me think. They have guns, and we have no way to defend ourselves. But we have to figure out how to escape."

I paced around the stall. It was empty except for the horse trough. The thick wooden stall door wouldn't budge. Then I noticed one of the planks in the floor was loose. So was the one next to it. But how to pry them up? A metal bar attached to the horse trough came off surprisingly easy. Prying up one end of the planks, I jumped on the other end and they popped loose. One leg slipped through a hole between the floor joists. I pulled my leg out and looked below. A mound of hay and manure was on the floor below. With all the strength I could muster, I pulled enough planks up to create an opening into the basement.

By now, we could hear whiskey bottles clanging against the metal trash can and the noise from upstairs getting louder and louder. The men up there were probably sloshed.

"Tony, we're getting out of here." I dragged his battered body to the opening in the floor. "Now brace yourself." He landed on the haystack and looked back up with a bloody smile. I jumped down beside him.

"Come on, we've got to run," I helped Tony to his feet, and we dashed toward the light that was coming from an open door leading out of the basement. Hearing the trickling sound of a creek, we made for it and just happened to see a square metal grate in the ground that was almost overgrown by grass. Somehow, we got the grate off, jumped into the hole, and managed to get the metal plate back over the opening. We were in an old abandoned steam tunnel, filled with rusted pipes. As we started crawling through the narrow, dark space, away from the carriage house, we could hear voices above.

Lefty yelling, "I *told* you we should've checked earlier!"

Luigi screaming back, "Quit bitching and find them or our asses are in deep trouble."

Then another voice, unmistakably Petrillo. "Find them, you idiots, or you'll both be beggin' for a bullet!"

We crawled down the steam tunnel until we came to another opening. I remembered hearing the trains earlier. The tracks couldn't be far from the house, and the trains seemed to pass fairly frequently. I decided to peek out. The tracks were just off to the left. Beyond them, the Delvecchio mansion and carriage house loomed. Lights were coming on and a car was pulling out of the big carriage house doors.

And then I heard the most welcome sound I've ever heard in my life – the low rumble of an approaching train.

I looked at Tony. "Do you have enough strength to run?

"Frank, I'm pretty beat up. I can try, but I don't know if I can make it very far." Tony grimaced.

"Maybe you won't have to run far. If we can hop on this train, we might be able to get away."

I peeked out of the steam tunnel again. The car lights were coming down the driveway. The sound of the train was turning into a roar, and it wouldn't be long before the whistle blew to signal its approach.

"Okay, Tony, let's go." I pushed him up and out the tunnel then crawled out behind. The lights of the car were getting closer, coming our way.

We jumped up and sprinted for the tracks. Suddenly, the car lights were on us, but by then the train was too close, and the Packard couldn't cross the tracks without getting hit. We ran for our lives.

"Tony, keep going. I know you can do it. Just a little faster," I yelled trying to synchronize our speed to the train. The train wouldn't stop. I reached for a grab bar on the boxcar with one hand and held onto Tony's arm with the other, leaped onto a step, and somehow managed to pull Tony's exhausted body up with me.

From the step, I could swing around to an open door of the empty car. I helped Tony through the door, and he collapsed onto the floor of the boxcar. Looking back along the tracks, I could see the Packard trying to follow, but the train track veered away from the main road.

Finally, I could relax and lie down next to Tony. We napped as stowaways all the way back to New York City. We were lucky. No one discovered us. And we were thankful to be out of the mobsters' reach for the moment. But both of us knew this wasn't likely to be the end of it.

# CHAPTER 26

The YMCA was several miles from where the train stopped in New York City. The church and Father Scott's rectory would be closer but still a long walk. With Tony's arm draped over my shoulder, I supported him as he hobbled to the church. By the time we reached the rectory, we were both exhausted.

"My God, what happened to Tony?" Father Scott exclaimed.

"It's a long story," I answered. "Can you help me clean him up?"

Father Scott brought wet towels and bandages, and we carefully dressed Tony's wounds. After a light supper, Tony fell asleep.

"You never answered my question," said the priest. "What happened to him?"

"We were just in the wrong place at the wrong time, Father."

He looked at me like he knew there was more to the story, but he didn't press. "Well, you boys need to rest. It should be safe here overnight."

Rest may have been needed, but I couldn't sleep well at all, worrying through the night about Tony and about what might be in store for us tomorrow.

Sometime around midmorning Tony woke me up. He had two black eyes and cuts on his face, multiple bruises on his chest and abdomen, but was able to walk, though with something of a limp.

"How did we get here?" he asked. "The last thing I remember is you yanking me onto that train." I told him the rest.

"What did you tell Father Scott?"

"Just that we got in with the wrong crowd. I was afraid he wouldn't approve of our stupidity."

"Yeah. I guess it wasn't the best decision we ever made. But I did enjoy spitting in Petrillo's face and kicking Lefty in the balls!" Tony laughed and then winced from the pain of laughing.

"You can laugh now, but that last maneuver almost got us killed."

"It was worth the pain," Tony said.

There was a knock on the door. Both of us froze, still on edge from the events of yesterday. "May I come in?" It was Father Scott's voice.

We both relaxed. "Of course, Father," Tony said.

"How about lunch at my favorite Italian restaurant? My treat," Father Scott asked.

We agreed, hiding the anxiety that the idea of going back to Little Italy triggered in our guts. The Mafia had its tentacles into everything in the city, probably even the Catholic church, and Petrillo would be looking for us.

On the way to the restaurant, our talk turned to baseball. "You can't get any better baseball than we have here," Father Scott said.

"I know." My enthusiasm banished thoughts of the mob for the moment. "On the road to a third World Series – it's unbelievable. My favorite player is Lou Gehrig. What a champ!"

As we walked the streets of Little Italy, I felt the hairs on the back of my neck stand up – that sensation you get when you think you're being watched but can't pick out the watcher. I glanced across the street and thought I saw a man turn suddenly to study the menu in a restaurant window. Did he look a little like Luigi? Hard to say without seeing his face. He was big enough. Of course, everybody here was Italian, and the area was a hangout for off-duty Mafia goons. With Tony's limp and black eyes, we'd be easy to spot. Even if it wasn't Luigi, word could spread quickly through the Mafia grapevine if Petrillo had made it known he was looking for us. I just hoped being in the company of a priest would provide us some protection. We needed to have lunch, say our goodbyes, and get out of town.

"My favorite Italian restaurant," Father Scott said as he held the door open for us. He seemed to know all the staff and half the patrons, judging by the number of people who waved or called out a greeting when he walked in. One man – young, clean-shaven, in a suit – came over to shake the priest's hand. He didn't seem concerned that a holster with a gun was visible when he held out his hand.

"Dominic, how are you? Off the beat today?" Father asked.

"Yes, Father. Just having some lunch before I head back to the precinct," Dominic replied.

"Well, meet some old friends of mine, Tony and Frank. You might have heard of them. They've been in the paper lately. Rode their bikes all the way from Texas," Father said.

"Yes, I did see an article in the paper about that. Welcome. That's quite a task. Tony, looks like maybe you had a spill and a meeting with the pavement," Dominic said.

"Just a little fall, but I'm okay," Tony replied.

We found a table, and Dominic met with his friends in a nearby booth.

"I recommend you have the spaghetti," said Father Scott as he motioned for the waitress to take our order.

While we waited for our food, talk returned to baseball. "Who do you think will give the Yankees a run for the pennant this year?" I asked.

"Red Sox are doing pretty well, but we can beat them." Father Scott seemed confident.

"I think Chicago could be a challenger. The Cubs are doing well too." Tony added.

The waitress brought out hot garlic bread, and we devoured it. Then a big plate of steaming spaghetti, served family style. We dove in.

Taking my last bite, I spied a tall man approaching the front door with something under his jacket.

"Tony, it's Petrillo!" I hissed.

Petrillo stormed through the door and pulled up his machine gun as he scanned the room looking for us. Lefty and Luigi were hot on his heels. Petrillo fired a short burst into the air to clear the room.

That was just enough time for Dominic to draw his pistol and fire. He recognized what was going down – a Mafia hit. Several diners screamed and dove under their tables for cover. A few made a mad dash to the kitchen. Those lucky enough to be near the front door hurried into the street. Tony and I threw the table sideways as a shield and pulled Father Scott down behind it with us.

Petrillo was caught off guard, not knowing a copper would be there. Dominic's shot had hit Petrillo in the left shoulder causing him to jerk his weapon upward and spray the ceiling with bullets again. Dominic fired a second shot and hit Petrillo in the chest. Lefty and Luigi got off a couple of rounds, hitting an innocent customer, before being shot by the other cops who were with Dominic. The screaming stopped when the shooting ceased.

The restaurant looked like a war zone. Three men lay dead on the floor. Tables were turned every which way, and bullet holes peppered the ceiling. The mirror behind the bar was shattered, and pictures on the wall hung askew, their glass broken. Waiters scattered to check on everyone, and one looked out the door and shouted for more police.

Dominic ran over to the priest. "Father, are you okay?"

"I'm fine – just a little cut from the table." He glanced over at me and Tony and we nodded. "Looks like we're all okay," the priest replied.

"Well, that was a shocker. I've been working undercover lately, trying to get some of these mobsters. We've been tailing Petrillo all over New York for years trying to link him to one of his crimes. He's weaseled out every time we've charged him and managed to avoid more than one prison sentence. He's even gotten to jury members and threatened them to the point they were too frightened to vote for a guilty verdict. When he pointed his weapon at this crowd, I had no choice but to knock him off. Sorry you had to see that Father."

"Me too," Father Scott said.

"And, Tony and Frank, what a welcome to New York!" Dominic said.

"Why do I feel you boys had something to do with this?" Father Scott asked gently.

I looked at Tony and knew he was thinking the same thing I was. We'd put innocent people in danger in our quest for revenge. Time to come clean with the men who'd protected us. So Tony told Dominic how Petrillo had killed our father in 1919 and gave him a rundown of yesterday's events. I filled in the bits Tony didn't remember.

Dominic listened intently. "Are you sure that's all?" he asked when Tony finished.

"Absolutely," we answered, more or less in unison.

"Then I don't think there's anything to charge you with, other than stupidity, which isn't against the law as far as I know. I don't think you caused this shootout intentionally. Luckily, there were no innocent victims with any serious injuries." He leaned in closer. "If it were up to me, I'd give you a medal for drawing this scoundrel out to meet his own consequences." By now, police cars with sirens blaring were pulling up to the restaurant and uniformed officers were beginning to cordon off the site.

Once out in the street, we walked a few blocks in silence. Finally, Father Scott said, "I hope you boys have learned a lesson here. I know you were dealt a bad hand when your parents died, but you were given another chance. Don't blow it. You came close here. Go back home and forget about your anger. I know it's tough, but it will make you stronger."

"Yeah, you're right, Father," I said "I think we'd better head home."

# CHAPTER 27

The next morning, we had an appointment at the mayor's office. We had to wait in the lobby until he arrived, a bit homely looking and grouchy. But we got his autograph along with several other big shots in the office—the chief of police, the chief of sanitation, and the head postmaster. None of them were particularly friendly.

It was time to move on. We said our goodbyes to Father Scott. "Safe journey, my sons," he said, making the sign of the cross. "May God give you a good and happy life."

The following morning, we packed up, ate a good breakfast, and checked out of the YMCA. We pedaled from 161st Street to 125th Street and took the ferry across the Hudson River. There were big battleships in the harbor and we caught a glimpse of the Atlantic Ocean. Standing by the railing on the ferry, we talked about what it must have been like for our parents to sail over the Atlantic and into the harbor with young children and only the belongings they could carry. "I wonder," mused Tony, "if we'll ever set sail back to the old country, back to the land of our unknown ancestors in Italy."

A visit to Washington, DC, had always been part of the plan. Then we headed west, across Maryland, Ohio, and Indiana and back to Chicago, where we picked up mail and some money from Teresita. South through Illinois and across northern Missouri took us back to St. Joe for another visit with our cousins. While we were there, we got to talking about what this journey meant. We'd learned a lot about what really mattered in life and about how to survive on our own. And now, the trip seemed more like a vacation. "What would you think," Tony asked, "if we didn't go home right away?"

"What do you have in mind?"

"It's only early October, we don't have jobs to go back to, we're as fit and strong as we've ever been . . . and if all this war talk turns into anything, this may be the only chance we'll ever get to do it."

"Do what?"

"See the rest of the country. We've got friends in Los Angeles. Whaddaya say we go to California before we go home? There's nothing in the bet that says we have to go straight back. We just have to get there before Christmas." And so that's what we did.

I kept working on the puppet, a little bit every night and a couple of nights after we left LA heading home, Tony exclaimed, "I finally see it! A wooden bicycle with a puppet man on it. Can those strings really make it work?"

By the time we got home, the bicycle puppet had working joints, moving wheels, and a detailed biker sitting on the seat. The strings were attached to the joints on one end and to the hand paddle on the other end. The string movement allowed the bike to be pedaled, which moved the wheels.

There was a big celebration at Gottlieb's Saloon the week before Christmas. Beer, sausage, and sauerkraut – and the whole town was there. John had our autograph books on display beside a number of newspaper articles about our trip. He made a big show of going to the safe and bringing out the box that contained the money. "All right now, everyone," the place went quiet, "is there anyone who wants to dispute that Tony and Frank here won the bet?" You could have heard a pin drop in the place. "Jack? Dieter? Billy?" All three of them just shook their heads. "Well, then, that's that." He pushed the box across the bar to Tony and the whole place broke into cheers and applause.

Even though the Depression was still on, the trip, the celebration, and the extra two hundred dollars made this Christmas seem particularly special. As always, the family went to early mass on Christmas morning. Florence insisted on sitting next to me, swinging her legs back and forth as the organist played while the parishioners found their places for the service. I tapped her knee and whispered, "You'll have to sit quietly once the priest comes in."

"I know, Frankie," she whispered back. "But it's just so exciting. I can't wait 'til we get back home and see what's in the packages under the tree. You got me a present, didn't you? I got you one."

Florence squealed like a baby when she opened my gift. She hopped up with the puppet in her hand, a huge smile on her face, and gave me a big hug.

"A long time ago," I told her, "my father made me a soldier puppet. Every time I was sad or missed him, I'd play with it, and it would remind me of him. I hope with this puppet you'll think of me and remember how much I love you."

•　　•　　•

No one said a word when Frank finished his tale. It was as if the quiet peacefulness of the autumn night and the enormity of what Frank and Tony had achieved combined to leave everyone awestruck. Finally, Ernesto asked, "So did you and Tony finally make peace with the past?"

"We did, sir. Father Scott was right – we couldn't let it ruin our lives. But I think it helped Tony to know that Petrillo had finally met his end."

# CHAPTER 28

*November 1943*

Vincenza buttoned her frayed winter coat as she walked the long hilly trail to the villa. Today, they were expecting more injured soldiers. The Allies had discovered a hideout where the Germans were holding Italian soldiers as prisoners. Many had been murdered, but those who might have had information were interrogated and tortured. The Germans had retreated so quickly they didn't have time to kill all the prisoners, so the Allies were able to rescue some survivors. Those that didn't need urgent surgery were being sent directly to convalescent nursing sites.

The head nurse met Vincenza outside, where there were numerous green canvas tents marked with giant red crosses. "I'm so glad you're here. The ambulances and trucks have been dropping off the wounded all night long. We have some more serious injuries from battles nearby." Attendants scurried between the tents and the villa, carrying stretchers.

Inside the villa, there was chaos. Stretchers everywhere in the foyer and the downstairs parlor. Wounded men moaning and asking for help. Some of them had head wounds wrapped with blood-soaked gauze. Others suffered from gunshot wounds. A few had missing limbs in need of dressing. It was overwhelming. There was nothing to do but jump right in. By afternoon, most of the triage had been done, and the men were situated in beds. A weary soldier with a broken leg asked her for a drink of water. His face was unshaven and his hair, long and ratty. He was still in his torn, dirty uniform.

"Thank you, ma'am." He took the glass she brought and gulped it all down. "I needed that."

"You're welcome."

"I've been watching you work all day and not take a break. Do you think you could sit down and just talk to me for a few minutes?" he asked.

"Yes, it looks like we have everyone attended to for the moment." She found a stool and brought it to his bedside and refilled his water glass.

"It's been a long week, waiting and waiting for help. The pain was so bad I couldn't walk to get help. I can't tell you what a relief it is to be here and see such a pretty face as yours. I don't mean to be insulting or flirting, ma'am, but you're like an angel with a face that reminds me of my wife." He gazed at her large brown eyes, flawless skin, and long brown eyelashes.

She took a damp cloth and wiped his forehead. "Are you having any pain?"

"Yes, but it's bearable. The pain medications just make me sleepy, and I prefer to stay awake. I never thought I'd make it out alive, and I want to know I'm not dreaming."

She noticed he had to take pauses between each sentence to catch his breath.

"Do you have any injuries other than the obvious?"

"Mainly, it's my leg. I had a chest injury, but I'm breathing a little better today."

"Do you mind telling me what happened – how you were injured?"

"I'll spare you the bloody details, but I can sum it up as a generalized daily beating. My leg was broken in an attempt to get information from me. The chest wound from a hard kick."

Vincenza cringed. "Oh my, how awful!"

"I'm one of the lucky ones. Most of the men in my unit were killed on the spot." He paused, closed his eyes and winced. "The Germans thought I might have information they could use since I was an Italian officer and knew Mussolini." He sat up to drink the water and the grimace on his face and sweat beads gave away the pain.

"Let me get you some aspirin. Be back in a few minutes."

"Okay."

When Vincenza returned, he was asleep. She set the aspirin on a tray next to his water. Most of the injured slept for days after the long, painful, bumpy ride away from the prison camp. She put a sheet over his legs and abdomen and let him sleep.

The next day when she returned, he was clean-shaven, in new pajamas, and sitting up having breakfast. He smiled as she walked in. "Princess, you have returned."

"Yes, and you look like a new man. Are you feeling better?"

"Never better." He coughed out.

"I'm gathering trays. Are you finished with your breakfast?"

"Yes, I don't think I can eat any more of this, but I'd like to keep my coffee."

She picked up his tray and saw the tissues on the bedside stand, stained in blood. She trashed them and told the head nurse. "The doctor's expected tomorrow," the head nurse replied. "I'll add it to the notes for that patient."

Vincenza went back to her routine. One of the last chores of the day was dressing the wounds, the most depressing of her duties, but she tolerated it knowing this might be her only chance of finding Fabio. She had seen horrific wounds, amputated limbs, and infections that weren't healing. The stench of the bad infections made her nauseous at times. She eventually found that putting menthol rub under her nose blocked the putrid odor of the pus.

Before she left for the day, she went back to check on her patients, replenishing water glasses and checking if they needed pain medications. The officer with the broken leg was sitting up in bed reading a newspaper. He was still coughing, but it didn't seem to bother him. He dropped the newspaper and motioned for her to come visit.

"Hello, how are you doing this afternoon?"

"Better," he replied. "I managed to hobble to the toilet. But I was a bit winded after that. Do you have time to visit?"

"I have a few minutes, but I have to leave soon to pick up my son."

"How old is your son?"

"He's four. How about you – do you have any children?" she asked.

"Two sons. My family is in Salerno. Or at least, that was where I last saw them. I miss them terribly. I wish I could just let them know I'm alive," he said, his voice cracking.

"Does your wife know you're here?"

"Doubtful. The military evacuation staff asked me who I wanted to notify and assured me they sent word of my wounded-in-action status. When I got to a hospital, another notification was to be sent. But you know the military. There's chaos in the lower ranks as the leadership shifts to a new command with the ousting of Mussolini and the arrival of the Allied forces. I have little hope those messages will get to her."

"I agree – it's a terrible farce. I've received no messages about my husband." A tear started to form but she decided to try to focus on helping this soldier. "Your home's not far from mine. If you tell me her name, I'll see if I can get word to her."

"Thank you," he said, his eyes glistening with moisture. "It would mean the world to me."

"You said you were an officer. Did you have a specific group of men assigned to you?"

"I was in charge of an infantry battalion, made up mostly of men from around Salerno and Sele. On the night of the defection from the Nazis, the men that were on duty, including myself, were arrested by the Germans and taken to their headquarters. We were forcefully interrogated and as I said, many of my men were killed if they didn't pass the Heil Hitler test. I refused the response so they threw me into a crowded cell. Slowly, men disappeared from the cell. By the third day, the chief interrogator dropped fifteen dog tags on the table in front of me. He made me look down the hall to see their bodies hanging from the ceiling, bloodied and battered. Then he said I was next if I didn't give him the information about the Italian army hierarchy and the Allied plan."

"What did you do?" Vincenza asked.

"I didn't have that information, so I just said, 'They're coming – coming for you.' The officer slapped me and had one of his henchmen break my leg with an iron rod. Then he threw me back in a cell with the dog tags and the dead men. I stared at them all night until I memorized all the names. They thought I'd break faith with the tags and the bodies."

"That must have been horrible."

"It was the worst day of my life. The faces, the blood, the broken bones, the smell of rotting flesh."

"How did you escape?"

"In the early morning hours, I heard the planes flying over. Not the usual German planes – these sounded different. I could hear tanks moving too. The Germans left quickly and didn't have time to take prisoners with them. As the tanks came down the road, I began yelling out the small barred window. An American soldier heard me and came to the rescue."

"Do you still remember the names on the dog tags?"

"I wrote them down, turned in a list to my superiors, and kept a list in my pocket."

"Do you still have it? Was there a man named Fabio?"

"Yes, I think so." He pulled out the list and handed it to her.

There – halfway down – was her husband's name. She closed her eyes and crumbled to her knees beside the hospital bed.

# CHAPTER 29

Another nurse's aide working in the room rushed to where Vincenza had collapsed. She lifted Vincenza up and made her sit on the side of the soldier's bed. Tears poured down Vincenza's cheeks as she sobbed quietly.

"Vincenza, are you okay?" the aide asked, reaching for a towel to dry Vincenza's tears.

The soldier replied, "She just found out about her husband's death. I'm so sorry, ma'am. This wasn't the right way to find out."

"There's no good way to find out. If I left it up to the military, I might never have known. And even if they told me something, I probably wouldn't believe it. At least this way, I know for certain he's gone."

"The Nazis showed no mercy, ma'am. I've got to get out of here and get back to the battle," he replied.

"You're in no shape to go back."

"I want to see my family and recuperate, but then I *will* go back. After what I've witnessed, I won't rest until they're destroyed."

"Vincenza, you should go home," said the aide. "I'll tell the head nurse."

Vincenza ripped her apron off, thanked the soldier, and grabbed her coat. She walked to the Perna farm, crying all the way. But she knew she had to get control of her grief before she saw her son. She had to be strong for him.

Ida saw immediately that she'd been crying. "Vincenza, what's wrong?"

"It's Fabio. He's dead." In between tearful outbursts, Vincenza told Ida and her mother what the wounded soldier had said.

"Oh my God, that's terrible. I wish there were something we could do. You can stay with us as long as you need," Ida said, looking at her mother for approval.

Carmela nodded and put her arm around Vincenza.

Tito came running in the room. "Mama, mama." He jumped onto her lap. His happy face brightened hers.

"Tito, did you have a good day today? Tell me about your adventures with Massimo."

His voice and excitement helped her compose herself and even lifted her spirits a little. She decided she couldn't bear to tell him about his father right now.

Frank came by that evening and played ball with the boys. Ida waylaid him before he went inside and told him the details of Fabio's death.

"Vincenza, I'm so sorry for your loss," he told her when Tito was out of earshot.

"I should have known. I received no communication from him after Italy renounced the Nazis. I wish I could have seen him one more time. Why? I don't understand . . . why did he have to be killed? He was a good man – a good father."

"Nothing makes sense in war," Ida said.

"We'll go after the murdering bastards, Vincenza. Our division will soon be joining in the efforts to capture Rome. We're close to clearing this area, but the Krauts are still sending bombers in support of a counterattack. Our reinforcements are arriving now and that should give us the force-strength we need to push the Germans back."

"I hope you kill every last one of them." Ida gritted her teeth and wrinkled her face with anger.

"I wish there was more I could do," said Frank.

"The officer who told me about Fabio was from Salerno. He has a family there. Do you think we could get word to his wife and sons that he's here?" Vincenza asked.

"Give us his name and information," said Ida. "We'll see what we can do."

The next day, when Vincenza returned to the villa, she told the soldier her friends would try to locate his family. Unlike previous days, his color didn't look right. He was wheezing and couldn't get out of bed.

"Vincenza, I don't know how to repay such a favor. If I could just see my family, it would mean everything to me. It would give me strength to get better," he said.

Ernesto managed to locate the soldier's family in Salerno through his contacts in the land improvement cooperative. The family found transportation to Altavilla, where Vincenza met them and took them to the villa. Her spirits were lifted just from knowing she was about to reunite the family. She stopped in her tracks when she saw his bed was empty. No. It wasn't possible. He couldn't be.

She rushed frantically into the corridor to find an aide. "What happened? Where is he?"

"Who?" asked the aide.

"The soldier with the broken leg and cough."

"His breathing and coughing got worse during the night. The doctor came by and sent him to the hospital in Altavilla to drain his lung."

By this time, Vincenza was so involved and so desperate to see the family reunited, she took them straight to the hospital in Altavilla. They found him in the post-op area, just waking up. Now, he was breathing easier.

The boys ran to their father, their mother behind them, all hugging him at once. He looked over their heads and saw Vincenza. "Thank you, angel. You are truly from above." He pointed at the ceiling.

Vincenza watched for a moment, knowing she would not have that experience but somehow comforted that she'd played a part in this family's happiness. Then she left quietly and went home to Tito.

# CHAPTER 30

*Late November 1943*

It was more than a week before Frank was able to return to the Perna farm. But when we did, he brought a bottle of wine – a thank-you gift from the CO for Ernesto's assistance. Frank was grateful for any chance to see Ida again.

Food was still sparse, but Carmela was a superb cook who could turn anything into a plate of mouthwatering delight. A few slices of tomato and cheese – "The last round until we can get a new cow," said Carmela, "so we're stretching it as far as we can." And then sausage and a few potatoes.

"But best of all," said Ernesto, "a glass of wine." He raised his glass in a toast. "I've pruned back the vines," he added. "Next year we'll be drinking our own wine again."

"Signora Perna, that was a wonderful meal. Thank you for allowing me to share it," said Frank as Carmela and Ida cleared the table and went into the kitchen to wash the dishes.

Ernesto poured a bit more wine in his glass and offered some to Frank, but Frank declined, knowing how much the older man relished this reminder of his normal life.

"I hope I can repay you somehow, someday," Frank said.

"We're happy to have you here, Frank. And it seems Ida has become very fond of you."

"Yes, sir, and I of her. Would you mind if I had a talk with her alone on the porch tonight?"

"I'm sure she would like that," Ernesto replied.

After the children were tucked in, Ernesto and Carmela settled in on the couch to talk. Frank was relieved to see they left the lights off. The last several nights had brought the sound of German planes and bombs exploding in the distance. The Luftwaffe was not giving up.

Frank beckoned for Ida to join him on the porch. They sat side by side in the swing, speaking in hushed tones, somehow not wanting to disrupt the peaceful silence of the evening. "I've never really thanked you for teaching the boys baseball and playing with them," said Ida. "They talk about nothing else now and ask me every day when you're coming back. Every day!"

"I'm glad they enjoy it. So do I." He paused. "But I'm even more glad to see you."

The night was chilly. Frank put his arm around Ida and held her close to keep her warm. She lay her head against his shoulder. "I'm glad to see you too."

"I can't begin to tell you how much the friendship of you and your family has meant to me."

"You mean a lot . . ." A loud squelch from the military radio in his jeep interrupted her. He usually rode a bicycle to the Pernas but his CO had allowed him to take a jeep tonight.

He dashed over to the radio to answer. His commanding officer gave him coded orders to move the villagers to safety; the Luftwaffe was approaching.

Frank ran his hand back and forth across his forehead as he climbed the steps back to the porch. He'd known this time would come. The German planes were flying closer every night. The chill he felt now was not from the night air but from knowing they were in imminent danger.

"Frank, what's wrong? You look worried," Ida said.

"The German bombers are getting closer and closer. They may reach this area late tonight. I have to go. I've been ordered to move the local villagers, especially women and children, to a place of cover."

Ida jumped out of the swing and ran to hug him, "I don't want you to leave."

"You can come with me to the safe location, but then I have to leave you. I'll have to join my squad when we get there. Let's get your family and have them follow me to the church. My commander thinks the

Germans won't bomb the church, but if they do, the stone walls should provide some protection for those inside."

Ida cringed, her mouth dropped, and her eyes opened wide.

"Frank, that sounds so dangerous. Can't we all just stay here together?"

"No. The army base is too close to your farm. It's a prime site for their bombers." Frank looked at her sternly. He wished they both could swing on the porch all night but knew that wasn't an option. Ida shrugged her shoulders reluctantly.

She quickly gathered the family for the short ride to town while Ernesto fired up the old truck. Frank checked his army pack and the action on his Browning rifle. He loaded the rifle and placed ammunition in the slots on his belt then put the rifle in the gun bracket in the jeep, so it would be ready for quick use. Ernesto loaded Carmela and the kids in the truck. Ida climbed in Frank's jeep. To the sound of distant explosions, they hurriedly drove toward Altavilla.

"Frank, can we pick up Vincenza and Tito? I'm worried she's alone and has no way to get to shelter," Ida pleaded.

"We don't have much time, Ida," Frank said as he shifted gears and tried to stay on the dirt road without spinning into the ditch.

"Please. She'll be so frightened. It's on our way," Ida said.

"Okay, but we have to hurry."

They stopped at Vincenza's house and Frank signaled Ernesto to go on to the church. "We'll catch up with you there," he told them through the open window as the truck went past.

Ida knocked on Vincenza's door. "The bombers are coming. We have to get to shelter," Ida said when Vincenza opened the door.

"I don't have anything ready, Ida. And Tito is sleeping."

Frank sat in the jeep fidgeting, tapping the gear shift, hoping Ida would hurry. He glanced upward at the sky and then back at the women at the door. And then the air raid sirens started up in the town.

Vincenza's eyes widened and she looked back into the house. Tito had woken up and was now crying at the sound of the sirens.

Frank looked at this watch, "We don't have much time. We have to go *now*," he said.

"I have to protect Tito. He's all I have left," Vincenza said.

"Then hurry," said Ida. "We have to go. You get Tito; I'll grab his blankets."

Frank drove quickly toward the town with headlights off to avoid being spotted by the bombers. Several ridges in the road caused them to swerve in and out of the ditches. The town was dark as they approached the checkpoint where the guard told Frank to beware. "There's been sniper fire in the area earlier tonight. Anybody in an army vehicle's likely to be a target."

Frank looked up at the sky, then headed uphill through the winding cobblestone streets toward the church, constantly looking from the road ahead to the windows of the buildings they passed. People were scurrying from their homes looking for a safe place. After a tense few minutes of trying not to crash in the dark or hit people running through the street, they could see the steeple not far ahead. In the darkness, there was a sudden tiny burst of red light from an upstairs window in an apartment a few blocks from the church. Almost simultaneously, a bullet hit the hood of the jeep causing Frank to swerve and turn into an alley. He could feel his heart pounding.

Vincenza screamed and Tito began to cry as they both were thrown to one side of the jeep. Ida tried to calm them and pulled the blanket over both of them for cover. Frank drove down the alley and stopped out of view of the sniper. "Don't panic. Just stay here in the jeep under the blanket and stay quiet. I'll be right back." He grabbed his rifle from the bracket, looked up at the sky again, and ran back to the street to see if he could fire back at the sniper. Unable to see anything, he hurried back to the jeep, knowing its occupants were vulnerable in the alley. A constant droning sound was getting louder. The bombers were coming. He drove quickly to the church and hustled everyone inside.

The Perna truck was parked by the church, so Frank knew the rest of the family was there. Visibility was low inside the church, but moonlight crept through the windows and a dim candle in the windowless part of the sanctuary allowed them to see people. The droning sound was now the blaring motors of aircraft flying over Altavilla. The building shook as the first wave of bombs hit at the edge of town. Some of the villagers were praying at the altar, others huddled in the pews with their children. An older woman lit a novena candle near a statue that was directly below a stained-glass window, causing the window to glow in beautiful bright colors. Ernesto hurried to extinguish the flame as the villagers pleaded with the woman, "Please don't light any more candles. The German planes will spot the light."

Ida ran to her family and hugged her brother and mother. They gathered in one of the side chapels. The first wave of bombers had passed, and there was a moment of peace as the dust settled.

"I have to go, Ida," Frank said. "I have to find that sniper and get to my squad."

She had a tear in her eye, "Frank there are Germans out there. They fired at us. Please stay here where it's safe."

"As much as I'd love to stay with you, no one is safe with that sniper out there. I have to find him and catch up with my unit. And it's safer for you here. I'll be back. I promise." She kissed him and whispered in his ear as she handed him a photograph. He smiled and placed it in his helmet. Oh, how he longed to stay and protect them!

Tito started crying. "He's hungry," said Vincenza. "I had only one potato, and he ate that this morning. And he needs water."

"Come on, Vincenza," said Frank. "The family room's at the back of the church on my way out. There should be a water fountain or sink there. Ida, stay here with your family." His tone was stern. He knew Ida could easily take it into her head to do something rash, and the last thing he wanted was for her to put herself in danger. "I *will* come back for you all as soon as I can."

He left Vincenza helping Tito to drink from the fountain. "Get back to the Pernas as quickly as possible," he told her as he made his way to the church door.

When he opened it, the distant drone of the bombers was approaching again. His palms grew sweaty with anxiety, as he was torn between staying at the church to protect the civilians and going out to look for his squad. He looked up at the sky. The sound of the planes was getting louder, but he couldn't see them yet. And then he spotted something – someone peering out the window from the lodging quarters above a store. In the moonlight, he recognized the shape of a German helmet. The sniper, also looking for his planes overhead.

"Vincenza, I have to go. I'll try to come back after the bombings cease. But right now, I can see where that sniper is."

He walked out the church door, feeling keenly the pain of leaving behind his love, his new family, and his friends. The noise from the planes was growing ever louder. He fingered the cross that hung around his neck with his dog tags. "Dear God," he prayed silently, "keep them safe. Mother Mary, watch over them in this holy place. Please don't let them be trapped like sitting ducks in a big stone building."

Staying low to avoid detection, he crept through the churchyard to the street then made a mad dash for the building where he'd seen the sniper. He found an entrance and pushed open the door. The hinge was old, and its creak was audible even above the noise of the planes. There were footsteps on the floor above. It was dark in the foyer, but his eyes adjusted quickly. The staircase was directly in front of him. The sniper would have the advantage of being at the top of the stairs, but Frank was sure he could take out a lone sniper if he could make surprise work in his favor. The planes were almost overhead now, and the noise would drown out any footsteps on the stairs.

Frank bolted up the steps two at a time, rifle at the ready, and made it to the landing just as a loud boom and bright flash lit up the window. The light lit up a German soldier, gun in his right hand, temporarily disoriented by the sudden burst of light in his eyes. Frank fired, hitting the man in the shoulder and causing him to drop the gun. The sniper ran toward a door on the other side of the room, leaving a trail of blood. As Frank gave chase, more bombs dropped from the planes, a ceiling support fell directly in front of him, and debris started flying. The German made it into the next room and slammed the door. Frank stepped over the beam and made his way cautiously to the door. Standing to one side, he turned the knob then pushed the door open slowly with the barrel of his rifle. He readied his weapon and stepped through the door. The German, holding a knife in his left hand, lunged full-force at Frank. Frank fired.

# CHAPTER 31

The sniper was dead. This was the first time Frank had pulled the trigger at such close range. But knowing how close the sniper shot had come to harming Ida meant he hadn't thought twice. He picked up the sniper's rifle and inspected it, clearly a better weapon than his. But he had no ammunition for it, so he dismantled it and chunked the parts into the street as he walked outside. He kept the knife.

The immediate threat was neutralized, but his relief was short-lived. The buzzing of another wave of approaching planes was rapidly becoming a roar. He wiped the sweat off his face and looked up at the sky. Black specks were visible in front of the clouds, growing larger and larger with each passing second.

He tried to run to find his squad but the cobblestone streets made it difficult to move fast without twisting an ankle. There was an eerie whistling sound followed by massive explosions as the bombs began falling from the planes. Then came a wave of planes strafing the town with machine-gun fire, a shrieking hail of bullets in straight lines down the streets, raining death on soldiers and civilians as they scurried from building to building looking for cover. The sounds were deafening: the exploding bombs, the engines of low-flying planes, the relentless firing of the guns, people screaming in the streets as they fell victim to the airborne assault.

Frank was breathing hard and felt his heart throbbing in his chest as he huddled in the shelter of a building trying to avoid being hit. The stone buildings were crumbling under the bombers' assault, and he barely escaped a spray of bullets down the street beside him. He started running for his life, sprinting in a zig-zag pattern in an effort to avoid the rapid-fire bullets.

Bombs fell on anything and everything, starting fires in the grassy park and inside the buildings they destroyed. High shooting flames created an orange glow in the streets. A man ran out of a building just ahead of Frank, his clothes on fire. Frank rushed to help him, and used his jacket to try to put out the flames, but it was too late. The man's body was charred beyond survival. There were bloody, mangled bodies everywhere, complete chaos as the planes circled for another pass. Frank ran for cover in a garage and paused to catch his breath. Several women and children were hiding there.

His thoughts turned to Ida. Had the church escaped the bombs? Or had those heavy stones come crashing down on the people inside? Losing her . . . it was beyond contemplation. He had to know. So when the roar of the departing planes subsided, he stepped out of his hiding place and back into the street.

The fires were shooting out of the buildings now, black smoke billowing above the orange glow. The air was thick with smoke and dust, and the smell of burning debris and charred bodies was sickening. He coughed, covered his mouth and nose with his handkerchief, and started running. Broken boards and burning debris rained down from damaged buildings, forcing him to stay in the middle of the street for safety. Looking right, left, up, straight ahead – anywhere danger might lurk – he failed to notice a loose cobblestone and tripped. His face hit the pavement next to a dead man lying in a pool of blood with his detached arm still holding a suitcase full of belongings. Ignoring the pain, Frank jumped up and took off.

As he rounded the corner, he froze in his tracks, his heart in his throat. The entire back wall of the church had collapsed. Where the entrance had once been, there was only a mountain of rubble. He could hear babies crying and people wailing inside. There had to be another entrance somewhere on the side, between the chapels. In desperation, he darted around to the west side in search of a door that wasn't blocked. More debris jammed that entrance. By now he was growing frantic. On the opposite side of the church, he found an unobstructed door and reached for the handle then pulled back his hand. What would he find beyond that door? If Ida was dead . . . he didn't think he could bear it. His heart pounding, he pulled the door open and stepped cautiously inside. This part of the church seemed unharmed. He rushed to the chapel where he'd left the Pernas . . . and there they were, huddled beside the altar, alive but clearly shaken. Ida turned at the sound of his footsteps. "Frank?" she asked hesitantly. Then she jumped up, ran to him, and hugged him for all she was worth. "*Grazie a Dio*, it *is* you! What happened to your face? And your jacket? *Dio mio*, I was so worried."

Tears welled in her eyes and ran down her cheeks. He grabbed her and held her tight. "I'm fine," he said. "Where are Vincenza and the baby?"

"She never came back after you took her to the back of the church. I wanted to go get her when the bombings started, but Papa wouldn't let me," Ida sobbed.

The image of what he'd seen from the outside flashed into Frank's mind. Without a word, he grabbed Ida's hand, and they ran to the back of the church.

The wall had collapsed into the room. Fallen pillars and stone from the walls had created a dangerous heap of rubble, with broken stones and wood piled haphazardly. Frank, Ernesto, and the other men started removing stones carefully, trying to prevent further collapse.

"*Aspetta!*" said Frank. Wait! He put a finger to his lips. "*Silenzio.*" And then he heard it again. A soft whimper that sounded as if it was coming from the bottom of the rubble.

"Dig faster. There's someone under this mess!" Frank shouted.

They began working frantically. Soon everyone's hands were cut and bleeding from pulling out broken rocks and fragments. The men lifted a large hunk of wall, and as they flipped it over, they uncovered a gruesome site. Vincenza's crushed body with her hands and arms stretched out, splayed like she was trying to protect something. The whimpering turned into a full-blown scream. Vincenza was dead, but Tito was under the small table she was lying over. Her body had held the table in place, just enough to keep the wall from crushing Tito.

Ida's suppressed scream turned into loud sobbing. Ernesto put his arms around his daughter and tried to block her view, as Frank gently placed Vincenza's bloody body on the ground. He tried to pull Tito out from under the table, but the child let out an ear-piercing scream. His small leg was wedged beneath some stone. They'd have to dig more to get him out.

While the others did the digging, Frank knelt down and put his head under the table. Tito recognized him immediately and reached out his hands. The look in the little boy's eyes broke Frank's heart – the child desperately wanted to be held and consoled, but his mother would never hold him again.

Finally, they got him free. When Frank pulled him out, he was covered with dirt and streaks of his mother's blood that had dripped onto him as she shielded him from the falling debris. He handed the boy to Ida, who cleared the dirt from his face and held him close. Then she and Ernesto took him back to the chapel.

Frank looked at Vincenza lying there on the ground. His throat was tight and he began to weep inside. He wished he had brought her back to the chapel before he left. He wished he had never left the church. He wished he had stayed to keep them safe. Would she have survived if they'd left her at home? It was all too much. He wanted to scream out loud at the senselessness of it all, but he couldn't. He looked at Vincenza and knew he would never forget her face.

He carried her body to the main altar and laid her beneath the crucifix, his eyes fogging with tears. Then he took a tattered curtain that had been pulled from the debris and draped it over her. At the bottom of the altar steps, he turned and looked at her, resting below the feet of Jesus, and knew he would never be the same again. He made the sign of the cross and prayed silently, "God, grant her swift passage to heaven."

He walked to the back of the church, communing with his thoughts, his gaze transfixed on the gigantic hole in the ceiling and the disintegrated wall. Two large support beams hung from the ceiling like broken branches ready to fall off a dead tree. A church that took men ages to build and that had stood for centuries was now destroyed in a single minute with a single bomb, leaving a small child orphaned. Tito was about the same age Frank had been when he'd lost his own parents. All the memories came flooding back.

And in that moment, his sorrow turned to resolve. He'd always known this war was important – that the scourge of Nazism had to be defeated. But now it was personal.

Back in the chapel, Ida was doing her best to comfort Tito. She had tears in her eyes as she held him and gently rocked him back and forth.

Frank embraced them. "I have to go," he said gently. Then he turned to Ernesto and there was steel in his voice. "This has to be stopped, and I have to be part of stopping it."

# CHAPTER 32

On the morning of Vincenza's funeral Ida woke up early, her eyes sunken with dark circles around them. Tito had cried most of the night, and she'd cuddled and comforted him until he finally fell asleep. Now she had to decide what to wear for this sad day. The few clothes she had were old and worn and no longer fit well. She found an old black dress and some faded, worn black shoes. Removing her nightgown, she looked at herself in the mirror. She'd gotten so thin. Her ribs were showing and her arms were like sticks. The dress, when she put it on, sagged on her like a child playing dress-up with one of her mother's frocks.

She woke Tito, found him a scrap of bread for breakfast, and took him outside on the porch to wait until it was time to leave. Frank had promised he'd be there. After the bombing, his unit had been assigned to search the rubble for survivors, and they rescued a number of people who'd been trapped in basements or in pockets in the piles of stone where they could survive but not escape on their own. But mostly, they found victims. The 36th Division was still on assignment to hold the valleys of the Sele and Calore Rivers and help the locals start to rebuild, but new orders were expected any day now. Knowing how valuable Frank's connection to the Pernas had proven to the division's mission, the CO gave him time to spend with the family whenever it didn't interfere with the army's needs.

Frank managed to get a jeep again that day so they wouldn't all have to squeeze into Ernesto's truck for the drive to the small parish church next to the cemetery. "Ida, you look beautiful," he said as he bounded up the steps to the porch. This was the first time he'd seen her dressed up.

She tried to smile but couldn't hold back the tears welling in her eyes as she rose from the swing, leaving Tito there holding onto his puppet for consolation. Frank put his arm around her and they walked to the other side of the porch. "Ida, I'm so sorry. It must be horrible losing your best friend."

"It's worse than that," she said quietly, not wanting the child to hear.

"What's happened?"

"Papa says we can't keep Tito."

"I'm not surprised." Frank tried not to sound harsh. "Think about how hard it is for him to support his own five children."

"Yes, I know. But what's going to happen to Tito?"

"Does Vincenza have any family in Altavilla?"

"No, her family moved away before the war. She stayed to be with Fabio. I never knew his family, but I think he was from Sicily."

"Well, let's talk to the priest after the funeral. Maybe there's an orphanage he can go to until the war is over and then . . ." He paused and found himself thinking of life after the war . . . of coming back for Ida and Tito. But now wasn't the time to be making plans for the future. Now was a time to grieve.

"It's *Tito*, Frank. How will he survive in an orphanage, in the middle of a war?" She retorted.

"He's strong – he can make it. And an orphanage might be the safest place for him, at least temporarily. If circumstances were different, I would take him, but you know I can't. Let's see if the church has a place for him."

She nodded and took his handkerchief to dry her tears.

He caressed her hair. "Ida, I only knew Vincenza for a short time, but I know she was a devoted mother. She would have wanted the best for him." Nothing about this was fair. Not Vincenza's senseless death. Not Tito being left an orphan. Not the deprivations of war that made it impossible for the Pernas to take him in. Not the perils Tito might face in an orphanage. But Frank had to give Ida as much comfort and strength as he could. And when the time came for his unit to move on, he had to do his part to put an end to the madness.

A number of families from the neighborhood joined the Pernas for the Mass and burial. The ceremony was short, as the priest had several of these sad duties to perform that day. Everyone was silent as they followed the priest on the short walk from the little church to the freshly dug grave. As the wooden casket was lowered into the ground, Ida stared at the box for a very long time. Finally, she made the sign of the cross and threw a flower onto the casket.

Frank and Ernesto took the priest aside to talk about what could be done for Tito. "There's an orphanage in San Pietro," he said. "Let me make inquiries."

"Thank you, Father," said Ernesto. "I would take him if I could, but these days . . ."

"Do not trouble yourself, my son. We do the best we can, and God will look out for the rest." Frank remembered how lucky he and his siblings had been to find loving families. Perhaps the priest was right.

It was customary to have a dinner after a burial for all the friends and neighbors to celebrate the life of the deceased. But with food so scarce, the neighbors understood and quietly went on their way. Frank took Ida and Tito back to the farm before returning to his post.

There, he discovered a mail bag had arrived, and he had a letter from Tony. It was the first time he'd smiled in days. He quickly ripped the envelope open and began to read.

*All is well here in Texas, Frank. I'm home on leave. Steve is in the Pacific. Mom said she got a letter from him last week, and he's doing fine. I'm being transferred to San Diego later this week and stopped to see the family on the way. Mom is well, but she worries about you constantly. Florence and Joey are growing up. They asked when you'll be home to play ball with them. Dad tries to stay busy farming, but his health is failing. I hope you're staying warm wherever you are. Mom says you met an Italian family. That's nice – hopefully a break from the barracks. I've heard rumors that the Germans have rounded up Jews across Europe. The stories are brutal. It seems they execute those who don't follow orders and have moved masses of people to work camps. Please be careful and be strong and fight for what you know is right. I hope to join you there soon or better yet, to have this war end and have you home for a long bike ride again. Love, Tony*

Oh, how he wished he could talk to Tony now! He'd tell him about the bombings and about Vincenza and about his guilt over Tito being orphaned. He'd tell him about the sick feeling in the pit of his stomach when he'd shot the sniper at close range. Tony had kept them together on the Orphan Train. Tony was the one who'd kept him going when he was too tired to pedal or too discouraged to go on. Tony would give him strength to see this through. And oh, he'd tell him about Ida too! He looked back at the letter, and Tony's answer leaped out from the page. *Be strong and fight for what you know is right.*

Frank put the letter in his pocket and went in search of his captain.

"I'd like to volunteer for the next reconnaissance mission, sir," he said.

The captain was older than Frank, but they'd been in training camp together back in Texas. They'd both survived the Salerno landing, but the captain had a few scars to show from the battle. A long scar on the side of his face said he'd been too close to some flying debris or shrapnel, but he'd been stitched up and was back in the action.

"Noted, Sergeant," said the captain. "There's going to be a major offensive – a big push to Rome. The plans are still being finalized, but it won't be long. For now, just keep doing what you're doing with locals. I'll let you know when we have our orders."

"Yes, sir."

"And Frank?" the captain's tone was less formal.

"Sir?"

"I heard it was you who took out that sniper. Nice job."

"Thank you, sir."

He grabbed several boxes of rations from the quartermaster – Massimo had decided he actually liked them and hoarded whatever Frank could bring. Frank, on the other hand, was eager for another of Carmela's home-cooked meals. He checked his sidearm, grabbed a bicycle, and headed for the farm. Along the way, he managed to kill a rabbit. They'd have meat for dinner.

# CHAPTER 33

And then the rains came. Monsoons that saturated the ground and kept on falling. Swollen rivers grew to five times their usual size. Roads flooded and bridges caved in. The whole Fifth Army was stuck in the mud, unable to mount an offensive. The only silver lining to the relentless clouds was that the enemy was stuck too.

When there finally came a day with only occasional showers, Frank knew their deployment orders wouldn't be far behind. The generals would want to get a jump on the Germans. He took advantage of what might be his last chance to spend time with Ida before they moved out.

She was cooking when he arrived. He gave her a big hug, getting a smile and a wink in return.

"Frank, I'm so glad to see you. We thought you'd be leaving soon."

"Now that the rain seems to be slowing down, yes – soon." She frowned. He pulled out the picture of her that he'd tucked into his hat and held it up for her to see. "And I'll keep this with me all the time to remind me of you."

The frown went away and she planted a warm kiss on his lips.

Frank looked around. "Where's Tito?" The boy had been clinging to Ida ever since he'd lost his mother.

"The child care authority came this morning. They insisted he had to be placed with a family member or go to a local orphanage. I was so upset, but they said I didn't have a say if I wasn't related to the baby. Papa didn't argue because we don't have enough food. They're working with the Church to get him placed."

"Which orphanage?"

"San Pietro – the one the priest who buried Vincenza told us about. The roads to there have reopened, so they took Tito to the church this morning."

"How will they get him there? There'll be Nazi barricades and checkpoints on the way, and there's no way to predict what kind of fighting there might be in the area."

"It's dangerous everywhere. But there are caves in the area, and the nuns and some of the local women care for the children in the caves. The priests are allowed through the checkpoints to go to the Monte Cassino Abbey and certain villages. The Nazis have allowed them access to say Mass at the churches."

Frank looked puzzled. "So Tito is being smuggled through with the priest?"

"Something like that. I went to the rectory to talk to the priest, but they told me not to worry. They've been doing this successfully for a while. There's a beat-up blue truck parked at the rectory that belongs to the church – it's what the priest will use to take him to San Pietro. They told me I was better off not to know the details."

"I've seen that truck. It doesn't look like it would make it around the block." He was worried about Tito, but there was nothing he could do. He was a soldier in the middle of a war.

"Frank, where are you going? Can't you give me some idea?" Ida asked.

"I couldn't tell you even if I knew, and we don't get our orders until we're rolling out," Frank said.

"When will you be back?" Her voice was sad and plaintive.

"As soon as I possibly can. I'll miss you, but the farther we advance from here, the safer you'll be."

"I know," she sounded resigned, "but it's just so dangerous. Let me finish up here, and then we can talk on the porch."

Frank retreated to the living room where Ernesto sat reading an old tattered magazine from before the war. "I like to remember what it was like before the Germans came," he said. "And now I can almost dare to hope that we might see those times again one day." He folded the magazine carefully and placed it on the small table beside his chair as

Frank took a seat on the sofa. "I saw the troop trucks arriving. I think that means you'll be leaving us soon."

"That's what we hear."

"Well, you're welcome to come back here anytime. You . . ." he looked down at his hands, not wanting to show emotion. "You've become like another son to me."

"Thank you, sir. I feel at home here with your family."

"Think of this as your Italian home, Frank."

"Actually, sir, I've been meaning to talk to you about Ida. I want you to know . . ." He paused and took his cap off, then looked Mr. Perna directly in the eye and said, "I want you to know that I love her. I want to come back and marry her."

Ernesto didn't seem in the least surprised. "I know she loves you too. You two haven't known each other very long, but you've been through a great deal in that short time. Those are the times that make us strong – the times when bonds are formed. When you come back, I would be proud to have you as a son-in-law."

They shook hands and Frank went out to join Ida, who was waiting on the porch step. "What took you so long?" As she turned to look at him, her hair flew to the side and her lips moved into a captivating smile. Her flawless olive skin glowed in the daylight. Frank's heart skipped a beat – he couldn't take his eyes off her. They sat down together on the porch.

"What were you talking to my father about?" she asked as he moved closer to her.

"There's something I want to ask you." He stared into her eyes for several seconds.

She nodded and looked at him inquisitively as if to say "Go on."

"Ida, I told your father, when I come back from this war, I want to marry you."

Ida stared at him, her mouth agape. Then she turned and saw her whole family looking out the window, all smiling. She was quite literally speechless. All she could do was nod her head and smile with the complete and total joy of it all. Frank took her in his arms and they kissed deeply and passionately, then clung to each other, not wanting the moment to end, knowing there was so much they had to face before they could be together forever – but happy as two people always are when they declare their love.

When they finally released their embrace, the family came running out the door, Clorinda and Maria squealing and jumping up and down and hugging their sister.

Frank stayed with Ida as long as he could, but the time came when he needed to return to base. He tucked her picture into his shirt pocket and put his hand over his heart. "This goes in my helmet in the morning," he told her, "so you'll always be in my thoughts." He gave her a long good-night kiss, and she clung to him until he finally had to say, "I don't want to, but I must go." He held her at arm's length. "If the worst should happen . . . if I die and never come back to you, look up at that star." He pointed to the brightest star in the dark blue night sky. "That will be me." Then he held her close for one more passionate kiss before walking to his jeep and driving off.

That night, he tossed and turned, worrying about Ida, distraught over leaving her, fearful for Tito as he was smuggled to the orphanage. He'd just lapsed into a deep sleep when reveille sounded, the prelude to the assembly where they'd find out what was going to happen next.

The CO didn't waste time with pleasantries. "The Fifth Army has a job to do. We have to control Route 6. Whoever controls this road controls Rome – and ultimately Italy. So we will take it and we will control it. That's your only priority – your only objective. And controlling Route 6 means we have to get control of the Liri Valley. That's the job that's been assigned to the 36th."

Frank looked around the room. He wasn't the only one who knew that the Germans controlled several mountain peaks where the road ran through the valley. He began tapping his foot nervously as he listened to the CO describe the plan and understood the danger they'd be facing.

"We need to take these hilltops here, here, and here," the CO pointed out the locations on the map, "and get ourselves established in San Pietro as quickly as we can."

"Did you say San Pietro, sir?"

"That's right, Sergeant, now don't interrupt. It's a mountain town that's the threshold to the Liri Valley. But it's heavily fortified by the Germans, so we'll have a fight on our hands. This rain has made a mess of everything, so you're going to be fighting in the mud and the muck. But we have a job to do. And it's the most important Allied operation yet. Be proud of the T-patch on your uniform!"

The room broke into a roar of cheers.

When the noise quieted, the CO resumed. "Officers and sergeants of the 143rd – in the chart room with me now. Everyone else, assemble with your unit commanders for instructions. Dismissed."

Eighty or so men crammed themselves into the small chart room behind the CO. "Your regiment's drawn the toughest job, men. Mount Sammucro sits just north of and overlooks San Pietro. That's one objective. The town of San Pietro is the other. We have intelligence that the civilians have been hiding in caves in the mountains around the town. There's also an orphanage there. G2 says the children are being protected in the caves, but we have to be careful."

At the mention of the orphanage, Frank's blood ran cold. He was sweating, even on this cold December morning, and his head pounded with every beat of his heart. Tito was going to be right in the middle of the battle. "Something wrong, Moster?" his captain nudged him.

"Nothing I can do anything about."

"Then listen up."

"We also have information," the CO continued, "that the men of the town are being forced by the Germans to help fortify a defensive line. You can expect plenty of land mines, so be on your guard. We'll get you as close as we can in trucks, but the terrain and mud are going to limit how far the trucks can go. You'll have to do the rest as foot soldiers. There's another regiment going after Mount Lungo to secure the south side of the road, but San Pietro is the key to our advance.

"Trucks leave at eleven hundred hours. Any questions?" No one spoke. "Very well. Dismissed."

# CHAPTER 34

*December 1943*

The column pulled out of Altavilla on schedule. Many of the troop transports had chains on the tires for extra traction on the muddy roads. But as truck after truck after truck passed, the weight of the vehicles and the action of the treads and chains churned the mud into an endless quagmire. They passed a few local vehicles that had been abandoned when they'd gotten stuck.

As the roads became increasingly impassable, the truck drivers struggled to avoid the worst of the mud holes. Lighter vehicles could take to the side of the road or follow a narrow track that ran along the side of a hill. Frank's vehicle eventually sunk axle-deep in a marshy mess. He hoped the priest carrying Tito to the orphanage had gotten through earlier – or better yet, had turned around and gone back to Altavilla. The men piled out to try to get the truck free, but nothing worked until a jeep towing a machine gun stopped long enough to set aside its trailer and help.

Somehow the truck managed to get them to the base of Mount Sammucro, but there the muddy tracks narrowed and steepened. Abandoning the trucks, their packs loaded with all the gear they could carry, they took off on foot, climbing over rocks, crawling under brush, doing what they could to stay dry in the cold and the mud. Frank's platoon was in the lead as the summit came into view. His lieutenant radioed HQ. "Objective in sight. Gerry outpost at the top."

The reply came back immediately. "Take 'em out. We need that vantage point now."

"Roger," the lieutenant confirmed then turned to his platoon. "All right, guys. Talbot, your squad takes the right flank – Reyes, the left. The rest of you on me. Grenades first, then we come at them from three sides. Moster, as soon as it's clear, get eyes on the valley. Any questions?" Silence. "All right . . . Talbot, Reyes, go. We'll give you five minutes to get in position."

Five minutes of silence. Five minutes when they could hear sounds from the valley below of the enemy reinforcing their lines. Five minutes for Frank to hold onto his father's cross and pray that Tito was already safe inside the caves with the nuns. And then the lieutenant stood up and lobbed a grenade at the little hut where the Nazis were dug in. Half a dozen more grenades followed and then the lieutenant's shout – "Go! Go! Go!" – as the platoon advanced on the outpost in a V formation.

It was over quickly. The Germans were outnumbered at least five to one. Those who got out of the hut ran straight into American gunfire.

Frank got his squad organized to monitor the activity below, assigning each man a sector to cover. Through his own binoculars, he picked out the main road and the church at the highest point in the town of San Pietro. He buttoned his jacket against the December cold then scanned all the sectors while he listened to his men report. "Pillboxes near the town, Sarge." "Yeah, this sector too. And they're digging trenches to connect 'em." "Looks like barbed wire everywhere." "Lots of action over toward Mount Lungo."

"Keep an eye on that, Sanders," said Frank. "Intel said they were reinforcing that hill." He signaled for the lieutenant and the radio operator, ready to give his initial recon report.

"They got a checkpoint on the road there just below the town. Bunch of vehicles lining up to get in. Reinforcements, I bet." Sanders pointed toward what he was watching. Frank trained his own binoculars on the spot. Sure enough. Trucks being checked then let into the town. More arriving. Then he shivered from his head to his toes, deep into his very bones. And not from the winter cold. There . . . on the road . . . headed straight to the checkpoint . . . a beat-up blue truck.

# CHAPTER 35

"Be ready to move out in five minutes," the lieutenant shouted. "The mortars will clear a path for us to advance on San Pietro."

The sick feeling in the pit of Frank's stomach deepened. Tito and the priest would be driving right through the bombardment. "Hey, Lieutenant," he called out.

"Yeah, what is it, Moster?"

"What's the plan to limit civilian casualties or rescue those in the line of fire?"

"We'll do what we can, but taking San Pietro's first priority. Got it?"

"Yes, sir. If you were thinking about detailing a squad to look after the civilians, I'm volunteering."

"Okay, so Intel says we got civvies hiding in the caves. You wanna try and get 'em out, go ahead."

"Looks like the caves are on the left side of the town," said Frank. "We can head around the left flank. That looks like the best approach."

"Sounds like a plan. I don't have a better one. The map looks like that's a decent starting point. Take five men with you on that route. I'll send another squad to cover the right flank." The lieutenant resumed barking orders as Frank prepared his men to take off.

Suddenly, Ray's hand was on his arm, holding him back. "Whaddaya think you're doing, Frank? Going into the line of fire? You friggin' crazy?"

"Somebody's gotta do it."

"Maybe, but does it have to be you? You've put your life on the line enough already, taking out that machine gun on the beach and then that sniper in Altavilla. Let somebody else be the hero this time."

Frank stopped and looked his friend in the eye. "Look, man, this is just something I have to do, okay? I'll find you when your squad gets into San Pietro. Now I've gotta go – my men are waiting."

"Keep your head down," Ray shouted as Frank trotted off.

The Germans still controlled Mount Lungo, so the winding road through the valley to the town was in the crossfire between the Germans on one side and the Allies on the other. Every yard gained for the infantry came with significant causalities. Frank's men were on alert, guns at the ready. Once or twice, Frank stopped to scan the area through his binoculars. The blue truck was still making its way, slowly and steadily, toward San Pietro. The Germans were reinforcing their defenses in the town, now setting up artillery sites behind rocks and sand bags.

Sixteen tanks had started the treacherous journey through the valley. Frank kept his men close to them, using the tanks for cover. The tension was unimaginable as they got closer to the town. Heavy artillery fire from Mount Lungo bombarded them, the sounds pounding Frank's eardrums, leaving a continual ringing in his ears. He and his men had to keep moving. He tried to counter the intensity by remembering better days. Picturing his brothers at home sparring with him. Remembering Ida's smile. Thinking of Tony and how he'd tell him to do whatever was necessary to free their parents' homeland.

The sound was deafening. Mortar fire. Blasts from the heavy German artillery. Buzz bombs exploding all around. Lethal shards of metal and shrapnel flying through the air. It was each man for himself now. Frank started using boxing tactics, stepping back from an incoming punch, to dodge the flying debris. The stench of burning phosphorous assaulted his nose. The sight of wounded and dead men lying in pools of blood and mud assaulted his vision. The 36th Division was taking heavy losses, with burned bodies, mutilated soldiers, and bombed out trucks crowding the battlefield.

Glancing to his right, Frank spotted a German soldier sneaking his way through the olive trees, trying to get to the tank he was using for cover. He knew if the soldier got close enough, he would try to throw a grenade into the hatch of the tank. He ran forward, using rocks and trees for cover, and crouched behind a smoking bombed-out jeep that was on the path the German would take to reach the tank. Even in the cold December air, a bead of sweat ran down his lip as he waited, out of sight, while the shadow of the soldier came closer. Just as the German reached the jeep, its jerry can exploded, shooting flames in all directions. Both men jumped away and saw each other at the same moment. Frank looked into the German's bloodshot eyes. The man held a grenade intended for the tank in his right hand, the pin already removed. His pistol was on his right hip, his rifle slung over his back. Frank knew he had the advantage, but could hear his pulse thrashing in his ears as he raised his rifle, aimed, and fired. It all seemed to happen in slow motion.

The bullet struck the German square in the chest. Knowing the grenade would go off in only seconds, Frank ran for his life back toward the cover of the tanks.

The Germans occupied the strategic side of the mountain but didn't have enough manpower to cover all sides. San Pietro villagers were being forced to help the Nazis. Women and children were scattering to get out of the town center, knowing the battle was headed straight for them. Most were rushing to the nearby caves, where there were intricate passageways and rooms to hide and where they had previously concealed food, supplies, and even people, knowing they would likely need a safe haven from the looming battles.

Only three battered tanks remained, churning their tracks through the muddy, bombed out battleground, firing blasts at the German front line. The enemy concentrated on the two tanks coming up the middle of the advancing army. The third tank – the one Frank and his squad were using for cover – was in a guard position on the left side of the city, having made it through the bombardment zone and out of direct firing range of the German artillery.

Peering around it, Frank could see the town center. There, inside the gated church grounds, he spotted the blue truck. Several nuns and children were running frantically around the yard. The Nazis were too busy fortifying their frontline to pay any attention to what was going on at the church. As Frank watched, two more nuns came out of the building next to the church – the orphanage, presumably – leading a group of children out into the yard. Another nun was speaking to a priest, who held the hand of a young child. Knowing who it must be and yet wishing with all his heart that it wasn't, Frank adjusted his binoculars to try to get a look at the child's face. It was Tito. The terrible sick feeling returned to the pit of Frank's stomach.

The other two tanks had made it through the broken German defense and now were getting into position to fire into the town center where the Nazi infantry was concentrated. The Allied tanks pounded a clearing for the troops to pass through the barbed wire and other obstacles. As they broke through and rushed into the town, Frank spied the path the civilians were taking to the caves. The nuns carried the smallest of the children; others rushed to follow them to the caves.

Frank knew they had very little time, so he and his squad rushed toward the nuns, who scattered at their approach. "It's all right, sisters," called the priest. "They're Americans."

"Let's get everyone into the caves quickly, Father," said Frank. "This is the front line for the battle and the caves are the only place they'll be safe."

"I didn't know this was happening when I left Altavilla. I've brought an orphan here to this chaos. By the Blessed Virgin, I would never have brought him here if I'd known what was happening." The priest was distraught.

"I know. I've been watching your truck pass through the valley. And I know the child – Vincenza's son, Tito."

"Yes, and I'm so sorry to have brought him to this danger zone."

The boy jumped and wailed with each loud noise, and tears streamed down his face. Frank's chest tightened as he struggled with memories of the day Vincenza died in the church bombing. His recurring nightmare would only get worse if Tito died now.

The 36th Division battered the Nazi headquarters, forcing German soldiers out of the town. Some were headed toward the caves. "Hurry, Father," said Frank. "We'll stay here and buy you some time to get to the caves. You too, sisters. There's no time to waste."

From their position on the path, Frank had a clear view of the riverbed in the gulley below. A group of about a dozen German soldiers were following the riverbed, coming his way.

"All right, men," Frank told his squad, "hold your fire. Let's let them get crowded up in the gully, then we can pick them off all at once."

Suddenly, he heard the unmistakable sound of the German screaming 88s. Leaving his men to deal with the Nazis in the gully, he dashed up the path toward the civilians. As he got close, his ears told him one of the 88s was heading right toward them. The priest looked back over his shoulder at Frank, who knew he only had a few seconds.

He leaped . . .

The squealing noise was approaching fast.

Frank's body collided with the priest and Tito, pushing them both into the cave.

The 88 strike landed on the rock outside of the cave, shattering off a large hunk of it. The rock debris and shrapnel struck Frank, throwing him across the path. A few seconds later, he was in agony amid the chaos, deafened and partially blinded by the blast. He was bleeding, and couldn't feel his legs. He passed out from the trauma and shock.

A small group of German soldiers were still making their way up the hill through the riverbed. Another 88 hit a few yards away and shook the riverbed. The loud noise and vibration were enough to pull Frank back to a semi-conscious state. He wiped the blood and dirt off his face so he could see. His vision was still blurry, but he could see the Germans coming up the riverbed and knew they would find the cave entrance if they made it out of the gully.

He looked back at the cave entrance and saw the priest holding Tito back to keep him from running into the line of fire. He waved the boy back into the cave, but Tito just stared. He couldn't shout – the Germans would spot them all and fire. Frank pulled his helmet off, pointed at the T-patch on his uniform, and then made the hand motions of the puppet. That was enough for Tito to recognize him. The little boy's face brightened, and he looked inquisitively at Frank as he put his helmet back on.

Frank put his fingers to his lips, telling Tito to keep quiet. Then he picked up two sticks and used them to make the motions of the walking puppet soldier, telling Tito that soldiers were coming and that he needed to hide. Tito pointed to the inside of the cave. Frank nodded back, and Tito ran back inside the cave.

Despite his broken, battered body, Frank was relieved the boy and priest had survived the 88 blast. But he had more to do. Wiggling his way into position, he peered down into the gulley. Taking two grenades from his belt, he pulled the pins and waited until the Germans were bunched up, then tossed them one right after another into the middle of the group. But four of them managed to escape the blast.

Retrieving his rifle using a tree limb, Frank fired the rifle at the fleeing soldiers, picking off three of them before he needed to reload. The fourth one took aim at Frank, but before the German could get off his shot, he was felled by a shot coming from a different direction. Frank let out a sigh of relief.

Now he could take stock. He couldn't move. His legs were paralyzed, and blood was oozing from one of his wounds. The blasts from the center of town were less frequent now, and he could hear voices coming up the path. English voices. He closed his eyes in relief. Help was on the way.

Joe Bezner, the medic from Frank's home town, was the first to arrive. "Stretcher!" he shouted, throwing his bag on the ground and putting a dressing on the worst of Frank's wounds. As the noise subsided, a few people started wandering out of the caves, Tito and the priest among them.

"Dear God," said the priest, running over to where Frank lay on the ground. "How can I help? This man saved our lives, Tito's and mine."

"Good work, soldier," said Joe. "You finished off some of the last Nazis here in San Pietro. We have control of the Liri Valley now."

As he was loaded onto a stretcher, Frank gave the boy and the medic a thumbs-up.

"Come with us back to the aid station, Father," said Joe, trying not to let his concern come through in his voice. The dressing he'd applied was already saturated in blood.

When Joe removed Frank's helmet at the aid station, he blurted out in surprise, "Frank, is that you?" He moved to where Frank could see his face. "It's me . . . Joe Bezner . . . from Texas."

Frank seemed to recognize him. He felt weaker and weaker as blood drained out of his wounds. He reached toward his helmet. Joe helped him, then Frank pulled out a picture. "Yeah, Joe, it's me. I don't think I'm gonna make it."

"I'm gonna get you some fluids and some morphine, and we'll get you patched up," Joe said.

"No morphine – not yet. I have to tell you this first. Look at this picture."

Frank's skin was pale, and his breathing was becoming labored. Between breaths he said, "It's Ida Perna. I met her in Altavilla." He took another deep breath and continued, "Tito and the priest – they know her well." Frank coughed and sputtered out blood. Through a haze, he saw them standing nearby.

"She's beautiful," said Joe.

"Yes, she is. I just want her to know that I love her. If I don't make it, please tell her. And most importantly, you have to tell my family in Texas to take care of the Pernas. Please, Joe, can you do that for me? Please tell Tony and Steve about her. Teresita, Florence, Joey . . ." he mumbled trying to keep his eyes open.

"Sure thing, Frank, I'll let them know. Hang on. We're going to get you back to the field hospital." Joe said as he struggled to get the tourniquet on tighter and the IV in place.

Tito and the priest listened and watched as Joe tried to save Frank. Frank closed his eyes and his breathing grew shallow.

Joe shouted, "I need more fluids. I need some help over here. Get me some plasma. This guy's bleeding out."

He opened the intravenous fluids up faster and then leaned over to listen to Frank's heart. He listened for a long time. There was no spontaneous air movement or heartbeat. Joe had done what he could, but Frank had lost too much blood. Joe looked at the priest and shook his head no.

"I'll see if a chaplain made it to the station to perform last rites," Joe said.

"If you don't mind, I will do it," said the priest. "I know this man and what he has sacrificed."

Joe nodded and knelt down next to Frank's body as the priest performed the last rites. Tito cried. The priest put his arm around Tito, and they walked away. Joe took the dog tags off of Frank and placed one of them in Frank's mouth and slammed the jaw shut. The other dog tag he would return to the commanding officer. There was a cross and a key on the necklace. Joe noticed the key had "Florence" engraved on it. He took the key to return it to Frank's family. Joe yelled to the retreating priest. "Father, wait!" When he reached them, he handed the necklace with the cross to the priest. "For the boy. I know Frank would have wanted him to have it."

# CHAPTER 36

*Muenster, Texas, December 1943*

Letters from the boys didn't come often enough to suit Theresa. So whenever she found something in the mailbox from Italy or California or the Pacific, she hurried straight inside to open it. She knew Tony was safe, being stationed stateside, but she worried constantly about Frank and Steve. The last letter from Frank had been so full of joy. He was going to ask the Perna girl to marry him.

As she flipped through today's mail, her brow furrowed. There was one from Italy, but the handwriting wasn't familiar. She turned it over and over as she walked back to the house and settled in at the kitchen table. The letter inside was in the same unfamiliar hand and in a language she couldn't understand. She phoned Teresita. "Let me get the washing in off the line, and I'll come over," Teresita said cheerfully.

Theresa went back to the stew she was preparing for dinner that night. Last week, she'd had enough ration coupons to get a nice roast and she'd managed to stretch it out for four days' meals already. Tonight, the last of the leftovers were going into the stew. Then it would be back to Spam while she saved up some more coupons. I'll bet, she thought as she chopped up an onion, that letter is from Frank's Italian girl, telling us they're going to get married. Maybe they got married already. People do that in war time.

Teresita came in the kitchen door, as she usually did, and shut it quickly against the blue norther that was rapidly dropping the temperatures outside. "The letter's on the table, dear," said Theresa. "I just know it has to be good news." She put the onions in the stew pot, rinsed and dried her hands, and joined Teresita at the table.

The younger woman's face changed as she read. "Maybe I should go get Papa Leo," she said as she lay the letter down on the table.

Theresa didn't hesitate. "No, don't go. Whatever it is, I want to know."

Teresita took Frank's mother's hand and began to read.

*Dear Mr. and Mrs. Moster,*

*Things are very bad here in Italy and I am beginning to wonder how we will survive. So before the worst can happen, I wanted to tell you how very much your son Frank meant to me and to my family. He took care of us when we were in danger, he brought us army food when we had little to eat, he taught my sons baseball, and best of all, he was going to marry my daughter. In the short time we knew him, he became like another son to me – like another member of our family. We loved him and miss him every day, as I know you do.*

*If we survive this terrible war, then perhaps we will meet one day.*

*May God be with you and bless you,*

*Ernesto Perna*

For a long time, Theresa was silent, her face impassive. "I'm going to get Papa Leo," said Teresita.

"There's no need, dear. Frank's unit must have moved on, that's all. Mr. Perna is in dire straits and just wanted us to know they loved our Frank while he was there." She went back to the stove and started fussing with the seasoning for the stew.

"Well, at least let me write it out in English so he can read it when he gets home."

"That's a good idea, dear. You know where I keep the paper in the drawer over there."

It was three more weeks before the telegram arrived.

*The Secretary of War desires me to express his deep regret that your son Sergeant Frank J. Moster was killed in action on 8 December 1943 in the initial assault on San Pietro Infine in Italy.*

*J. A. Ulio*

*The Adjutant General*

Leo was overcome. He sat in his living room chair, holding the telegram, staring off into the distance, and he was still there when Florence, Joey, and Tommy came home from school. "You children go get cleaned up," Theresa admonished, "and don't be bothering your father."

The boys ran down the hall to their room, but Florence tiptoed into the living room. "What's wrong, Daddy?" she asked quietly. When Leo didn't answer, she took the telegram from his hand and read it . . . and slumped to the floor, put her head in her father's lap, and sobbed inconsolably. That shook Leo out of his trance. He stood her up and took her to the sofa where he held her and cried with her.

Theresa came in from the kitchen. "Now, now, you two. It's not for certain. We all know the army makes mistakes all the time. And until they send us his body to bury, we can't be sure of anything."

When the Christmas package they'd sent Frank came back a week later marked "Return to sender, Addressee deceased," Theresa remained unconvinced, refusing to attend the memorial service or light a candle for him.

But everyone else knew. Every night before she went to bed, Florence would stroke her bicyclist puppet and whisper "I love you, Frankie" before crying herself to sleep.

Teresita took on the sad task of writing to Steve and Tony. "Tony'll be devastated," she told Leo. "But I think I know what he'd want to do."

"What's that?"

"He'd want to do something nice for the Pernas because they cared for Frank. Ernesto's letter sounded like they were near starvation. You know, if we pool our ration coupons, we can come up with enough to send them a little food package with a thank-you letter. Maybe even send a few dollars to buy a little more. Whaddaya' say, Papa Leo?"

"You take care of it, Teresita. And write a nice letter that they can read."

"You write the letter, Papa Leo, and I'll put it into Italian."

Three days later, Teresita had everything organized and the package ready to go. She'd managed to get some dried fruit, sausages, flour, sugar, dried meats wrapped for preservation, cereal, and four chocolate bars. Leo's letter and twenty dollars went in the box last.

*Dear Perna family,*

*We are sorry that we didn't respond to your letter sooner. The news of Frank's death shook us badly. It was weeks later before we finally received an official notification from the US War Department that our son had been killed. We want you to know how much it means to us that you welcomed Frank into your family and that he was happy there in his last months alive. His letters to us were filled with stories of the time he spent with your family and his growing love for Ida. We know she must be heartbroken as are we. His spirit will live on with us as we pray for Italy and for our countries to survive this war. We hope you will accept these gifts as our thanks for providing such a wonderful friendship to Frank in his short time there.*

*Sincerely,*

*Leo and Theresa Moster family and the Sicking family*

As the winter wore on, Leo's health deteriorated – so much so that Theresa wrote to Steve and Tony urging them to try to get leave to come home. Toward the end of February, there was another letter from Italy.

*Dear Leo and Theresa,*

*We were so excited to hear from you. Words cannot express the appreciation we have for what you did. The food you sent was a godsend. We were able to make it last for several weeks by using it with the food rations that finally started coming from our government. We are starting to believe, at last, that we will not starve to death after all.*

*The money you sent went farther than you can ever imagine. With American dollars, we could buy a cow, three chickens, and a pig. Frank told us you have a farm, too, so we think you can understand just how much this means. The Nazis took everything from us. Now we have milk and eggs, and we will be strong enough to plant a garden in the spring. We will forever be grateful. May God bless you and your family, and may our countries win this war together and never have another one.*

*Ernesto and Carmela*

When Teresita finished reading the letter, she said, "We did a good thing, Papa Leo."

"We must do it again," said Theresa. "If Frank is still alive over there, that's where he would go. So we should help the Pernas as much as we can."

# CHAPTER 37

Whether it was Frank's death, Leo's illness, or the family hardship of having all their sons serving, no one ever knew. But the result was that Steve and Tony managed to get thirty days' leave at exactly the same time in early summer.

Despite the shadow of Frank's death and Leo's illness, the reunions were joyful, especially the one between Steve and his fiancée, Mary. On the train from the West Coast, Steve and Tony had hatched a plan. Their leave coincided with the first hay harvest of the season, so they planned to hire themselves out with neighboring farms and make some extra money to see the Mosters through if Leo couldn't work that summer.

They got Frank's bike out of the attic and fixed it up; Tony's was in the garage in good condition. And then they biked all over Cooke County and southern Oklahoma helping with the harvest. When they were working close by, Teresita and Mary would pack their lunches and bring them cold lemonade in the afternoon, and they'd spend the night at home.

As they wrapped up a day's work not long before their leave was up, Steve said, "Hey, why don't we stop by Gottlieb's bar on the way home and have a beer for Frank?"

"Yeah, he'd have liked doing that," Tony replied.

The place was not as busy as before the war, but Gottlieb himself was as expansive as ever. "Tony! Steve! Heard you were home. What'll you have?"

"Coupla beers, John," Tony replied.

"Comin' right up. And it's on the house for you military boys."

When John brought their drinks, Steve asked, "Hey, is that Joe Bezner down at the other end of the bar?"

"Yep," Gottlieb replied. "Home on leave before he gets reassigned. I hear he's had it pretty rough – first Salerno then Monte Cassino, Rapido River, and Anzio. He was a medic – probably saw a lot. He's been at the church, sitting in the back praying."

Tony and Steve took their beers down to the other end of the bar to talk with Joe. "Glad you made it back," said Tony.

Joe's throat made a swallowing movement, and he looked down at the ground. He could hardly speak when he looked at the brothers. He shook their hands, smiled, and looked back at Gottlieb, who'd come down to join the conversation. Tony waited for Joe to say more, but he was awkwardly quiet. John broke the silence. "So, Tony, anyone tell you we had a little memorial here for Frank back in February? Lots of reminiscing about that bicycle bet you guys won. Not a dry eye in the house when we drank a toast to him at the end of the night." Joe gulped his beer down and stepped away from the counter.

"That was a little strange, don't you think?" Tony whispered to Steve.

"Yeah, but after everything he's seen, I can understand," Steve said. He'd seen his own share of fighting in the Pacific.

"Has Joe had too many beers, John?" Tony asked Gottlieb. "He seems a little off."

"Nope. What you saw was the only one he had."

The brothers finished their beer while Joe sat at a table by himself. Suddenly, he picked up his hat and left the bar.

"Thanks for the beer, John," Tony said then turned to Steve. "Let's go see where Joe's headed and see what's eating him."

They followed him several blocks to the Catholic church in the center of town, where he went inside. Tony and Steve waited a few minutes before following. After all, it could be nothing more than Joe wanting some quiet time to pray. When they went inside, Joe was kneeling in a pew near the back of the sanctuary. They sat two pews behind him. The church was empty except for the three men. The silence was reverent.

At long last, Joe said, "I know you guys followed me here."

"We just wanted to be sure you were okay," said Tony.

"Well, I'm not. But I'm glad you came. The bar wasn't the place to talk."

Joe moved to the pew in front of Tony and Steve and turned to face them. His eyes were moist, his expression serious. He looked into each of

their faces, then swallowed heavily again. "I was with your brother when he died."

Steve and Tony glanced at each other and then back at Joe.

"I was the medic that found him," Joe could hardly speak now, the rims of his eyes turning red as he fought to hold back tears. "He told me that he loved you all and how much you meant to him. He took out a picture of Ida and told me to tell you how much he loved her and how important it was to help her and her family survive. There was a key on his necklace that has "Florence" engraved on it. Can you give this to her?"

Tony looked at Steve, both wondering why he hadn't told someone sooner.

"I was a medic, so I'd seen horrific injuries and death from the moment we landed on those beaches, but when I saw Frank with his body blown up . . . I was in shock. I never expected it to be someone I knew." He wiped his eyes and continued.

"I couldn't talk about it . . . couldn't sleep for days. Every night the vision of Frank and his injuries haunted me. I went on with my duties for months by avoiding looking any of my patients in the face and limiting conversation with them. I think I'd have cracked up completely if I'd lost another person I knew.

"I wanted to tell your parents, but I couldn't face even the thought of telling them what happened to him. So I avoided them. I knew they'd ask. Everyone does."

Tony and Steve remained silent, looking up at the altar and the crucifix above it.

"He was hit by a buzz bomb. His injuries were devastating. There was nothing I could do, but God knows I did everything I could. I'll never forget the look in his eyes as his soul departed this earth. Maybe you can take some consolation in knowing he most surely had a quick passage to heaven. He died saving the lives of an orphan and a priest."

# CHAPTER 38

Florence and Teresita had cooked supper and had it waiting when they arrived. When the meal was over, Tony asked the boys to go outside and play. "Something's on your mind," said Leo. "You hardly said two words all through supper."

"Let's go in the living room," said Tony.

"Just let me clear the table and set the dishes to soak," said Theresa.

"That can wait, Mama," said Steve. "It'll be dark soon and the boys will have to come back inside."

As gently as he could, Tony recounted Joe's story of Frank's death, leaving out the gory details of the buzz bomb injuries. Leo was stoic. Florence and Teresita hugged each other, sobbing. Theresa's eyes glazed over, and she started rocking herself back and forth in her chair.

Tony said, "Florence, Joe Bezner brought this key back from Italy. It was on Frank's necklace chain with his dog tags. Looks like he meant it for you."

Florence knew what it was. The locked box under Frank's bed. Somehow that helped her deal with the grief. She went to her mother, put an arm around her, and spoke softly, "Come with me, Mama. Let's get you to bed."

Theresa offered a feeble protest. "I can't sleep knowing my Frankie's gone. I just can't believe it."

"I'll stay with you, Mama, and we can cry together and pray and talk about how much we loved Frankie. And then tomorrow we can send those nice Pernas some more food like Frank wanted us to." Still in a daze, Theresa let herself be led away.

As soon as Theresa was asleep, Florence went to get the box and unlocked it. Inside, his favorite whittling knife, some cash, and a life insurance policy made out to Florence. She sobbed quietly, not wanting anyone to hear but completely overwhelmed by Frank's gift – by just how much he had loved her and how much she would miss him always.

When the end of their leave arrived, Steve and Tony gave Leo a packet of money they'd earned working the harvest. It wasn't as much as Leo thought it should have been; but then again, this was war time and folks didn't have a lot, so maybe that was all they could afford to pay for harvest help. In any event, it would be enough to tide them over until he was back on his feet, so Leo was grateful.

Seeming to finally acknowledge the fact of Frank's death, Theresa became obsessed with what had happened to her son's body. "If he's dead, then there's a body and they should send it to us," she told Teresita every time the younger woman visited. She wrote letters to the Graves Registration Service, but her pleas went unanswered. She wrote to the Pernas asking if they could help. And while she waited, she sat in her rocking chair, vacant eyes staring off into the distance, mumbling Hail Mary's. Weeks, then months passed with no answers. When Tony or Steve came home on leave, she'd acknowledge their presence, but her depression only seemed to grow worse. She never left the house except for Sunday Mass and Wednesday Novena.

A year after Frank's death, Tony was discharged and returned home. When he went over to check on Theresa, he found a newly arrived letter on the kitchen table. It was from the Pernas. Inside were a photo of a military burial site and another of a single white cross. Rummaging in a kitchen drawer, he found the magnifying glass Theresa always used to read the tiny print on aspirin bottles and such. He held it up to the photo of the cross and there was the name – *Frank J. Moster.*

Leo was on the couch talking to Theresa, who seemed a bit more responsive than when Tony was last here. "Mama Theresa," he said, "I opened the letter. I think you finally have your answer." He handed her the photos.

She hugged them to her chest and wept. "I want him back here, Tony," she sobbed. "I won't believe it until I see him. Bring him home . . . please."

Tony looked at Leo. "She'll never be at peace until he's here," said Leo.

"I know, Papa Leo. I'll look into it."

The American Graves Commission told them they had a choice: leave the body in a grave near the battlefield or bring it back home. But Tony's requests to the War Department for repatriation went unanswered. Ernesto wrote that Ida visited Frank's grave twice a week and left flowers. But that proved no consolation at all to Theresa.

When the war ended and Steve came home, he immediately asked Mary for her hand in marriage. The City of Muenster welcomed him home, too, by hiring him as the City Supervisor. The city hall was only a block from his mother's home, which allowed him to check on her twice a day. At first, it seemed this might be enough to bring Theresa out of her depression, but it was only temporary. "One of us will have to go over there," Steve told Tony over a beer one night at Gottlieb's.

"Can we pull together enough money?" Tony asked.

"Do we have a choice?"

They both knew the answer. "You should be the one to go," said Steve.

"Why me? You could go."

"Your Italian's better than mine. And besides, you and Frank did that long trip together. Seems like you should be with him for his last trip home." He paused for a swallow of beer. "Anyway, I couldn't get away from my job long enough, and you'll have a break once the harvest is done."

Theresa continued her pleas to bring her Frankie back. And so, when harvest ended, Tony agreed to go Italy. He took the train for New York and set sail for the land of his ancestors.

# CHAPTER 39

*Italy, 1946*

When Tony stepped off the train in Battipaglia, Ernesto recognized him immediately. "*Benvenuto, Antonio, benvenuto. Siamo molto felici che sei venuta.* Welcome, Tony. We're so happy you've come.

"*E sono felice di essere qui, Signor Perna.*" And I'm happy to be here.

The two men embraced, shared joy and shared sorrow drawing them together as if they were long-lost friends.

Ernesto was still using the same old farm truck. "There wouldn't be anything newer to buy even if we had the money, so Massimo and me, we take good care of it and keep it running. Things are getting better, but slowly." He swerved to avoid a series of holes in the road. "Every time it rains, they wash out even more, but it will take a long time to repair everything."

As they left the town behind, Tony kept turning his head all around, looking out every window of the truck at a landscape that was unlike anything he had ever seen. "It's so beautiful, Signor Perna."

"Please . . . call me Ernesto."

"Even with the scars from the war still so visible, you can tell that the vineyards are coming back and that the soil is rich, and the fields will produce as soon as people can work them properly. Frank wrote home about how beautiful the hills are and he didn't exaggerate."

They passed a compound surrounded by a tall fence topped with barbed wire. Its grounds were meticulously kept and a neat row of jeeps was parked in front of evenly spaced buildings. "That's the army base where Frank's unit was stationed before they left for San Pietro," said Ernesto. "Now it's just the American base for this whole area."

Tony got a lump in his throat, knowing that now he was on the same road that Frank had biked so often on his visits to the Perna farm. As they turned up the lane to the farmhouse, he almost choked up. The small vineyard. The big barn. The tan stucco house with green ivy crawling up the sides and a porch that overlooked the fields below. "I see why my brother was so happy here. It's so peaceful. So remote from the destruction below." He spoke almost reverently.

"And soon, I hope," said Ernesto, "the farm will be like it was before the war." As he pulled the truck to a stop in front of the house, he turned to look directly at Tony. "Without your family, I do not think we would be here now. The only thing we had left in that terrible winter was the vines and they were near to dying. Your help saved us, and I will never forget it." Ernesto's eyes were gleaming with moisture.

"It's what Frank would have wanted."

"His death was hard on Ida. Even after all this time, she still grieves. My wife and I try to help her, but sometimes she still has moments of deep despair."

Just then, the front door burst open and three boys came running to the truck, all talking at the same time. "You're back!" "We've been waiting." "Did you bring Hershey bars?" "Can I carry something?"

"All right, all right," Ernesto tried to calm them down. "Massimo, take Antonio's duffel bag up to the room your mama made ready for him."

Tony climbed out of the truck and turned toward the house. There, on the porch, was a woman on crutches, her long, thin face accentuated by enormous brown eyes and a captivating smile. He knew immediately this was Ida. And he knew immediately why Frank had fallen in love. As he walked toward the porch, her smile turned to an open-mouthed stare.

"*Dio mio! Sei proprio uguale a lui!*" she said. You look just like him.

Tony smiled and stepped up onto the porch. "Maybe, but not quite as tall." They laughed as an older woman came out of the house.

"Tony, my daughter, Ida, and my wife, Carmela," said Ernesto.

Carmela embraced him at length. "Ida's right," she said. "I'd have known you anywhere for Frank's brother. Now come inside. You must be hungry. And this year, we finally have some of our very own wine like before."

"She's been cooking all day," said Ida as Tony held the door so she could work her way through on her crutches.

"What happened?' he asked.

"It's a long story, Tony," Ernesto quickly intervened. "Better for Ida to tell you after we eat."

"I hope you like pasta. We made it special for you today," said Carmela.

"I've been looking forward to some real Italian food. I remember what Mama's food tasted like in New York. We can't get that in Texas."

Before they sat down to the meal, Ida beckoned the youngest boy to come to her. "Tony, meet Tito. He's my friend, Vincenza's, orphaned son."

The little boy studied Tony carefully for several seconds, as if unsure what to make of him. Then his face broke into a huge grin, and he hugged Tony tightly around the legs before turning back to Ida. "Like Frank," he said. Tony tousled the boy's hair, and he scurried back to stand close to Ida.

"He's alive because of Frank," said Ida.

Carmela called them to the table. "We should eat while it's still hot."

Over the meal, they talked of what things had been like since the war. "We were so desperate that first winter after the Americans came," said Carmela. "We were finally free of the Nazis, but we had nothing to live on. Massimo hunted, but the winter was so harsh he could rarely find any game. Ernesto insisted the children have what little food we could scrape together. He was getting so weak, I knew he wouldn't be able to work the farm. And when the government finally started issuing rations, what they gave us was barely enough for two people, much less eight. We tried to claim extra rations because of Tito, but since we weren't blood relatives, they said no. I cried all day when your first package arrived. God had finally answered my prayers."

"Tell me about Tito," said Tony. "What will happen to him now?"

"The priest brought him back here after Frank died saving them," Ida replied. "It's a good thing he did. The orphanage – in fact, the entire town of San Pietro – was totally destroyed in the battle. Our neighbors are helping us care for him for now. I'd love nothing more than to take care of him myself. But as you can see, with these crutches I'm having trouble managing everything. There's no way I could chase after an active young boy."

"Did you have a fall?" Tony asked

"I was foolish. After Frank died, I became reckless. I was involved with the resistance when Frank arrived here. Frank and Papa convinced me to give it up, and I did . . . for a while. But when I learned of his death, I had to do something. I had to fight back, so I went back with the underground."

"I tried to stop her, but it was useless," said Ernesto.

"After I lost Frank, I didn't care whether I lived or died. If I died, at least I could be with him. So I took all the dangerous missions. And one day I fell and broke my leg and it never healed right."

"I can't imagine you in the resistance," said Tony. "You look so innocent!"

"That's why I could get away with it. No one suspected me. I was a delivery girl, riding my bicycle, collecting documents, and passing them to the Allies. That's how Frank and I first became close."

"I can just imagine it! We took a long bike trip together once upon a time."

"He told us all about it, and I so loved to hear his tales and watch him play baseball with the boys." Tears started streaming down her cheeks.

"I'm so sorry," said Tony. "I didn't mean to open old wounds."

She took a deep breath, "And I didn't mean to cry. It's just that you look so much like him."

"It's been a long day," said Ernesto. "We all need some rest. And I think maybe tomorrow, we should all visit Frank's grave."

"I'd like that very much, sir," said Tony.

Ida looked directly into his eyes, and her gaze pierced deep into his soul.

# CHAPTER 40

Tony tossed and turned that night, unable to fall asleep. Ida's look. Was she seeing him or was she seeing Frank? He felt as if Frank's spirit was still here. When he finally dozed off, his dreams were vivid. He and Frank on their bike ride. The night they talked about the girls they would marry. Frank calling to him, "I found her! I found her!"

And then the crow of the rooster jarred him from sleep. His heart was racing. It had all seemed so real.

Carmela had breakfast waiting when he came downstairs. She was serving him a plate of eggs when Ida hobbled in with a basket full of flowers. "For Frank," she said.

The route to the military cemetery gave Tony a closer look at the devastation from the war. Piles of rubble alongside the road, bomb craters in the middle of pastures, fences broken and unmended. They passed small groups of people in ragged clothes and torn shoes, looking down at the road as they trudged along.

"Who are they?" Tony asked.

"Locals looking for jobs. They walk from town to town, looking for work, scraps of food, whatever they can find." Ernesto shook his head.

"There are so many," Tony said sadly.

"Yes, we are blessed to have the farm." Ernesto made the sign of the cross.

The cemetery was a latticework of white crosses covering the green grass. They walked quietly down the rows, Ida limping along without her crutches so she could carry the flowers. At the grave, she reached down, pulled the wilted flowers away, and replaced them with the fresh ones.

"Hail Mary, Mother of God . . ." Ernesto began to pray, and they joined in the prayers for the dead. As Tony's eyes began to glisten with tears, they left him alone to commune with his brother. Ida waited at a tree nearby. When Tony finally turned away, Ida took his hand and they walked slowly back to the truck.

No one spoke during the drive back to the farm. As they turned into the lane, Ernesto asked Tony, "Would you like to visit the barracks? I can get you in."

Tony hesitated, then said, "Yes, I think I would."

"I'll stay here, Papa," said Ida. "I've had enough long walks for today." The younger girls dashed out of the house with Ida's crutches and helped their sister inside.

At the barracks, they learned what all was involved in the arrangements for Tony to take Frank home. "It looks like I'll need to stay longer than I'd planned," Tony said on the way back to the farm. "The paperwork's going to take far longer than I thought."

"Stay as long as you need to, Tony. I think Ida would like that."

"Do you think she'll ever get over Frank's death?"

"It's been hard for her. First Vincenza's husband, then Vincenza, then Tito almost getting killed twice, and finally Frank. Each one crushed her spirit more than the last. She feels responsible for Tito now, but she has to deal with her own physical and emotional trauma first. I just don't know if she'll ever truly get over it all."

As the days passed while the Army's paperwork machine slowly ground away, a new pattern of life emerged at the Perna farm. Each evening, after one of Carmela's delicious meals, Tony and Ida would sit on the porch talking. At first, they cried together when they talked of Frank, but then they began to talk of the good times and even laugh at each other's funny stories. Sometimes, when Ida wasn't too tired, they'd walk around the garden. Now and then, they'd take the truck and go into town.

One evening, they joined a group of Ida's friends for dinner and a dance. There was lots of American music – boogie-woogie, swing, even a Charleston. Ida's friends asked Tony to dance and he politely accepted, but what he really wanted was to dance with Ida. Toward the end of the night a slow dance was playing. "Ida, if I promise not to let you fall, could you hobble a dance with me?"

Surprised by his question, she thought about it, then replied, "Sure, I can try."

She left her crutches against the chair and joined him on the dance floor. He wrapped his arms around her and she leaned into him for support. And as the music played, she seemed to lose herself in the moment, melting into his embrace, and laying her head on his shoulder. When the song ended, she lifted her head and gazed into his eyes. It was obvious she wanted him to kiss her, but he hesitated and then pulled away. He took her hand and they left the dance floor.

On the way back to the farm, they rode in silence for a while. Finally, Ida touched his arm gently and said, "I'm sorry if I made you uncomfortable."

"I'm fine."

"It's just that . . . well . . . it's just . . . this is the first time I've been able to escape my depression. Since Frank died, I haven't been out to a dance or anything like this."

"I'm glad I could help. You're a very attractive woman, Ida. I'm sure there are lots of men chasing you."

"That's nice of you to say, but I don't feel that way. I have a reputation for being strong and stubborn . . . you know, having helped the resistance and all. Lots of men are turned off by that. And then there's this darn limp."

"Ida, if there is one thing I know, it is that you are the most gorgeous woman I have ever seen."

She blushed and looked away.

"Have you had a doctor look at your leg?"

"Yes, but we don't have the money for the surgery he suggested." Even in the dark, she could see Tony's frown. "There aren't many doctors, and the more serious war wounds are attended to first. The clinic told me I'd have to wait, and they talked to Papa about the costs. I know he can't afford it."

"That's too bad. Surely there's something that could be worked out?"

She answered with a smile, and Tony felt himself caught up in her spell yet again. God, he wanted to kiss her! But he held back, uncertain how she'd react. He didn't want to spoil the magic of the night.

Ernesto was sitting on the porch when they got home. "I think I'll sit with your father for a moment," Tony said as he held the door for Ida.

"Good night then," she replied and went inside.

Tony perched on the edge of the porch.

"What's on your mind?" asked Ernesto.

"Do you have a hospital or doctors in Altavilla?"

"We have a small clinic that functions as a hospital."

"Could we drive into town tomorrow and take a look?"

"Sure. If you want to." Ernesto didn't pry.

At the clinic, Tony managed to convince the nurse to let them talk to the doctor between patients. "But you'll have to wait until I can work you in," she said. The lobby was overcrowded. A young man whose leg had been amputated. A line of men with assorted bandages, waiting their turn as, one by one, a nurse called them back to change dressings and check their wounds. Coughing children, crying in their mothers' laps. Mothers looking worried that their child might not be seen that day. Two hours later, the nurse called Tony and Ernesto back.

"How's Ida doing?" the doctor asked, hurriedly escorting them into his small office.

"She's not much better," Ernesto replied. "She never complains, but I know her leg hurts with every step she takes."

"Can you tell me about her injury?" Tony asked.

"I believe Ida has osteomyelitis, an infection in the bone from bacteria introduced at the time of the fracture. The vagaries of osteomyelitis significantly complicate recovery. Most surgeons don't have the experience to treat it, but I know a military doctor who's had good outcomes with a combined approach of antibiotics and open bone wound debridement." He paused, realizing his words didn't mean anything to these two, then started over, explaining in a way they could understand. "The infected area within the bone has to be cleaned out and a path created for drainage and removal of the bacteria. The success of the operation depends on obliteration of the cavity so that the infection doesn't come back. Penicillin can hold the infection in check for a while and it's worked for Ida up to now, but it's not a cure. She'll need surgery eventually, and that's best done by a surgeon who has experience with this sort of thing.

"I spoke to my friend about the severe injuries I'm dealing with here and asked if he's willing to help me. I would have to fund the equipment and probably his trip here, as he's in great demand. But you can see from my waiting room, I have my hands full. Ida's not the only one who could use his help."

"So, let me see if I understand," said Tony. "What's causing Ida's pain and her limp is an infection inside the bone, at the site where her leg was broken. What happens if she doesn't have this surgery?"

"Well, the trouble with osteomyelitis is the chronic infection. If the bacteria remains trapped within the bone, it will continue to destroy bone and the limb can become useless. But that's not the worst thing that can happen. If sepsis sets in, it can overwhelm the immune system and lead to death if left untreated."

Ernesto's face dropped. He rubbed his forehead then put his hands in his pockets and looked out the window as if searching for an answer.

"If we could raise some money to pay for the equipment, do you think you could convince your friend to fix Ida's injury?" Tony's sense of anxiety came through in his voice.

"I don't know. He's very busy," the doctor replied hesitantly.

"Doctor, this is important to me. I'll do anything to make this happen," Tony said.

"Very well, I'll look into it. I think the penicillin will buy us a bit of time. But I'm not promising anything. Maybe, if we can arrange a day of multiple surgeries including Ida's – having several in one day – maybe if we can use his time wisely and some of the other families may be able to help with the costs. But so many of these families are poor and can't afford to help."

"I'll take that as a positive answer on your part." Tony smiled.

Driving back to the farm, Ernesto said, "I don't think we should get Ida's hopes up until we're sure this can happen. It will take a lot to raise the money for her."

"I agree. Let's not tell her yet. I have some ideas. I'll need to talk to my family in the States. But I assure you, Ernesto, we can do this."

# CHAPTER 41

The Army paperwork to repatriate Frank's body was stuck. No one could say where or why or when it might get unstuck. "You'll have it when it gets here," was the best they could offer. But that gave Tony time to put his plan in place. The barracks CO took pity on him and let him use their communications to contact Steve and arrange for some money to be wired to Italy. Only after the funds arrived did he tell Ernesto what he had in mind.

"We're going to bootstrap your operation so you can start making some money. How many more cows can we buy with this?"

Ernesto gasped when he saw the money. "*Dio mio*, Tony. What have you done?

"What I wanted to do. Now how many cows can we buy?"

"Five . . . maybe six. But how would we manage that many more? There's the milking and then we have to figure out how to sell it and . . ."

"And that's where I come in. You know the local markets, so you can figure out how and where we sell. I'll get the dairy up and running. Massimo can help when he's not in school."

Ida had wandered into the room while they were talking. "I can help too. I still know how to milk a cow, you know."

"I don't know." Ernesto shook his head, still skeptical.

"We can do it, Papa." Ida's enthusiasm was contagious. "Lots of people need milk but can't afford their own cow or don't have a place for one."

"How can I argue with two of you?" Ernesto capitulated. "All right, Tony, let's go see if we can find some cows to buy."

And with that, another new pattern of life was established. Morning and evening, Tony and Ida did the milking. Then Carmela and the girls would rush to get the milk and cream ready to sell while Tony tended the cows and turned them out into the pasture to graze. By midmorning, everything was loaded into the truck and Ernesto was off to the local market. And by early afternoon, Ernesto was back with money to add to the growing sum he kept in an old biscuit tin. During the day, Tony worked around the farm, helping Ernesto with repairs to the barn, building a new chicken coop so they could get a few more chickens and supply eggs to the market as well, and generally tidying up from the neglect of the war years.

Evenings, though, still belonged to Tony and Ida. Walks in the garden and endless talks on the porch. After a few weeks, the walks were becoming shorter, and Tony could tell the pain in her leg was coming back. She seemed to enjoy their time together, and he loved listening to her stories of narrow escapes on her resistance missions, including the time she and Frank hid in a hillside cave while a battle raged above them. "I think Frank was more frightened than I was," she laughed. And she begged him to tell her about Texas and life on that far-away farm. In spite of himself, Tony knew he was falling in love.

The next morning, Ida didn't appear for milking. Tony was worried. He and Massimo rushed through the task, and he hurried back to the house to check on her before turning the cows out.

He knocked on her door. "Ida, are you awake?"

"Yes, come in." The minute he stepped inside, his fears were confirmed. "I'm sorry," she said. "I just couldn't get out of bed this morning."

Tony sat down beside her, and she struggled to sit up. There were beads of sweat on her forehead. "The pain in my leg is much worse than usual, and I just feel weak."

He touched her forehead. "You're burning up with fever." She lay back on her pillow. "I'm taking you to the clinic." He carried her down the stairs, calling for Ernesto to bring the truck around.

The doctor examined her and shook his head. "You need to stay here for a few days," he told her, "so we can give you antibiotics again."

While the nurse took over and got Ida to a bed in the ward, the doctor gave Tony and Ernesto the bad news. "It's worse than I wanted to let on in front of her. I'm afraid sepsis is setting in in the leg. The antibiotics may keep it at bay for a while, although I fear they may not work this time. That surgery I told you about is probably going to be necessary to save her leg."

"Then that's what we have to do." Tony was emphatic. "We've got some money now. It's probably not as much as you need, but we have our dairy business going and will work to pay for this. Please . . . please ask your friend to help her."

"You can have all of it," Ernesto added, handing the doctor a thick envelope filled with cash, "and your family can have fresh milk and cheese from our dairy for the rest of your life."

The doctor looked in the envelope and frowned. "This might be enough for the surgery, but afterward, she's going to need more medications, nursing care . . ." He looked up at Ernesto's pleading eyes, and his expression softened. "But let me see what I can do."

Tony was in despair. What were Ida's chances if they didn't have all the money? Would the surgeon take pity on them, or would he have no choice but to first help those who could pay? He needed to get word home fast. His thoughts went back to the bicycle trip with Frank – how Teresita used Western Union to wire them money and how they could let her know the same way when their plans changed. As they were leaving the hospital for the day, he asked Ernesto, "How do I send a telegram?"

"The post office."

"Can we go there on the way home?"

The next week was tense. There was no news from the orthopedic surgeon. One evening, when Ida's fever was so high she actually thought he was Frank, Tony knelt at her bedside repeating the Our Father over and over.

When they went home that evening, Massimo greeted them at the door waving a yellow envelope. "A telegram, Tony. It came while you were at the hospital."

Tony grabbed the envelope and ripped it open.

*I have some money. Wiring what you need for Ida thru US Army. Know what you will say, Tony. Save your breath. Must do this for Frankie. Florence*

Tony crumpled the paper in his hand and stepped back out onto the porch, his mind in turmoil. How could he allow Florence to deplete her nest egg for a woman she'd never met – probably never would meet? He stared out over the pastures and rubbed his forehead. But how could he allow Ida to die? He smoothed out the telegram and read it again. Frankie. The only other time since his death that Florence had used her pet name for Frank was at the memorial service. She was telling him what to do.

He folded the telegram carefully and put it in his pocket just as Ernesto stepped out on the porch. "Tony? Is something wrong?"

"No, Ernesto. Everything is very, very right." Tony's voice choked with emotion as tears came to his eyes. He embraced the older man, then stepped back. "We have the money. Everything is going to be all right."

• • •

On the day of the surgery, the hands on the clock seemed to crawl as Ernesto and Tony waited. They barely spoke, neither of them wanting to give voice to their fears. After several hours, the surgeon finally came out to speak to them. "She came through the surgery . . ." Tony and Ernesto exhaled in unison, their relief palpable. ". . . but she's not out of the woods yet. It looks like we have the bone cavity cleaned out, but she'll need more antibiotics to clear the sepsis and allow for healing. That will take a while, so she needs to stay here for now. I'll leave the drain in and come back next week to check on her."

"Can we see her?" Tony asked.

"She's only just coming out of the anesthesia, and she'll be groggy the rest of the day. Let her sleep and come back tomorrow. By then she'll be alert and will really benefit from having you cheer her up."

• • •

One morning, when Ida had been in the hospital for two weeks, Tito didn't show up for breakfast. No one could find him in the house, and there was no sign of him outdoors. "When did you last see him?" Ernesto asked his wife.

"When I put him to bed last night."

"And he was sound asleep when I went to bed," said Massimo. The three boys shared a room.

"Ida would never forgive us if something happened to him," said Carmela. They fanned out looking for him.

Tony found him in the loft of the barn, sitting in the hay playing with a puppet. He recognized Frank's handiwork immediately. He sat down beside the boy. "What are you doing up here, Tito?"

"Playing with my string toy."

"Do you remember who gave you that soldier?"

"Sure I do. Uncle Frank."

"What do you remember about him?"

"He was very brave. I didn't want him to go. But he went anyway, and he died."

"Why are you hiding here in the loft?"

"When I'm sad, I come here and play with my string toy. Frank told me he had one just like it, and when he was sad, his soldier made him feel better."

"Why are you sad?"

"Ida's not home. Just like my dad . . . just like my mom . . . just like Frank. They never came back."

"Ida will be back," Tony assured him.

"Last time she came back, she was hurt."

"This time she'll be better. The doctors are fixing her leg."

Tito sniffled as he concentrated on working the puppet to make the soldier walk.

"Would you like to visit her?"

Tito looked up with tears streaming down his face.

"Could I?"

"You'll have to be brave and strong for her, like Frank. Can you do that?"

"I can be brave," Tito replied, a smile replacing the tears.

When they got to the hospital, they found Ida walking in the hallway. She opened her arms, and Tito made a dash to her, almost knocking her over in his excitement. She wrapped him in her arms and picked him up. Tony watched as she twirled him in a circle, the enormous smiles on both their faces revealing their shared joy.

"Looks like your leg is much better," Tony said.

"It is. The doctor said I could put weight on it now, so I've been walking today – and not limping."

As they walked back to her hospital bed, Tony told her about Tito's retreat to the loft.

"Did he have his puppet?" she asked.

"Yes."

"He's had such a difficult time. He watched Frank die, you know, and he told me how Frank told him to be strong. Imagine losing both your parents in such a short time, and then Frank."

Tony closed his eyes and looked at the floor.

"Oh, dear." Ida put her hand to her mouth. "Tony, how thoughtless of me. I know that's exactly what happened to you and Frank."

"And I understand how he feels. It takes a long time to learn to trust again that you really have someone you can depend on, something stable in your life. It's tough. He's lucky to have you."

# CHAPTER 42

Four weeks after her surgery, Ida came home. Her improvement was remarkable. She still had pills to take and doctor's orders for regaining her strength, but she followed them to the letter.

A week later, she asked Tony, "Can we go to the beach? I want to walk in the sand." He hesitated. "Don't worry. I've already talked to Massimo and he'll see to the milking this evening."

When Ernesto returned from his trip to the market, they took the truck and headed for the beach. There were still so many places where relics of the invasion reminded them of sadder times, but they finally found a secluded spot where it seemed the war had never intruded. They took off their shoes and walked hand-in-hand in the sand. It was late afternoon and the sun was slowly setting through a bank of thin clouds on the horizon. Brilliant shades of orange and pink lit up the blue sky.

"Look at that sky," she said. "Just seeing it makes me happy to the depths of my soul."

"And I feel very lucky to be enjoying it with you."

She stopped and turned to face him. "Tony, I don't know how to thank you and your family for all you've done for me . . . for us. I don't have the words. And I know we can never repay you."

"I didn't do it for repayment. Frank wrote to me that meeting you was the best thing that ever happened to him. Now I know why."

She smiled. "After everything . . ." She paused, choosing not to put "everything" into words. "I didn't know if I could ever feel anything but sadness and pain again. But now, it seems as if a great weight has been lifted off me." She took his hand and led him to a piece of driftwood, and they sat down together. She leaned against him and he put an arm around her. "You've given me back my life, Tony. Shown me I can be happy again."

Brushing her hair out of her face, he gazed into her eyes and then kissed her lips. She wrapped her arms around him.

"I know you have to take Frank's body home. But, Tony, I want you to come back. My family has grown quite attached to you, and I . . ."

He put his finger to her lips. "I know. And there's nothing I want more than for you to come to America with me."

She kissed him, a long passionate kiss that neither wanted to end.

When she spoke, her voice was barely above a whisper. "I want that too. But how can I leave Tito? You said yourself that what he needs right now is someone he can depend on. It's . . . just not the right time for me to leave."

"It's difficult for me too. I feel my brother looking over my shoulder and that makes me feel guilty for having fun with you . . . for wanting to kiss you . . . just for being here in what was supposed to be his place."

"You mustn't feel that way, Tony. Frank and I lived through a terrible time and perhaps our love was doomed."

"I know. I just wish he could know that all he did wasn't in vain."

He kissed her again, finally able to pour into it all the love that had been building in his heart. And he knew, by the way she clung to him, that she felt the same. He also knew that their love, too, was doomed – that they might never share a moment like this again. But they would always be bound together in their love for Frank.

# EPILOGUE

*Italy, 2010*

"You ready, Papa?" Ernesto called from the front door. "We don't want to be late. You know the trains in Italy . . ."

"Always run on time," Massimo finished his son's sentence as he came into the living room from the kitchen. It was their little private joke – a nod to the older man's memories of the sad times during the war. At eighty years old, Massimo was still spry, even if he could no longer run as fast as he did when playing baseball with the American soldiers back then.

"The car's out front," said Ernesto.

"Just let me put on my jacket."

Ever since they'd received the letter from Signorina Bracaglia saying that the lady from America wanted to visit, he'd had a spring in his step. Could it really be that, after all these years, he was going to meet some more of Frank's family? He had tried to hold his excitement in check. After all, she could be just some distant relative who never knew Frank or Tony. Or it could all be a hoax. But today, he'd find out.

They were waiting on the platform when three women disembarked from the train – one obviously Italian, one a blonde with a friendly face, and the third a brunette. As the women approached, the Italian one asked, "*Signor Perna?*"

"*Si,*" Massimo replied.

"*Signor Perna,*" she repeated, extending her hand to Massimo and Ernesto in turn, "*mi chiamo Danila Bracaglia. E questa è Susanna e la sua amica Julie dal Texas.*" I'm Danila Bracaglia. And this is Susan and her friend, Julie, from Texas.

The blonde woman's face lit up with a beautiful smile as she stepped forward to shake hands. "*E questo è mi figlio, Ernesto,*" Massimo introduced his son.

They stowed the luggage in the trunk of Ernesto's car and headed back to the farm. During the drive, Danila explained Susan's relationship to Frank and Tony. Massimo thought he might just burst with excitement. After all this time, to have a member of Frank's family here in Italy! What a celebration they would have today!

As they drove up the lane, Susan gasped. "It's exactly as I imagined it!" The classic Italian farmhouse, beautifully laced with ivy, was perched on top of a hill overlooking the farm. "Just like Tony described it."

"It's been my home all my life," said Massimo. "We have a few kitchen appliances that we didn't have during the war. And indoor bathrooms now! Best of all, the view from the porch is still the same one your uncles would have seen. Come, let me show you."

The vineyard was not expansive, but the lush vines promised a nice harvest. "We still make our own wine," said Massimo. "My father taught me, and I taught Ernesto. He's named for his grandfather, you know. And there," he pointed to a small expanse of lawn, "is where we used to play baseball." Massimo still loved baseball and had taught his son and grandsons to play, but somehow, they didn't quite share his enthusiasm. Maybe that was because they'd never experienced the magic of hearing the stories about DiMaggio and Gehrig firsthand. "Now, come inside," he said. "There are some things I'd like to show you."

Ernesto showed the women into the living room and introduced his mother while Massimo disappeared upstairs. He returned carrying a photo album and sat beside Susan on the sofa, so she took her own album out of the satchel she'd been carrying. "Frank came here every chance he got," said Massimo. "He'd eat with our family and play with the children."

They opened the albums simultaneously and then looked at each other in amazement. So many of the pictures they had were identical. Frank . . . Tony . . . Ernesto . . . Massimo as a young boy. "This is Ida," Massimo pointed to a photo of his sister. "Frank truly stole her heart. She remembered him till her dying day."

"And my family – especially Frank," said Susan, "loved her and all your family."

They went through every page of the albums, with Massimo telling stories about all the photos. Danila somehow managed to keep up with the translation as Massimo and Susan shared the joy of this reunion.

When they'd been through the photos twice, Ernesto looked at his watch. "Enza will be waiting for us. She'll have lunch ready by now."

They all took the short walk over to young Ernesto's home, a more modern house overlooking the valley where a huge herd of water buffalo grazed in the lush Campanian fields. Nearby were massive barns. "For the farm equipment," Ernesto explained, "and for the milking and cheesemaking. We're one of the largest producers of mozzarella in the district."

Ernesto's wife, Enza, greeted them at the door and led them to the dining room where a veritable feast covered the table. Over salad, a pasta course, a meat course, and finally dessert, they talked about Susan and Frank's family in America and how she had discovered all the artifacts from Frank and Tony's famous bike trip and letters from the war and from the Pernas. As Enza served coffee, Massimo's eyes welled up and a few tears began to flow down his cheeks. His wife patted his arm and spoke quietly to soothe him, but it didn't seem to help. "What's wrong, Papa?" asked Ernesto.

"I think," he replied, wiping away his tears with his napkin, "I think she doesn't know the rest of the story." Danila translated.

"I'd like to hear it," said Susan. "Will you tell me?"

"Your family . . ." Massimo began, getting control of his emotions. "Your family, they sent us gifts. Even after the war, the packages kept coming. Every day, my brother and I would run to the mailbox to see if anything had arrived. And at least once a month, there would be a box.

Sugar, flour, cereal, food in cans . . . But my little brother, he'd grab the Hershey bars first." Everyone laughed.

"There was always a letter inside. Sometimes, there would be small sums of money for us to buy things. The Italian currency was worthless at that point, but a few American dollars went a long way. And then one day, when Papa opened the envelope, he completely broke down and dropped the envelope and everything inside. Then he picked it up slowly and handed the check to my mother. They hugged for a long time, both of them completely overwhelmed. The letter said that Frank's brothers had worked extra harvesting hay and the family had saved enough to send us this gift.

"Papa never told me how much money it was, but it was enough for him to buy a dozen buffalo and some more pigs and chickens. It didn't take me long to realize that your family's generosity completely changed our lives. Those buffalo started the herd that you see out there now. And with Tony's help, we were able to afford Ida's surgery. Susan, your family gave us hope during a hopeless time. They breathed life into the operation we have today, and now we even export our cheese to America. It's some of the best in all of Campania."

"Actually," said Susan, "I think there's another part of the story that *you* don't know, Massimo. The money for Ida's surgery. That actually came from Frank. You know that key he wore with his dog tags? It was the key to a small box he'd left at home with instructions inside that Florence was to get his bank account and insurance money if he didn't survive the war. And Florence insisted there was no better way to honor Frank than to put that money toward helping Ida."

Tears welled up again in Massimo's eyes. Susan rose from her seat and walked over to embrace him as he dabbed them away. "I'm so very lucky to have found the people who meant so much to Frank," she said.

Returning to her chair, she asked, "Do you remember Vincenza? And what happened to Tito?"

Massimo beamed and gestured to Enza. "Vincenza was my grandmother," she said. "When I was a child, my father never tired of telling the story of how his mother died protecting him as the bombs fell and how your uncle and the 143rd Regiment saved him and pushed the Nazis out of here."

She was interrupted by the sound of someone coming in the front door and footsteps hurrying toward the dining room. A young man walked over to Enza and kissed her on the cheek. "I'm sorry for being late, Mama. The wholesalers wanted to haggle over the price of cheese!"

Enza took his hand and patted it as mothers do when forgiving a child a small transgression. "*Susanna*," she said, "*questo è mi figlio.*" This is my son. "Francesco."

# AUTHOR'S NOTES

This work of historical fiction is based on a true story. Most of the characters in this book are real, though some have pseudonyms. I have added a few fictional characters either to complete the story or because I didn't know the name of the actual person. I have taken certain artistic liberties to present the story as I believe it to have happened. Where the narrative strays from the purely factual, my intent has been to remain faithful to the characters and to the essential drift of events as they really happened.

Working with the US government reinterment department, Tony arranged to have Frank's body sent back to his grieving family. They held a proper funeral mass at last and buried him in Sacred Heart Cemetery in Muenster, Texas.

After a stateside posting in Louisiana where he met his wife, Anna Mae, Joe Bezner returned to Lindsay, Texas (near Muenster) and raised a beautiful family. As of the date I am writing this author's note, he is still alive at 101, residing by the Catholic church, where both priest and parishioners regard him as something of a spiritual guardian. Although it was very difficult for him to talk about it, he was a main source of information about Frank's death and the military experiences of World War II for this book. Other sources include the many letters between the Pernas and the Mosters during and after the war and the daily diaries kept by Frank and Tony during their bicycle trip.

Ironically, the town of Lindsay was near a German POW camp (Camp Howze) that housed prisoners from the Italian campaign – the very same men that Frank and Joe fought against. Some of those

German prisoners remained in this German settlement in the United States after the war and started their new lives there.

Tony worked the family farm near Lindsay and Muenster. He thought of Ida, the Pernas, and Frank often. He wanted to spend time with the Perna family; but thoughts of Italy only brought back the painful loss of his brother. He knew in his heart that Ida had to stay there and take care of her family. He never married.

Ida married an Italian man but died of cancer at a young age.

Ernesto and Carmela Perna had a total of eight children, five of whom appear in the novel.

Vincenza actually had four children. She died in the bombings, protecting her youngest son. To highlight the special bond Frank undoubtedly felt for the young orphan, I took the artistic license of limiting the narrative to Vincenza and the child she gave her life to protect.

The four siblings – Tony, Frank, Steve, and Theresa (Teresita) – were the children of Pasquale and Catherine Peccaro. Pasquale was murdered in New York by the mafia, and Catherine died of influenza in the 1919 pandemic. The siblings arrived in Texas on the Orphan Train in 1920.

Tony and Teresita died in the 1980s. Her real name was Theresa, but to avoid confusion in this book, I've referred to her as Teresita – the diminutive and loving name used by her Italian parents. Steve returned to Muenster after his battle tour in the Pacific islands, and he and Mary adopted two sons – Frank (named for his uncle) and Chris. Steve died in 1991. Florence Moster Grewing cherished the memories of Frank and kept her gifts from him, which brought her joy until her death in 1999. Every Christmas, she brought her many family members together to celebrate the magic of the season and taught us to be happy and appreciate the life we have.

Leo and Theresa Moster were my grandparents. Believing they'd never have children of their own, they did what people did in the days before advanced fertility treatment and IVF – they adopted two boys. And then, as so often happens, once the pressure to have a family was off, they had four children of their own. Joe – called Joey in the book – was my father.

I grew up hearing stories of the great bike journey but never really put much stock in them. It all seemed too preposterous – like a family fish story that got more and more exaggerated with every telling. Then, when Steve's wife, Mary, died in 2009, I discovered the evidence. The daily journals – "scholastic notebooks" with daily notes describing everything about the trip. The Hawthorne bicycles, starting to rust but with their odometers still intact. Boxes of photos. The autograph books. A typed transcription Mary had made of the journals. Frank's diaries and letters home. The correspondence between the Perna family and ours. Suddenly, what had seemed implausible came alive.

I read it all – even plotted the bicycle journey out on a big US map.

In 2010, I decided to find out more about the Pernas and how they actually fit into the family folklore. And that story turned out to be just as remarkable as the tale of the bike ride.

Theresa, my grandmother, was never able to fully come to terms with Frank's death. Even after his body was reinterred in Muenster, she continued to question whether the Army had made a mistake. Until her death at the age of ninety-five, she continued to believe that Frank had somehow managed to survive his injuries and had chosen to live out his days somewhere in Italy. Perhaps she wasn't completely wrong. There's no doubt at all that his spirit lives on even today at the Perna farm.

# ACKNOWLEDGMENTS

I have deep gratitude to all who helped me make this book possible. Thank you to my family, Julie Johnson and Nicholas and Benjamin VanWey – especially Julie for her unwavering motivation and encouragement along with being a great travel spouse to visit the many places we traveled to put the pieces together. To my mother, Emma Pelzel, for supporting me and helping me make the connections to make this book possible, including Joe Bezner, for whom I hold a special place in my heart. Thanks to Baylee Moster, my niece, for reading and re-reading my drafts and to Robert and Patsy Johnson, the best cheerleaders in the world, for their wisdom and help with editing.

I owe so much to my editor, Pamela Taylor, who went above and beyond the call to help me with edits and direction. Her continual belief in my project inspires me. I wish her so much success.

Many thanks to Dr. Danila Bracaglia of Monte Cassino Battlefield Tours for her expertise with Italian battlefields and her knowledge of the 36th Division of the US Army in the invasion of Italy. We spent many days traveling Frank's path from Salerno to Altavilla to San Pietro and many other villages along the way. Through Danila, I was able to find the Perna family and make the connections that Frank had found over seventy years ago. To the Perna family, our lives have been forever bonded—thank you for you all you did for Frank and for your insight to the events. Also in Italy, Kate Little, thank you for helping with research and travel through Italy and Sicily. Our travels to Corleone and Palermo were an adventure!

To my fellow writers at SMU for their continual encouragement and support, I wish you success in your writing careers: Suzanne Frank, Heather Ellett, Scott MacLaren, and others. My book club friends and Dolph Haas—thank you!

I must acknowledge Frank, Tony, Steve, Mary, Florence, and my grandparents and parents for their documentation of this journey, their inspirational lives, and their service to our country. We owe a great deal to those who have served our country and to those who lost their lives doing so in order for us to have our freedom. Please remember history and let us not repeat the mistakes of the past.

**Beach landings at Salerno**
Transport ships offshore, LCTs stopped short of the beaches so men had to wade ashore into enemy fire

**T-Patch**
Uniform patch of the 36th (Texas) Infantry Division
Black "T" on blue arrowhead

DEDICATED TO THE SOLDIERS WHO CAME TO THE AID
OF OUR COUNTRY AND OUR HOME:

THE 36TH (TEXAS) INFANTRY DIVISION (REINFORCED)
WHO FOUGHT AND DIED FOR OUR FREEDOM

"THE NAME OF SAN PIETRO WILL BE REMEMBERED IN
MILITARY HISTORY...WE PICKED OUR WAY
THROUGH FIELDS RIPPED BY MORTARS AND SHELLS
AND THE STILL BODIES OF DOUGHBOYS WHO FELL
IN THE BLOODY, SAVAGE FIGHTING... [IN] THIS GRAY,
LITTLE TOWN OVERLOOKING THE VALLEY APPROACHES
TO CASSINO. THE SOLDIERS CALL IT DEATH VALLEY
BECAUSE DEATH WAS ON THE RAMPAGE FOR FORTY-EIGHT
HOURS AS THEY STORMED THIS ENEMY FORTRESS RINGED
BY FORTIFICATIONS, DUG INTO TERRACED SLOPES
COMMANDING THE LIRI VALLEY"

143D INFANTRY REGIMENT OPERATIONS REPORT, DECEMBER 1943

*The siblings in 1920 and as adults*

Frank, Theresa, Steve, Tony

# The Bike Trip

Tony

Frank

## Detroit Free Press
## August 11, 1938

### Windsor Is Reached by Texas Bicyclists

Bound for Callender, Ont., and the Dionne quintuplets, Tony Sickey, 25 years old, and Frank Moster, 22, arrived by bicycle in Windsor Wednesday from Gainesville, Tex.

Pedaling bicycles which have gear shifts for climbing hills, the young men left Gainesville July 5 and have traveled 2,078 miles, they said. They will continue their trip Thursday.

### Pulitzer Winner Is Hired

N.Y. Yankees
Paul Andrews
Steve Sundra
Johnny Murphy
John Schulte
Art Ogara

Lou Gehrig

To Lucy
good luck
Jack Dempsey
9/4/38

# ABOUT THE AUTHOR

The daughter of a Gold Star military family, Susan Gayle is an avid lover of history, a charter member of the New Orleans WWII Museum, member of the Texas Legislative Ladies and a physician. She completed the SMU Creative Writing Program in Dallas. Though her previous writing was medical articles, she turned her hand to fiction when she discovered the source materials that led to *The Caves of San Pietro*. She enjoys relaxing weekends at the lake with her family.

# NOTE FROM THE AUTHOR

Word-of-mouth is crucial for any author to succeed. If you enjoyed *The Caves of San Pietro*, please leave a review online—anywhere you are able. Even if it's just a sentence or two. It would make all the difference and would be very much appreciated.

Thanks!
Susan Gayle

Thank you so much for reading one of our **Historical Fiction** novels. If you enjoyed the experience, please check out our recommendation title for your next great read!

*The Reckoning* by Jeffrey Pierce

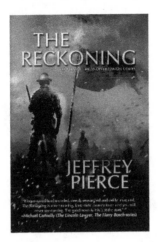

"Eloquent and hard muscled, deeply researched and deftly imagined, *The Reckoning* is an entrancing, fantastical journey to an end you will never see coming. The good news is it is just the start."

**-Michael Connelly** *(The Lincoln Lawyer, The Harry Bosch series)*

View other Black Rose Writing titles at www.blackrosewriting.com/books and use promo code **PRINT** to receive a **20% discount** when purchasing.

CPSIA information can be obtained
at www.ICGtesting.com
Printed in the USA
LVHW111343230821
695905LV00005B/65